TWO GENERATIONS
A Novel

TWO GENERATIONS
A Novel

MALLIKARJUN PATIL

ATLANTIC

ATLANTIC PUBLISHERS AND DISTRIBUTORS

Published by
ATLANTIC PUBLISHERS AND DISTRIBUTORS
B-2, Vishal Enclave, Opp. Rajouri Garden, New Delhi-27
Phones : 5413460, 5429987

Sales Office
4215/1, Ansari Road, Darya Ganj, New Delhi-110 002
Phones : 3273880, 3285873, 3280451
Fax : 91-11-3285873
web: www.atlanticbooks.com
e-mail : info@atlanticbooks.com

ISBN 81-7156-972-2

Typeset at
APD Computer Graphics, Delhi

Printed in India at
Nice Printing Press, Delhi

DEDICATED TO

LORD MACAULAY

and

RAJA RAMMOHUN ROY

Who made English a Medium of Education in India

PREFACE

The art of writing is really a mind-boggling one. It demands a writer to be well-versed in language and in thoughts. The writer has to be good at wielding his pen as much as giving a beautiful shape to his ideas and feelings, lest his production should not get him a good readership. Really, he has to explore the beauty and truth of human domain in his image of life.

Today, novel of all forms of literature has acquired a place of pride as it is handy in entertaining and enlightening all types of readers. So, like cinema, it is hypnotic in engaging human attention.

A word or two must be said about Indians' writing in English. Though English is not our mother tongue, we dare to write in it, for two reasons — one writing in it introduces us to a world readership and two it facilitates the writer for a broader intellectual interaction taking him close to global lyceums. Besides, if his writing is good, he will earn some money or fame or both.

My real knowledge of English dates back just to the year of my graduation. Like Conrad, I learnt English lately and like him, I started to make a profession in it. Indeed, I have taken the job seriously and I believe, I will succeed there.

Writing a novel in English means learning many things from many people. Intellectuals in many walks of life have encouraged me in my endeavour. First, I thank Prof. S.P. Hiremath, Vice-Chancellor, Kuvempu University, Shimoga, Prof. Ujwala S. Hiremath and Prof. M.V. Nadkarni, Vice-Chancellor, Gulbarga University, Gulbarga for their supporting of my literary ventures. I am beholden to my friends P.G. Javalgi and Mohammed Zaheer Basha and many more whose names I cannot reproduce here, for their encouragement and suggestions. Likewise,

I cannot forget my artist wife, Dr. Nanda M. Patil, for her toleration of my absence at home, which is rather memorable and I thank M/s Atlantic Publishers and Distributors, New Delhi, for publishing my work world-wide.

MALLIKARJUN PATIL

PART I

Holidays were always amusing. It was a Sunday morning and all were free to spend their time and money for sportive activities. But farmers and labourers worked at fields and farms to eke out their living, while most others killed their time or spent their money for slavish pleasures. They played dice, gambled away their earnings or slumbered deep. Since it was the month of February, the sky was crystal-clear — no black or blue clouds hovered across the pale-blue heavenly sky. The weather was pleasant and calm, the sun was hot but tolerable, while the climate looked serene, but pleasant and warm.

'I must get my rank anyhow this year,' Harish spoke to Umesh, his boyhood friend, while he was eating roasted groundnuts given to him by the other's kinsfolk.

'I hope you'll,' replied the other leisurly. Both exchanged smiles and threw warm glances at each other just in a sheer boyish pleasure. Now they started eating sugar cane.

'How is the taste of it?' Umesh spoke.

'A nice piece,' came a trite reply.

The friends were walking on the carttrack in Umesh's field at Telsang, a big village near the historical town Bijapur. They trode on the dishevelled road which had been roughly hewn with stones and gravels during the previous year. The village lay thirtytwo kilometres North of Athani on the way to Bijapur. It was an old village with its own history, culture and modern facilities. Umesh's field was well irrigated and it was full of greenery. The canecrop had been grown enough just to be harvested. But the uninterested sugar factory owners did not yet issue their order for Tukaram's yield. Other crops too displayed every mark of maturity. They looked like newly-weds ready for their appointed honeymoon.

Harish was given another piece of sugar cane — very long in size, black-coloured but sweeter than the earlier one. Harish looked at it marvelling and smelt it to confirm his childish conviction. No doubt, he was fond of things sweet. Already the other had finished his piece of cane, while Harish was still doing his overjoyed. The time they finished eating it, they felt gumminess on their body, — tired. Now, after eating, they began chatting about their classmates. They spoke of Susma, a favourite of their class, while Shobha fascinated Harish more than any other belles of their college. Nobody knew why. Harish had loved and admired Shobha for her fair skin, round face, straight nose and radiance that was rare and bewitching. They attended their classes regularly. However Umesh accompanied his friend to college, his general interest did not lie in studies. He lacked Harish's aptitude for higher-education but he developed to become a prosperous farmer.

On the other hand, Harish was a man of different mettles. Unlike Umesh and Govinda, his everloving admirers and well-wishers, he studied well; he missed no classes; and engaged himself even in sports. A healthy boy always, Harish was a good runner. Taller than the two, wiser than them, Harish was a prodigy of refined culture. He was a handsome fellow always cheerful, jovial and active. He loved walking — walking in evening dress; and his gymnastic exercises included many other things. No wonder, physical activities kept him hale and hearty ever afterwards.

Harish had a flock of associates — a nice thing for youngsters. On account of his humour, oratory and good-studies, Harish was a leader par excellence. Pleasant was his company. Social, warm and fruitful, his worldly activities. This quality made him a boy-hero. Besides, he maintained cordial relationships with everyone at home and outside. His clear-headedness, indeed, made him par social. But he had also been an enigmatic figure — talkative, gloomy and more unintelligible too. Maybe for this reason those who loved him assessed him variously. His college principal talked of him in superlatives, while his English teacher encouraged him merely in admiration of his careerism. The latter thought he would become a writer. This had hatched an alarming envy in Raviraj, a hack-writer of the college. Of course, the budding writer Raviraj hated him for the silliest reason that one day Harish might eclipse him. But his was a mere predilection — unreal, an imaginary fear. But a few, due to their imaginary dread, harboured malice towards others only to be drowned themselves in the water of their futile enmity. Raviraj belonged to this class.

While the college clerk Shantappa's estimation of Harish had been more realistic than any other's in the college staff. The clerk held the view that the boy, of course, would become a man of letters, he would be a die conservative. Nobody knew Shantappa's meticulous observation of Harish's ways with women. When he told Raviraj about the young man's weakness, the latter summarily dissmissed it as uncredulous. However, there were certain reasons for Shantappa's crude calculation. He had based his supposition upon Harish's apparent relationship with a variety of college ladies.

Harish after a due leave from Umesh, began his homeward journey. Umesh's absence quickened his eastward walk. He saw the canecrop, the groundnut, the onion and chilly and numerous other things blooming brightly. Some of them, he found, had already been ripe for harvesting. So ripeness was all. Among them the cane and groundnut were in the forefront. Harish passed them one by one quickening his pacing. He did it rather unconsciously. It had been a part of his nature to walk past when he had been alone. On the way, he heard, and he loved birds' chirping, beasts' wandering and the crops fluttering in the gentle breeze. After seeing maize, no doubt, he wished he had eaten them — very natural for a foodie boy.

Now when Harish had been on road, an old idea returned to his mind as an invalid depending upon his protector. It was the same idea — the idea of winning Gold Medal in his B.A. He was ambitious to fetch it. In fact, in B.A. I he had obtained it. But wholly owing to his college-politics, he could not retain it during the next year. He simply stood second which hurt his affectionate mother who helped him fastidiously for his higher education. Now he determined to get the coveted rank. No doubt, his preparation with this sole end in view had been soundly underway. Although he was annoyed by Raviraj, in his all study activities, he was liberally abetted by the principal. The young boy resolved to defeat Patil, the teacher's daughter who scored highest in the second year. Harish knew it well that a cross section of lecturers had a hand in his deprival of prize. So he had been vehemently pursuing his enterprise in the forthcoming days.

Presently Harish joined 13 number State Motorway on which buses sped fast with passengers from Athani and Miraj and Kolhapur and the other border areas of Maharastra. He saw many vehicles but none of them stopped on his request. They ran fast towards Bijapur, 40 kilometres away from Telsang, the village of Harish's birth. This historic name of Bijapur brought many memories and recollections to the growing boy. He had read in the history books about the Adilshahs' rule of Bijapur. Their pomp and glory had not been less magnificent than that of the Rayas of Vijayanagar. Whenever Harish went to Golgumbaj, he read edicts, and inspected the forgotten events. As a history student, his knowledge of Bahamani architecture and the cause of its construction was sounder than many others'. The oldsters of his village had, at times, told him tales about Bahamani kings and their village raids. Could he forget Adilashah's beseizing of Telsang either? His villagers had also talked of Ramba's love for a Bahamani Sultan, very pure and constant. Several events of the Shahi dynasty and its destruction of the glorious empire Vijayanagar reminded him of the past. But Harish was not a youth who could not think about matters of love, romance and adventure. So the tales of village raids included Sultans' raids for peasant women of the days. These flickerings of ancient days worked in him dismal changes beyond his boyhood years.

The wide countryside that lay in front of Harish looked vaster in the absence of any fellow wayfarers. However buses, lorries, tractors and cars passed by him interminably on the road, they gave him no providential pleasure. Occasionally some two-wheelers appeared but only to disappear. The winter winds were calm and cool. During the day the sun was hot and clear but his rays were unbearable. But the shade of neem or mango was cool and pleasant enough. So the solitary walkers on the long way never reached home without one or two sittings beneath them. Only a few people liked acacia or tamarind as their shade was either insufficient or covered with dirt and thorns. The endless countryside was unterrainous as it had been a large tract of table land where the woodland was very scarse. Only short bushes and undergrowth of cactus spread there uncontrolled. The countryside was similar to the descriptions of any desert area. The presence of big trees however few and far between added a kind of misshape to it ironically. Or were there any hills to offset the distortion of topography? The rarity of rivulets if not valleys and the dearth of sufficient rainfall turned the region into a kind of barren land mostly halfcultivated. Only the rich had borewells irrigation, while the poor, like beasts, laboured long like anything.

Harish came home. It was six o' clock evening. The shadow of palm in front of his house was stretched longer than the palm itself. He got into the house but found his mother in a mist of brazen dispair. The reason, as he hearnt it later, was that Harish was not attentive to his studies. So he wasted no time in convincing his mother that due to intrigues he could not surpass everyone. He consoled her that he would get it this year. His mother but a rigid woman took much time to believe it. She advised him to pass his final B.A with highest score. This strengthened the boy's morale and ambition. Thereafter, his mother served him food and both, after an hour of chat about the superb beauty of her brother's eldest daughter, retired to bed.

Time passed while the wheel of it turned. Within a month, Harish's exams were over along with the pressure it generated thereby. Likewise as anticipated the results came in Harish's favour.

He had stood first to his college. Everyone turned overjoyed. The happiness of his widowed mother had been boundless. Harish was duly appreciated for his talent, hardwork and sincerity of purpose. Umesh's admiration of the gold medalist was especial. Though he failed, Umesh congratulated him warmly without any ill-will. So was Govind, a poor boy.

A common nature of people in a village like Telsang was to praise or flatter the rising sun. No matter whether the man in the field was laudable or not, if once he got a name, flattery and praising of him was astoundingly begun. In this regard, people in countryside were as perblind as the urbanities. Most of them respected important persons only on appearance. While the stark reality of the rural phenomena was invariably different. No wonder, this the rustics inherited from their ancestors. Whatever they found worthy of heroworship, they continued it without any enquiry in the matter. Therefore the blind beliefs and rituals persisted in the gentry who were always at a loss of understanding the inner details. This rose because of their lack of clear-headedness.

So is the case with Harish Pattan. As Thomas Hardy says, persons with any weight of character carry, like planets, their atmosphere along with them in their orbits, Harish, the favourite of the old village carried with him an air of boyhood fame. Most of those familiar valued him, the less merely admired his talent and the least simply respected him by maintaining certain distance. Correspondingly the village laity lettered or not, talked of him in superlative degrees. The more educated advised their children to study in the line of Harish. Some of those who were closer to him spoke of his brilliance always. In fact, a hero, he looked to them. The love, affection and regard, the people amply bestowed upon the wizard of weight became a folk narration. People's admiration of the boy had been varied too. Some said he was a genius, while others spoke he worked hard for success. There was also a class of rustics who attributed his fortunes to *daiv* (an unknown force) that brought him worldly truimph.

One day the college principal sent Harish a letter about the college gathering. The function was arranged to honour the retired professors. The letter also stated that a programme to felicitate the rank holders was arranged. At once Harish left his village to attend the function and the friends accompanied him included Umesh, Govind and a score more.

The college gathering began at five in the evening. This was arranged in an auditorium of the institution. A large number of students, the teaching and non-teaching staff and their spouses, the VIPs of the town which included the District Collector, the District Ministers, the local MLA and MPs had adored the gorgeous hall. Soon the function began. The retired teachers honoured, received their shawls and prizes. The principal appreciated their service and spoke of their students. Thereafter, he called Harish to the dias for receiving a medal, and a cash award of Rs. 10,000 was announced for him. Harish, then an M.A. student of Pampapati University stepped up while the studentfolk, for a minute or two, clapped their hands cheerfully. No sooner he appeared to the eyes of the multitude than the girls had a fine look at him. A few of them, naturally eyed him with an eye of love. There was a moment of stock stillness in the hall. The andience enjoyed the sight and expressed their words of appreciation. But none could have beholden the wizard more devotedly than Shobha, a local MLA's daughter. Believable or not, Shobha's eyes were directed at the gold medalist only. The DC and other dignitaries sat admiring the boy's merit. Someone briefed them that the boy stood highest not only to the college but also to the University. This had already appeared in local dailies. Soon afterwards, the DC got up to address the gathering. He spoke very less but his words carried more weight than the whole verbosity of the college principal. He advocated the view education in India should be made secular and liberal. Meanwhile the media-persons busied themselves to note down the remarks for their next day newspapers.

The time the programme was over, the audience turned homeward. But Harish and his friends amid admirers' thanks and well-wishes moved about there till the crowd could melt away sufficiently. Thereafter, they left Bijapur for their homes over joyed and proud. Now Harish looked like Tensing Norge, a super character. Both the savants and simple could not help admire him, the day's hero.

Back in the department of Kannada, Pampapati University, Harish was highly respected. But with his friends, went the number of his enemies too. No doubt, there were Ravirajs with their own axes to grind him. However, the malice of a few did not enerve his determination. He passed the first year of his post-graduation with a good score. This made him more respectable in the campus life.

PG study gave Harish more knowledge than pleasure. Really a very good thing. It helped him plenty of wisdom. Education given in university, the highest seat of learning was aptly wholesome. The standards, the syllabus, the quality of research were quite systematic and effective and beneficial. After all, the university stood for higher education and streamlining human energy towards creative thinking and activities. As a centre of human choice, thought, knowledge, discussion, the University of Pampapattan refined human faiths and practices. 'The real university,' F.R. Leavis says, 'is a centre of consciousness and human responsibility for the civilized world; it is a creative centre of culture and civilization. Pampapati University where thousands of students graduated was really a place of quality-education and research. It was, undeniably, a live centre where a large number of youths were made aware of a past that shaped their present and sharpened their sensibility. It imparted liberal education and in Matthew Arnold's phrase produced 'sweetness and light.' People from far off as well as nearby places came over there; they valued the university greatly and compared it to Oxford. They knew the education given there gave them a life. Sure it maintained democratic values and fairness. None could blame the centre as its standards had been high and intact and useful.

However, it should be borne in mind that everyone who had a degree of Pampapati university did not succeed in getting a job or in attaining an orderly life. The children of wealthy people came over there just to get more delight than knowledge or wisdom. They fell headlong in revelries of joys and pleasures. They thought the secret of life was joy instead of peace. The way of life they led, or the manner of studies they carried on, fell below the lines. The rich attended classes without an interest while the poor laboured long. What can the spoiled youngsters do in a place like this? So the students of indisciplined mind simply wasted away their money, energies and interest. Instead of learning, like rabbits, they roved in quest of sheer fleshly pleasures.

Indeed, the students of improper conduct pursued cheap extravaganza and unhealthy sexuality. Some of them chose their beloveds in the campus. Even a few daring became illegitimate fathers and their sweethearts victims of carnal villainy. They mixed up with girls of their choice and understanding and met them at parks, in laboratories and outside lecture halls. And nobody knew or could tell why some boys accompanied girls to city, to theatres and to frequent walkings. A few boys even flirted with ladies at Pampapateshwar temple just outside the campus.

Harish too did not remain an exception. How can he as he ate the salt others did? When he was in graduation itself years ago, he had befriended Shobha, a celestial bride — now a fair maid. Now, two years after, their courtship continued. However, Harish did not dally with her in public as he was careful of his character. This fellow had inherited certain foxy features. His weakness for flesh was glaring however. Notwithstanding, his familiarity with Shobha in the class was limited to his studies alone. But he, for her, had already developed an inner attachment which could never be shaken by any winds. His occasional gesticulations carried the flickers of his in-depth love to his sweetheart. He talked to her much of the time but in privacy. Careful was his undertaking of every precaution to conceal the lusty affair. In fact, his tactics were invisible.

It was dusk when one day Shobha had been her way to hostel in blue-tinted nighty alluring. Harish happened to meet her at a crossroad. The bewitching beauty was going her way with her own thoughts smiling occasionally. This coaxed Harish's pent up emotions. At once to trap her he made a frightening sound and the next moment she turned to him for safety. Soon each found the other consoling.

The University Park that was beside Ladies Hostel was called Lover's Shade owing to its soothing features, green lawns and nice turf. The park cum garden was very extensive and it had been sequestered as the authority reserved it for ladies alone. But the fairsex rarely relaxed there as the end of it was covered by bomboo thickets and woodland bushes full of snakes and animals. Many flower plants, crepeers, trees, had refurbished the area splendidly. The arrangement of light had been dismal as it did not cover the whole area. The back side of the park that was almost half in size by any measure was covered with wild undergrowth. Indeed, the garden had been a fine place for those souls who could workout their ways for a union of bliss.

Harish arrested Shobha's fulsome interest at once by engaging her in a slipshod chatting. No doubt, he pretended her as if he were to reveal her some mysteries of glorious life that had long vanished away from the earth. This encouraged the dame to turn towards him nearby a neem tree. Good or ill, the lady led by his mellow company walked in response to his feelings. The nature of talk they held took them not only to the neem tree, but to the guave grove at a farther end. Throughout the walk each was tempted by the other. Because of her beauty he followed her, while his inducement, led her astray. The two seething souls then stood abruptly somewhere beneath a shade where none could notice them.

'Have you got any letters from your father?' Harish spoke gently.

'Not yet,' smiling upon the other, Shobha enquired him about his mother's health.

‘She’s well,’ Harish returned her a smile with an added interest. She writes me only to study. That’s all.’

‘Tell her not to bother about your future. I know you’re a brilliant chap. Soon you finish your M.A., I’m cocksure, you’ll get a job as well as a wife whom you’ve already chosen,’ spoke his companion nourishing a feeling of love.

‘What d’ you mean?’

‘You’ve already fallen in love with someone.’

‘Someone...Already...Whom?’

‘Oh should I tell it?’ She remained hideous.

Harish remained silent as he could not comprehend her. He was at a loss of understanding the situation. But his silence was voluminous. It did not quench the maid’s anxiety, while she was curious of reading his heart. She had, at times, noticed him unloving her. Their *tete-a-tete* continued. Soon they sat down under the shade of a mango tree which grew terribly wild. It was large — full of branches covered with rugged leaves. Now Harish’s silence began deadening her. Shobha was staring at him as ever before, while his smile-lit face was downcast a little. Admittingly he had been deftier than his dame in stirring the emotions of her heart but his love for her was not as strong as hers for him.

‘Shall I know your lover?’ Shobha could not help entreating him.

‘Why you’re so insistent on this?’ smiling upon her, Harish turned irresponsive. In turn, he was sure that she would not leave him without extracting the truth. Then why he turned non-responding? Truly he did it for teasing her. He knew Shobha was persuasive enough to trace the unknown and thereby for him become a pleasuresome item.

‘I want it dear,’ Shobha became anxious as her heart throed and throbbed. As she was short-tempered, she could not control her whim. Meanwhile a woodland creature suddenly crawled near. It was a small snake passing somewhere. No sooner she glanced at the moving object than in sheer dread she embraced him. What a thrill in fear? A romantic touch? He took her aside and asked her to be at ease. The embrace she gave him was warm and sensational. However the snake had disappeared, Shobha still sat to him body to body to find a reply. No doubt, the tremor of her body began thrilling his heart for the first time.

'Why you get frightened at small creatures?'

'First answer my question,' she held the ground. Already she had forgotten the creature, or she valued his response greatly.

'The answer is not yet ready,' he smiled.

'Don't pretend. I'd know it,' Shobha shot instantaneously.

'Is it your urgent aspiration?'

'If you don't tell a lie,' she cut it briefly laughing at him. Her dress specially the frock was slightly scattered now.

'I'll answer you but subject to a conditon...' He saw the part of her body uncovered.

'Conditon? What's... that?'

'You'd not question me further about my love-affair,' Harish expressed it giggling. Presently he put his hand upon her which thrilled her inwardly.

'Alright,' said she conscious of his hand.

'Don't you ask me anymore?'

'It depends upon the nature of your reply. If truth is spoken no questions further,' she burst out into a peel of laughter. Her voice carried an assurance. Occasionally the way he saw her with love quenched her inner fury.

'What d' you mean by this?'

'A simple demand for truth.'

'Ok. Already you know I'm loving someone. Take it for certain that I'll marry her with whom I've already fallen in love.'

Harish deftly abridged the assertion but that left her swimming in a river of confusion.

'I know that you're loving someone and I also know that you'll marry her alone, but tell me *whom* you're loving?' Shobha broke her word of promise.

'See you're a naughty lady. You don't stand by your words.'

'But tell me the truth,' Shobha sticked to the point. Her ears had been closer to Harish's face. She was curious to scan his heart and go home delighted.

'You want to know it in advance?

'Yes in advance,' she fingered his hand.

'Why yes?' he spoke back. Their hands were scanning each other's shoulders.

'Come on with reality,' she appealed him fervently.

'Didn't you understand me when I uttered it ?' Harish eye-teased her. 'Ladies are foolish — not quick in appreciating things,' he added it sardonically.

'Shall I think you love me?' Asked she turning anxious. Her face turned more bestirring than the face of angry moon who to do his duty had just arisen in the western sky.

'You want to know whom I love, don't you ?' asked he.

'Yes.'

'Certainly; I love you,' Harish kissed the dame really. It's a master stroke.

'Hai,' she screamed kissing him.

Shobha turned joyous. No wonder, she kissed him at once and found an ecstasy which she had never felt so far. He kissed her and she kissed him again. Both kissed each other for many more times. In fact, the delactation induced each to fall into the other's arms.

When the portions in the department were over, the dreadful process of examination followed. Soon the results came blessing. The fate of many was decided by then. Some were destined to become teachers while most others not. Fate had betrayed them if not their disinterested endeavours. It had issued orders for them for following an odd number of jobs. Most of the students scored impressively, while many others had just passed the frightening exam. The limited group of students who pursued their education sincerely succeeded to a fair extent, while others who squandered their money because of their roguery had lost their blithe chances. However, most of them had passed — mostly in pass class. On the other hand, the fate of those who fell below the line was worse than of those who simply got passed. Be it as it may, the failed were not pessimistic as they believed in the Providential Man — Him who helped everyone weak and erring.

Glad were those who passed; gladder were those who passed well; and gladdest was Harish who had scored highest. What a lucky chap he had been! He got the first rank and distinction. The Gold Medal was his till then his greatest obssession. He had become an intellectual champion of his department and had silenced those who maliciously disliked him. People apprised him for his excellences. None hated the look of him. His pronounced enemies stood outside stockstill blaming their fate or cursing themselves. But those who had loved him without any caprice exalted him whole-heartedly. Harish, soon he had got the news, met his professor and friends and showed them his sincere gratitude. Likewise Shobha who too had passed in first class, accompanied her wouldbe companion to see the chairperson.

'Good morning, sir,' Harish spoke, while Shobha and others intoned the phrase simultaneously. The scene was touching.

'Oh! you've got your result?' the Head of the Department said it with an air of extraordinariness. There was a smile of contentment on his fiftyfive year old face.

'Yes, sir...,' the young voices broke out in a tone of humility and delight.

'Who stood highest, Harish or Ganesh?' The chairman put it enquiringly. He did it because he was not assured of Harish's victory as some villainous hands worked against him before they dwindled into decay. However, none could deny the stark reality *Satya meya jayate* (Ultimately Truth Triumphs). All including the administration staff, the man who wished to set Ganesh against Harish and Ganesh himself knew this. But the head for another reason, had asked this to avoid hurting Ganesh who was one of them standing before him. Anyway Shrishailappa, the Head was in an euphoria today.

'It's Harish,' said Ranganna, a common friend.

'Doesn't matter. I'm jubilant, for you've obtained your MA degree. I hope many of you'll get jobs immediately,' he smiled upon all those gathered. Now, the ones who had secured an eligibility turned cheerful, while others who did not, stood worried. Shortly the Chairman nodded the boys — a nodding to go away.

It was the month of May, the hottest sun had not yet stopped burning. His heavenly rays were seething enough to burn all dry things. There was no sign of rain-bearing clouds in the eastern or western sky, and in the paramount absence of cool breezes, everything was blistering. However, people of *maidan* lands of South India were largely accustomed to it. As the month of May had never been the cool one, it provided them rest for leading quite a leisurely life. The abundance of mangoes and bananas gave the robust sons of soil coloured juice to drink; and the longer leisure days facilitated them to work indoors or play at inns. So many of them had cultivated the habits of listening to popular radio songs, watching cricket matches on star TVs and gambling away their stocked finance. This did not mean they had no worries or vexations. Most of them who had their daughters particularly aged never slept comfortably. They knew it best that ladies aged more would be of lesser value in matrimonial alliances. In India this is still implicit in every house — rich or poor, cultured or heathen. Even the tribals marry off their girls when they do not yet reach the level of maturity. Matrimonial alliances of young girls particularly in countryside had been in vogue and it was not criticised on any grounds. It is because of this baby wives and girl-mothers were many among the country-gentry.

Exactly this was the state of affairs at Shobha's house when she had returned home post-graduated. Her father, a former MLA had been on decline economically then. His property, though large, due to no addition to it every year, was on the way of gradual erosion. Mr Satish, Shobha's father who had been then in his sixties had married off his first daughter. Shobha was his second and Karisma stood last in the line. Mr Ravindra, Satish's only son had been an engineer well-settled down in the far off city of Bangalore. So virtually Satish had the responsibility of marrying off Shobha and her sister. However Shobha had just obtained an MA, he was not sure of her finding a good job. Still his greater fear lay just the other way. He wondered whether she could remain virgin because she had many boyfriends. Though she was certain of marrying Harish and had revealed it to her parents, Satish was not certain of that dreamy eventuality. Therefore one cool morning, he summoned Shobha to his chamber when all the kith had gone off to bazaar.

'What is your M.A. score my dear?' Satish asked her.

'I've scored sixty-five percent daddy' she put it proudly.

'A very impressive score,' replied the old man shaking his head.

'Shall I think it'll help you to get a job?' he enquired. He was looking at a picture of an M. Com holder in a photo who had driven his car when he could not find a suitable job in the last decade.

'I'm sure about it,' the girl replied politely.

'Alright... what about your marriage? D'you think Harish whom you love would marry you hundred percent?' the old man stopped for breathforce.

'Yes, hundred percent. He's assured me that he'd come here for a bride-show ceremony at the earliest soon after he gets his mother's consent. He'll be, I'm sure, my life-partner.'

'Oh! does it mean a marriage?' the elder threw a glance at her for confirmation.

'Yes. Marriage and Happiness,' she replied gently.

'See; whatever may be your relationship with him, make it clear to me by June first. Otherwise, I'll arrange your wedding with a distant relative,' the all concerned father said it decidedly. She knew he was firm of mind. Soon when a guest intruded, Satish rushed out to welcome him. But the dame sat there a little longer and when her daddy did not turn up she retired to her bedroom.

Marriage in Indian context is a sacred rite, a holy ceremony and a social endorsment. To Indians marriage is said to have been made in heaven. It is only-once happening phenomenon in life. Therefore, much importance is attached to the event of wedding. Parents, while they search out brides for their sons will be fastidious enough about their choice. A good bride or groom is carefully selected. The event of wedlock is arranged by parents of both parties. First a ring ceremony is initiated and then the final event of uniting the bride and groom with a holy thread will follow at the appointed day and place. So the people kindred attend the celebration and bless the newly-weds.

But this is a traditional method of conducting marriage. Today everything has undergone a change — a sea change, uncertain and varied. A boy of marriageable age who is sufficiently educated, selects a girl himself right in his college days. Most of the time, the boldests take a hard decision to marry their respective beloveds. Today owing to the impact of western culture, new education and civilized mannerism, many Indians neglect the suggestions of their parents regardless of their relative commitments and well-wishes in the matter.

Wedding to the people of this nature is very simple, economic and satisfactory. They choose beloveds and after a due familiarity, start their jolly courtship. No doubt, the next step to them is nothing but preparation of marriage through love and romance. But in India, unlike the westerners, people fail frequently in love-marriages. This is attributed to their steps hastily undertaken. In a country like India where multiplicity of caste, race, religion, culture and languages, prevail beside a low level of knowledge, love-marriages fail due to one or other's individual limitations. In this regard, none denies the relative role of social codes of conduct which are quite harsh and objectionable.

Yet another reason for the failure of love-marriages is hasty steps taken up by wedding people in the heat of their sexual gratification. Aspiration for beauty is also a genine cause. They do not think 'love at first sight usually ends with divorce at first slight.' They utterly fail to know the point that marrying someone for her beauty is like a poker game. Most of the marrying do not understand Adrian Anderson's remark : "The thing that counts most in the pursuit of happiness is choosing the right travelling companion." Some people marry either for beauty or for wealth, while those who wed for the first commit an unretrievable harm first for themselves. Do they understand the fact that to marry a woman for her beauty is like buying a house for its paint? Correspondingly one should not marry for money too. Despite the fact, it could be worth to associate with wealthy women and fall in love. But in Thomas Hardy's view 'marrying in haste and repenting at leisure' is something unendurable. When man and woman come up of age and search for their beloveds, they must choose persons of adjustable character, of good taste and temperament, status, culture, beauty (if possible), wealth (if indispensable), job or some work that can provide them a living. Usually boys commit the same errors which ladies follow. When one goes either for beauty or wealth, regardless of conjugal bliss, he or she is destined to making their lives meaningless.

On retiring to her bed-room, many thoughts occurred to Shobha's tender mind. Without changing sides on the milliflorous diwan, she pondered over the issue of selecting a man. Sometimes she thought though her father could try to arrange her marriage with a distant relative, like Pritwiraj, Harish would come up and take her away as his wife. But this was not an era of chivalry. Though she never heard of a distant kin, her father mentioned, she could not brush off him aside. She knew he was a man of instant action.

However, she was confident that she could not yield to any one in the matter of her nuptial. At some moments she also wished to consult her mother who could give her a sound counsel. But always the image of Harish more as her beloved than a classmate whom she loved beyond measure, danced on the tableland of her tumultous heart. 'Can I avoid Harish? No, no, no...' she said to herself. A war about the pros and cons of the matter took place in her warm bosom. Soon a cool breeze of reason came and everything turned apparent and clear. He belonged to her own community; he had been better qualified than most others to get a job; and his mother was shortly to approve her as her daughter-in-law. All things were to balance the ripple caused by her father. She went on nursing her thoughts at times and again. But to her wonder she found something still outlandish and missing.

It was six o'clock evening, when Chandramma, the landlady returned home with Karisma, her third daughter not more than twenty-years old. They came in an auto. After finding the mini vehicle the outsider who till then held a talk with Satish prepared himself to go off. He had so far talked over an issue which as his appearance showed was rather confidential. The vehicle sound alerted the master and the latter changed the matter. Consequently, he did not encourage the hesitant outsider to continue his talks any further. Meanwhile, Shobha who had till then been meditating over her issue rushed out. Anxiety-stricken, she looked. However her father would not oppose her desire outright, she had rather been uneasy today. She was, no doubt, eager to consult her mother. Both drew out to welcome Chandramma and Karisma who smiled upon the two souls who had to their surprise been in an ocean of their tempests.

'Get indoors. Why you came late?' Satish enquired his wife gazing at the setting sun in the western sky.

'No; we've come back in time,' Karisma spoke on behalf of her mother who was picking up things that fell down.

'Alright,' the father went in.

'Mummy why you didn't take me to market?' Shobha being bored asked her mother.

'You're not here. I think you'd been to your friend's house. So we couldn't help going ourselves,' the mother replied affectionatey.

'Anyway, you've come,' she sighed.

'Why?' D'you have any urgent discussion?' Chandramma broke in interrogation.

'Yes,' Shobha moved inside with an air of aloofness which beset the other. So without a minute of loss soon after dumping luggage in a storeroom, even relegating her desire to see her husband, the landlady rushed to Shobha's room smiling. Several thoughts gripped her then. Chandramma had known the nature of her daughter. As a sensitive woman, she never annoyed the sentiments of Shobha or any others. The questions before her were: 'What might be her problem now? Did she have a talk with her father? In that case did he behave with her high-handedly or left her high and dry disrespecting her desires?' Many thoughts about Shobha's future flowed down. No doubt, as it was a high time, Chandramma took the matter seriously.

Presently she went to Shobha with a plate of fruits that included seedless grapes and pomegranates plentily grown in Bijapur district and some dry eatables.

'What's the matter?' the mother broke the silence by placing fruits on an exquisite tipoy lain by a good looking sofa. She sat near her.

'I want to talk to you,' the younger burst drily.

'I know,' Chandramma smiled at her in an amiable manner. This she intended for consoling the unhappy girl. She knew, that at times her husband used to talk harshly and this time, she guessed his speech to her in a hard way.

'Let me know your problem,' Chandramma arrived to the point.

'Have you ever thought of my marriage?'

'Certainly. We've already discussed the issue and taken a decision too.'

'Decision...Already... May I know it ?' the dame beseeched the elder out of curiosity.

'You said you've loved Harish and given us certain details too. If he comes with a job, we're glad and ready to approve your wedding with him,' she stopped for clearing her throat.

There fell a heavy silence.

'However, we're parents, the final say in the matter is exclusively yours. I hope you know this. Our only duty is to help and encourage you to get a job and to get a benevolent husband. Ours is to teach you how to catch fish but not to teach you how to eat it. So you can find out your own ways towards happiness,' the matron finished her say comically.

Finding the maid silent over the issue, the mother sat calm and composed entertaining many dry conjuctures. A volley of doubts milled her mind. The questions, 'Has Harish not wanted to marry her? Or does she have any problems in this regard? Is her love-affair riddlesome? Why she is introvert over the matter?' etc. boggled her overgrown sensibility.

'You remained silent?' As an elderly person, the old woman tried to explore the hedious mystery of the lass's heart.

'Mummy I've loved Harish truly and if at all I've to marry I'll marry him only. But he's not yet found a suitable job which you expect of him. Nor like us does he have any independent income to support a family? He's definitely been from a good stock however his father left the family in troubles when he died fifteen years ago. Now the mother and son live on his poor pension. Then how can he marry me at once?' Shobha stopped soon in anticipation of a kind reply from her benigh mother.

'Is it very difficult for him to get a lecturer post in spite of his excellent records and marry you within a year or two?' Prompt was the mother's enquiry.

'I think that's possible... A nice solution... Good for both'... the maid turned keen in the matter.

There was a moment of silence.

'May I know whether he is quite sure of marrying you when he finds a job?' the old lady broke the silence. There was a concern in her voice most natural for an elderly woman.

'Yes, very much,' came the voice firmly.

'Then you do one thing. You drop him a letter urgently asking him to meet us on 18th next Monday. As your daddy won't be here, we can work out a plan.'

'Alright,' Shobha said assured. There was a smile of satisfaction on her gloomy face as her mother explored a salvage.

'How d'ye work out this enterprise of my marriage?' She enquired the other yet curious. Still a doubt lingered long in the tenderest heart of the maid.

'Let me help him in case he decides honestly to marry you. I'll ask my brother, the President of Sangmeshwar Education Society to give him a lecturer post. D'you think I won't do anything for your welfare?' the matron looked hearty.

The ladies turned glad and chatting.

It was five o' clock evening. January sun was not yet fully settling down. The sky was clear and blue. The highschool building where Harish and his friends were playing cards had been very vast but uneven throughout. Many school lads and lasses were at play on the western side of the ground. The playground was fully skirted by a wide hedgerow of tall evergreen trees which had been planted during the British Raj. Now after many decades they had stood majestically giving much pleasant shade to the tired people. Birds of different natures, colours and shapes chirped in them and rested in their finely built nests. The common brids that flew over the village sky were pigeons, cuckoos, crows, parrots and a numerous others whose names were unknown to the villagefolk. Below the old trees and undergrowth animals of all distinctions — class, creed. colour, shape, size, — gathered for relaxation during the day times. Stray animals like dogs came there to take vengeance upon their enemies. Besides the village playground, existed a big village tank as the biggest source of water both for humanfolk and animals. The tank's water was used by villagers for washing their clothes too. Women in large came there to draw water, to wash clothes or for other unnoticed reasons. Those who washed their clothes tied their sarees upward to avoid cold and wetness. They bent down for doing their work. This scene was blissfully attractive and spectacular. The village activities either at the waterfront or beside the temple were substantially diverse and wide-ranging. But the way the activities were carried on was still traditional and rustic. However, the folk led a plain life unlike their urban counterparts. Indeed, because of their few wants, they were the happiest people.

The time a boy was sent for Harish, the latter was playing cards. Already he had won some rounds and had established his superiority over those who eagerly played with him. The company he was thirsted in consisted of people of diverse tastes. But all did not busy themselves at playing. Some of them were playing curiously, while most others, specially those who had no money to throw, gazed at them unintentional. The interest of onlookers in the card game was as intense and emotional as the interest of those dexterously playing. When Harish won the round again, there was a sparkling applause. One companion with a short nose said he was lucky, while a few others supported the baldest assertion. A few of the souls, like stone bowlders, had been asleep all the while. No wonder, the majority of them had taken some country wine and as a result of that often they turned vulger and merry-making. Their language was aweful.

'Harish you won it again?' a fellow with matted hair broke down.

'Yes,' Govind replied him on the man's behalf.

'Our Hari is a brainy,' Siddanna poked his nose. Meanwhile Kallappa, a sturdy boy quipped the irksome chap for silence. But

Siddanna, the adamant waif repeated his folly of interefering into other's activities. The game was hilarious.

The dice play went on until Harish and Kallappa wished to stop it. Suddenly Harish left the folk for his home. Already he had been informed by a neighbour to rush home as his kith had arrived.

Harish Pattan's family was not a big one in Telsang. Unlike the Pishes, the Patels, the Jamadars, the Pattars, the Biradars, the Kattimanis, the Kulkarnis, the Hirematħs, Pattans had been people negligible in numbers. Although Harish's ancestors had been the unforgettable royolets of the village and for a considerable span of years had dominated the village politics, at present Harish alone had survived. Harish's credulous mother attributed this oddity to a wench's fervent curse upon the family. The mystery of this misfortune over them was strikingly interesting. Harish's great grandfather Guruputrappa Pattan who had been the village royolet in the first third of nineteenth century when the British Raj throve had been all sound — educated, wealthy and powerful. He led a luxurious life as the overlord of village, while his wife Badramma had been a sober doyenne. All villagers — the haves and have-nots alike submitted to the all powerful Pattans in humbleness. Really the whole village administration was in his hand, and whatever he did, the local British resident did not oppose him. In fact, the resident did not know what crimes and follies the baron committed. Therefore, however atrociously he lived, the vagaries of his nature did not get any criticism.

Nonetheless Guruputrappa, the village lord was good, in matters of sex, at times, he behaved badly. In the heydays of his youth, he did anything to enjoy — gambling, sporting and flirting. He ate all sorts of food which his own kindred shunned. The event that brought the family a dreadful curse was related to his sex crimes if not to his political atrocities. Although he had a wife and several kepts for his nighttime revelries, he did not appear satisfied. One day when he was inspecting his village at dawn in connection with law and order situation, he saw a beautiful Venus bathing as naked as a child in the backyard of his surrounding. As the houses in those days were poorly built in consideration of the prevailing facilities, the villagefolk had their bathrooms entirely in their backyards. Of course, they bathed in early mornings. This was more true in case of women whose only outward behaviour was confined to hutment walls. So Guruputrappa, the David, that day went near his Bathseba, a disrobed and bewitching figure who had been unfortunately widowed the previous year. When one day her only son had been out of station, by chance, she did not get up early and had started her bath at about six or so in the morning. It was but a moon-lit night yet. As she was hardly in her forties and bore a very good health and looking she looked all enrapturous. Besides, her nudity made every part of her slender body look shiny and radiant. Her breasts were like fresh apples as they had not yet been fully used. They looked neat and trim. In her face, the glow of her entire beauty mirrored like anything. The woman's big brown eyes, slender waist, soft balm, round sides, black hair and the brimming thighs looked like inviting anyone who glanced at her presently. It is because of this reason she bathed daily at about five o' clock morning but on that unfortunate day she made an inordinate delay.

Guruputrappa who stood very near to her relished the scene to its fullest extent. He had a fine look at her nudity. Greedily he saw the way his Bathseba washed her breast, belly and southern parts. The rapturous scene enraptured the baron and with all his lust he made a move to drink the dust of her nakedness. As the roughly-hewn huts were secluded, the yard was wholly covered by thatches. The next moment gathering all his courage he took her inside her house. No surprise, the widow who was hungry enough or knew the purpose of the man, did not find any meaning in sheer protesting. Her dictum was that 'when rape was inevitable it should be enjoyed.' So she calmly bore the circumstantial boon.

Guruputrappa's love for Gauri, his neighbour lingered longer than she had expected. The pretty bride withstood the Gauda's affair, for she had not enjoyed it sufficiently. In fact, fate had blundered against her leaving her barely satisfied. Over and all, she was not strong enough to brave the feudal lord who had been notorious in the matter. So the affair between them flourished inevitably. But one day, Gauri's son who learnt the volpone's illicit relationship with his mother, decided to send him to hell. He determined to murder him in his own house. But Guruputrappa who smelt the inimical danger, finished the enemy before he could rise up. Verily he murdered Gauri's son. Nobody knew hence what happened to the village Hamlet. Nor could anyone suspect the hands of village knight either? Like the rustics, the Gauda too mourned over the early death of the young guy. But how can a truth be hidden forever? One day smelting her paramour's blunder, Gauri burst out into wild tears and cursed the cunning criminal. She said, 'thereafter, like the Odeyas of Mysore, the Pattans ought not to get any male issues in their progeny.' Indeed Gauri's affair with him ended thereafter as she moved to her brother's village far off. No wonder, thenonwards the curse worked wonderfully well and in the coming years, Guruputrappa lost his sons one by one. But miraculous enough due to a holy swamiji's honest blessings, the curse did not work after a hundred years. Therefore, Harish's father as well as the boy Harish survived the anathema. But the creeper of the family did not grow tall and wide and subsequently the Pattans lost their way over the village politics.

Ramachandra, Harish's maternal uncle who came to his house just had been Harish's ony relative. He lived at Kakamari, a nearby village in Athani taluq of Belgaum district. He had been a prosperous businessman and had his daughters well-educated. Indeed, Ramachandra had been Gangamma's only brother dearest or disliked. However, Ramachandra did not come to Harish's home as often as as a relative he was expected of. Only recently he had shown some interest in the matter apparently for the reason Harish had obtained good education. He knew Harish had reached a marriageable age too. But his wishes behind his revival of interest had still been undisclosed. Like a clever choir-master he posed his face as a well-wisher of his sister Gangamma and her only son.

'Oh! Hari come indoors. My dear knight,' Ramachandra called in Harish with an enforced affection, while the latter was shortly to step indoors. Although he heard the news of his kin's unexpected arrival, Harish had not yet prepared to face the situation. At once he heard the welcome, he got a bewildering feeling, a variety of thoughts, a thrill — 'Had he come to disturb our harmony? What must be his axe to grind us? Does he wish me become his son-in-law?' However, his immediate concern was to see the man without any malice.

'How're you uncle?' getting in Harish spoke.

'I'm fine, tell me how you're,' Ramachandra smiled upon the blue-clad youth in consideration of his credentials — a Gold Medal or an eligibility to secure a college job. A brilliant achievement! When he heard that Harish was about to get a job his round face flowered like a heavenly redrose.

'Shall I think you'll get a job soon?' the kith intruded eagerly to confirm the news. As he was a businessman he would enquire others twice or thrice, though the other parties were annoyed by his overgrilling.

The youngster made a nod in a positive way uttering no words.

'How much salary will you be entitled to then?' the uncle asked the scholar, while his business like manner persisted in each of his enquiry. He was earnest to know the figure of salary, Harish was possibly to receive. But when Harish turned reluctant to leak out statistics, the old man displayed his deepest annoyance.

There was a pause.

'I'll get ten thousand rupees per month,' Harish at last respected the volpone's crude sentimentality.

'Oh! it'll be quite sufficient for your family,' Ramachandra spoke giggling.

As Gangamma and Harish had already dined late, and as the guest too had taken something soon he reached home, nobody bothered about eating anything there and then. Since it was not yet a time for their supper their lively chatting prolonged. Nor did they think of any drinks like tea, coffee or Sarbat or any light tiffin either? Gangamma who had succeeded in her politics by inviting Ramachandra, her brother to think about Harish's future, had been delightedly triumphant today. She was very happy on this starry evening.

'What about your mother if you get a job somewhere away?' Ramachandra burst out unaffected.

'She'll be here,' Harish spoke briefly glancing at his mother who expressed her displeasure to stay behind.

Throughout the heart-to-heart talk about this and that, the words 'marriage' and 'family' were frequently articulated. Harish desired to stop taking any further interest in the matter. He wished he should have not been there. On the contrary, the woman kept on abetting the two to talk over the issue of his future. This made Harish look shy and occasionally reserved. He hardly succeeded in exploring the truth that was hidden behind the conspiracy of elders.

When Harish withdrew to his room, a volley of disconnected ideas occurred to him specially about his marriage. It was natural, he thought. No wonder, then he had been twentysix, certainly a marriageable age. Round in health robust he was. He had already begun to think about his career and family and decided to mould his future on a strong base. Truly he had decided to marry Shobha, his sweetheart. Albeit, he had a singular doubt about it. He wondered whether his mother would approve his wedding with that exquisite maid to whom he had already subscribed his heart. The reasons were not unknown to him or to his mother. Already in her view, Lalita, Ramachandra's daughter was born for him. He remembered his mother's occasional descriptions of Lalita's talent both at home and school, her nymph-like-face and rare splendorous glitter. The mother had compared her to Sita, Savitri, Mandodari and those hundred others whoever had been the great beauties of Indian myths and legends. Perhaps she did not compare Lalita to Helen and other Grecean Venuses, as she did not know their names. Whenever Harish had unresponded to her queries, she would tease him by saying that soon after his marriage Lalita would teach him any lessons. No wonder, Gangamma's concern was to maintain her family ties which had then been on decline. Besides, she wanted a less educated girl of her own caste to become her daughter-in-law. Another factor the old woman believed was that a daughter-in-law of her own choice would serve her better than an outsider. Indeed, more worried she was about the urban girls most of whom she supposed had lost their chastity prior to their wedlock. Occasionally she thought highly educated girls did not work at home, nor obeyed their husbands. Even she felt they would dominate their men and if time demands, would desert them for their paramours. No doubt, the old Gangamma had seen and heard many of such crude village events.

However, in the absence of Harish, the hectic talk between Gangamma and Ramachandra continued. Each of the two looked at Harish who went into his room without respecting their feelings. In his absence they discussed about the viability of matrimonial alliance and its consequences in case Harish declined the offer.

'Would you think he'll marry Lalita who is ten years junior to him?' Gangamma asked her brother sardonically.

'Age does not matter, sister. What matters is money, worldly status, family ties and tradition,' Ramachandra spoke pointedly in a business like manner.

'Maybe true brother. But today-boys dislike girls who are too junior to them. However, you think that money and status can compensate the age difference, don't you?' she spoke complainingly.

'Yes; but have you forgotten the fact that you married my uncle who had twelve years been senior to you?' he gave her a smile. Besides, without allowing her to reply, he went on harping upon the matter.

'Did any one of you have any problems of unhappiness about your age? No, not at all,' he himself added it comically. He was sure she did not turn incredulous.

'No, but due to modern education, everything is changed today. As my knowledge goes,' Gangamma continued, 'these days no boys or girls marry persons of too much unequal age differences. Of course, some men marry even women of higher ages,' replied she. Presently her talk was interrupted by him.

'Is it really true?' he asked curious.

'Yes,' she said definitely.

'Now let's take a close view,' burst he coming to the matter. 'Can we think Harish will like Lalita?' Ramachandra came to the point of immediacy.

'See Ramachandra, you're not an outsider nor is Hari an indifferent boy? You're both my kindred. In this regard, I favour you as I favour him. You know I'm already seventyfive, however, I possess good health. As his mother, what I wish is that he'd marry soon and set up a family. Also he'd marry a girl less educated but from our own clan. Surely what I'm telling him time and again is to marry Lalita as I wish her to be my daughter-in-law. So I want my kinship flourish together,' so spoke the elderly woman anticipating her companion's views.

'Have you enquired him?' her brother burst sporadically. He was much intent upon the matter.

'I've done it but he has not yet agreed.'

'D'you mind if I ask him personally?' Ramachandra turned earnest. As he had solely appeared there to strike out an alliance, everytime, he displayed gestures of impatience which his sister could not know as she was a simpleton.

'However, you are too curious to know, it is not a good time for us to enquire him now. Let's think about it in the morning tomorrow,' she tried to pacify the business tycoon.

There was a striking silence.

But Ramachandra felt it should be now or never.

'Don't worry, my son is a man of round and clear character and he has never disobeyed me,' Gangamma mollified the annoyed bull. Her consolation worked but only until all dined at nine in the evening. Occasionally she idolized her son while she did not neglect her brother to maintain balance. But during the next hour, they were busy and engrossed again in the matter. If Harish was cool and calculating, Ramachandra was nowhere but in his dreamland, while the old woman struggled hard to balance the scale of their emotions.

When all of them finished supper it was nine o' clock, the time for retiring to bed. But because of her brother's persistent insistence to hold a closet with Harish then itself, she changed her routine. She asked Harish to sit beside her and closed all doors and windows. This was done in a bid to avoid neighbours' overhearing of their discussion which could slaken the family image.

'Hari, your dear uncle has come here to wish you happiness and prosperity in the days to come. Wait, wait till I finish,' she quipped him when Harish hurried to say something of his own. 'As he loves you,' she continued, 'he has decided to give you Lalita, the beauteous dame in marriage. So it'll be a nice thing for all of us if you accept this proposal of wedding,' she finished her say strenously unaware of the masquitoes swarming over her.

'Let me think about it later.'

'How many days d'you need my boy?' his uncle could not discontinue his business tone.

'Lo, ever since you're born, I have been advising you to marry her. So it's left to your goodself to take a good decision soon. And bear in mind that it's a high time for that now,' the elderly lady broke in anticipation of a positive reply.

But Harish who was at cross-road sat still as if he had not heard anything.

There was a long silence followed by the old woman's coughing.

'Tell me whether or not you want to marry my daughter,' Ramachandra who believed more in frankness than in somehow persuation, put his nephew a final question.

True Harish was surely embarrassed. He became more confused than ever before. He could not understand the intricacy of situation. Nor did he detect elders' plot. There was Shobha in his heart, while Lalita came before him. Whom to marry? How to avoid the other? The mother and uncle pressing there, while Shobha held her own sway. Anyway he had not harboured any ill-will towards Ramachandra. Since he held his mother very dear he was not to oppose her. Quite well he knew her love and affection for him. His genuine concern had been to respect her at any odds. As he could not rebel against her, his desire for Shobha began melting away. So he could not resist those Herculian figures before him. However, he thought, questioning her at least once was worth a try for his own welfare.

'Mother d'you have to wish me marry her?' There was an utter dismay in his face and his entire body shuddered.

'Why not? D'you have anyone in your mind ?' the righteous mother struck him boldly.

'Yes.'

'Oh! who's that?'

'Shobha, a very good girl, beautiful, virtuous, humble... My good friend and classmate throughout my education career. If you don't mind, I'd like to marry her,' Harish turned aside shrinking.

Natural enough both Gangamma and Ramachandra turned shocked, spellbound and bewildered by Harish's rebellious desire to marry someone else, while there was one in their own clan, own class, own caste, indeed in the same family circle. She wondered whether he did not see the fruit that grew fresh in her own garden. Failed was she to apprise the harsh fact that he did not like the homebred melon. For a moment or two, Gangamma remained in a state of coma. But when she collected her inward vigour, she turned fully aware of the old tradition. Then she decided to hammer the hot-iron at the right moment. Indeed, the ball was in her own court.

'My son, d'you know that I'm your mother?' began she gently.

'Yes,' he burst mildly.

'Then d'you acknowledge me as a person who can ask you to follow her sincere advice?' she asked him imposingly. There was, no doubt, a mark of wisdom in the line of her argument.

'Certainly I obey you,' he looked all faithful.

'Then why you said you'd marry someoneelse whom we have not seen, not heard, not liked, not even imagined or thought of?'

'No mother; don't mistake me. Simply I expressed my honest wish. But let me make it clear that I didn't tell you that I must marry her,' he spoke diffidently. His face turned downcast.

'Is it really so?'

'Hundred percent!'

'Alright,' she began, 'you know I'm your mother, an experienced person, and a person whose words you're not supposed to disrespect.'

'That's right,' the boy bore the mother's vigorous stance.

'Then will you marry Lalita?' she stopped abruptly expecting the only word 'yes' and nothing more.

'Yes,' Harish gave the expected word of obedience. He could not go against her whether in personal or family matters.

'Thank you a lot. Truly you're my son. Indeed, my life is successful,' the jubilant matron expressed her declamation.

'Sons must be like Harish sister. See how he obeys you,' Ramachandra gave a word of appreciation to his future son-in-law.

'Okay, it's already ten-thirty night. Now you can go to bed,' the mother told them affectionately. But returning no words of reply, or a nod, Harish retired to his bed. The mother and her brother who failed to understand the boy's heartfelt desire, sat there discussing about the success they attained during the hour long persuation. The tradesman appreciated the elderly lady's defty argument and unfailing persuation, while he praised Mr. Harish for his conformity to tradition that had been inherited by all. This day he was extremely happy as his mission was nearly fulfilled. No doubt, Gangamma too was gladdened for the reason she could get a right daughter-in-law. Then she expressed him her desire to see Lalita, the adored girl of her mind whom she had not seen in the recent years. No doubt, after a little while discussion, both decided to go to Kakamari the very next day. Anyway Harish's mother had taken the decision in her own interest. So she determined to see Lalita and stay with her for a week or two. By this she meant that she should fix up the ring ceremony, the wedding day and the responsibility of marriage.

However, the next day dawned only to enerve Harish who had already been agitated by the development of latest events in the house. It was to affect his life undeniably. It was a sort of failure for him. Marrying an unwanted young girl in the event of a beloved fulsomly ready to embrace him, looked genuinly awkward. So he felt ashamed of this. Anyway, it was not even nine o' clock morning, his mother having arranged everything for her son, left the village for Kakamari, her birthplace. Ramachandra was there to take her over there. However, it all took place in a casual manner. But they knew not Harish was very much disgusted by the binding. At times even he toyed with an idea of rebelling against his mother's indifferent decision. But his respect for tradition subdued him. As he had his mother alone alive, in the paramount absence of his father who lost his life in a motor accident, he never liked to lose her by frickling her with his distressing problem.

It was not more than four hours his mother had left for Kakamari in the company of his uncle, there came a village postman. By the time Harish had rushed out just to go towards the village market, a shrill voice came from the Carpenter's club of Kumbar Street. It was Sangappa, the village newsman who had brought him a registered AD. So Harish stood awaiting it.

'Sir, you've a letter,' Sangappa said in a hurry.

'You could've dropped it in the box outside there,' spoke Harish lightly.

'It's a registered post, sir. It might be something very important,' the other cut it seriously as if he had brought some urgent news.

'Alright where should I sign?' Harish asked the other humorously.

'Here sir,' the postman pointing the space, handed over the letter to Harish and within a minute or two, like a wild species, he disappeared. As the letter had been from Shobha Harish dropped his decision of going away. He got indoors. The letter bad the following note written by his dearest :

Shobha H
D/o Satish K, Former MLA
"Shantiniketan"
1005, Opp. Ravi Ray's House
Gol Gumbaj Road
Bijapur-25

To

Harish Pattan
Near Carpenter's Club
Pattar Street
Telsang.

Dear Harish,

I'm well here. I hope you must be well in the company of your benign mother.

The present letter is of utmost importance. I've to talk to you very urgently over the urgent issue of our marriage. You know you've loved me and I know I've loved you but what about this affair? Already it is two months over we met each other at the Old Relics near Bijapur. I don't feel you'll tolerate the recent developments that're taking place in my house. My daddy has asked me to finalize our matrimonial alliance within a month and he has warned me that if you want to marry me you should come to our house for the brideshow formality. Otherwise, I'm sorry to say, he thinks he'll marry me off to a distant relative. No surprise, my mother has asked you to come here soon to set right the possible deadlook. You need not worry about your unemployment. She is ready to help you in getting a job which is not impossible for us. Indeed, if you marry me my parents'll be all glad.

Hence, I earnestly request you to visit us within a day or two. You don't know how my days in your absence have become longer than years.

I'm looking forward to see your presence.

With Best Wishes.

Yours ever lovingly,
Shobha H.

The letter did what it should. It wonderstruck the man who presently read it with all his heart set earnest. Though he had anticipated it, his mother's binding upon him had enerved his impulses and, like a withered grass, he had sat down sapped of his self-assertive energies. Presently Harish spoke nothing; he moved no limbs of his for a while and the emotions of his resolute heart stopped their motion. He was at a crossroad. He did not know whether he should choose Laxmi or Saraswati. Both mattered most — but one to him and the other to his family. Lalita, the Laxmi had already been selected as his bride if not by himself, but by his care taking mother. But his love lay for Shobha and certainly he wanted to get her as his life-long companion. But today destiny looked to have scored an upper hand against him at the current critical juncture.

Fate, Harish felt, had no regards to his wishes whatever. Meanwhile, many thoughts occurred to his humbled mind. Like Hamlet, the Denmark prince, he became a vexed gentleman, serious but awkward. He knew he did not possess sufficient strength to rebel against the Mother-Force. The questions 'what I'd do? should I go to her without any waste of time and strike a deal? or should I follow the mother, the tradition, the meaningless lot? troubled his weakening heart. He found many questions but no solutions to anyone of them. So riddles remained riddles. Timid words came from his timid heart. Harish got up and began walking in the house. He saw various articles — urns, furniture, books, selves, calender, photos, wall-paintings etc. — but all looked as if speaking about his utter cowardice. He turned right and articulated something to himself. Things turned to him to be in a muddle. Thereafter, he walked to frontyard and then to backyard but only to enhance the quality of his indecision. Was he conscious of anything at the moment? Although he was deadtired of his walk, he did not aspire for a relief. His house looked like a madhouse. Despair struck him strong. He did not think of anything until he sat down tired on a cot nearby. However, within an hour, he found himself fast asleep. Presently as the Greeks say he was a brother of dead.

The afternoon sun was still in the western horizon burning and shining. Dense clouds had gathered a good deal. Rain was not unlikely to downpour within an hour or two. People were busy in collecting their corns, grains, clothes kept in the sun to dry. The crowd at the nearest temple where a marriage was underway was afraid of the dark climate that was likely to trouble its business. But the happiest of village folk were neither the people at temple nor the elders but the children — joyous and sportive in the open. They were playing games such as hide and seek, Ganga and Jamuna, Kabaddi, anipini etc. Even some of the elderly boys were at field for cricketing though they knew no rules of it. The hustle-bustle of these miniature adults was a medlex of sounds quite inarticulate. They were in their own world of revelry and merry-making. None dared to disturb them in the outdoor air. Even it was worthwhile to see their ventures. Particularly a section of women had partaken special interest as most of their younglings were in their sportive entirprizes. The joy of these young mothers was unbounded. Besides, the blue sky, the frequent thunderbolts, the rainbearing clouds, the absence of sun as it was hidden behind clouds, the coolest breeze, the watery smell were obviously exhilerating to the tenderminds.

The pleasant atmosphere, indeed, made the rustics happy at homesteads.

The summer rain had hardly begun when Sangappa, the village postman arrived to Harish's house once again. So on the same day, the same postman. He ran helter skelter when he found none at the lane. There was an apprehension of some danger in his face. He straightway jumped into Pattans' frontyard and knocked on their door. But to his surprise nobody gave him any sounds of response. Anyway he found the door unlocked. He saw a fan whirring inside. Thereafter, tension stricken, he knocked the door violently. Yet no sound. However, at the repeated knocking, a voice in a low key was heard and within a minute or two he found the door thrown open.

'Your, sir, your.... 'Sangappa who stepped in stammered.

'Who're you?' At once a man cried. Harish who was just awaken had not yet been in his senses. But within a short while, he identified the fragile figure intruding. He saw Sangappa who had already delivered him a letter in the morning.

'Sir... Your, Sir... Your,' Sangappa's inarticulation continued but that did not help the yawning figure comprehend any message. Nor did he display the telegram he brought with him either? Indeed, Sangappa kept the paper in his pocket and endeavoured to inform Harish, the news of his mother's death in a gruesome bus accident.

'What you're telling Sangappa?' Harish irked by his inarticulation, urged him anxious

'Sir, your mother.'

'Yes, what my mother?'

'She dead... bus... accident, Sir,' Sangappa burst into tears himself first. As he had been very close to the family, he began sobbing a great deal, while Harish turned sorrowing. At once, their blubbering reached the neighbourhood. In consideration of some apprehension of disaster, the vicinity people hurried there at once. So did the children merrily playing outside. Instantaneously the whole locality was filled therein. When the telegram was read and reread and the news was briefed and briefed again to the bystanders who were a multitude most of the gathered turned atearful, asorrowful and asobbing. A few of the womenfolk stood aside could not help weeping. Since they were friendly with the family, always they shared their joys and sorrows. Soon some relatives hurried there and began the next preparation. Mr. Yashavantrao, a village doctor with a car, took Harish and his friend to Kakamari where the calamity had taken place.

The time Harish reached his uncle's village he went to the spot of casualty which had occured because of a lorry collision to a KSRTC bus in which the poor brother and sister had travelled together. It was told to them later that when the bus was overtaking a lorry which was driven by a Sikh drunkard, the collision between them happened. The bus, people said fell in a rivulet drainage. But to men's surprise, the only persons died in the accident were three villagers of Kakamari that included Ramachandra and Gangamma, while others had simply lost their limbs; some, their legs; some got their arms fractured; and a few received fatal internal injuries. Already the dead bodies were rescued with the help of local people and they were transported to the Government Civil Hospital, Athani, the taluka headquarters of the region. The time the postmortem was over, the dead bodies of Harish's relatives were brought back home. The accident, indeed, had taken the villagers by a big shock. The kindred of both the dead and injured had rushed to the spot and had been greatly mourning over. The ghastly tragedy had befallen the small village. Soon Harish, Umesh and the doctor rushed to the house of Ramachandra where the two dead bodies had been on a grand display. The whole funeral ceremony was conducted by the deadman's relatives. When he saw the holy mother's body, Harish burst into distressing tears — quite emotional.

'Oh! Mother,' Harish broke down aloud 'mother you went away in spite of my obedience to you.' Umesh also sobbing consoled the bereaved son. As the bodies had already been kept for a long time, the village elders decided to arrange the funeral soon. Already the kith, kin, and dear ones of the family had appeared for the last rite. The lack of any relatives on the part of Harish, did not delay the last rites of the dead who were presently to retire to the burial-ground. Within an hour, the *Puza* of the bodies was performed and the people akin to them, paid their last respect to their departing favourites. When the dead bodies were lifted up by pallbearers, Harish's sorrowing increased manyfold and it did not lessen until the mother's body was placed in God's acre, along with her brother's. Then, like cattle, people began scattering homeward. The hysterical outbursts of relatives had already been waning as the dead were no longer in their presence. The dismayed men and distressed women started to get back home. However most of the villagers were uneducated, they pondered over the issues of life and death, the two ends of human strife. The aged people were talking to one another in groups of twos and fours and occasionally in more numbers. They spoke about the futility of human struggle. One of the elderly persons burst to the gathered that life is a long labour in a purposeless universe.

'See how Ramachandra and his sister joined the rank of eternal absentees today,' an old man spoke like a seer-commentator.

'But death is certain,' his companion muttered.

'True but fate should not summon us premature,' said another. There was, indeed, a grain of truth in this man's predilection. The mourners simply nodded to the oldman's mark of wisdom. Intermittently a dead silence swept over the multiple. So the muttering sounds were heard and unheard, found or not found any answers to the riddles of life. Some young people heard only questions, while a few old people spoke and spoke endlessly. This continued until the large crowd disappeared and a deadly silence overpowered the graveyard.

Now, after an adequate mourning was over, Harish was with the companions with whom he had come there. Soon they asked him for the return journey. At this time of parting with his relatives, the latter gave him abandant consolation. Now Lalita was also one amid those who gave him solace. She appeared singular to his grieved soul. But he showed no signs to talk to her. As he was disgusted with the family, he made no moves even to support them. Naturally Shobha's recent letter had perverted him. So in this moment of despair he neither tried to talk to her nor thought of assuring her anything. The whole situation had disheartened him. His mood was tragic if not pessimistic. The atmosphere was then looked to him slipping away. He saw only pain and agony ruling the world. Now and then he felt of lying down to weep fulsomely until his soul could turn purified. But the idea did not look practical. Soon he wished to part with relations. So Yashavantrao and Umesh took him to the car and within a few moments, they left the village of Kakamari once forever.

The village to village journey was over within half an hour.

When the car reached Telsang, it was evening. Harish who had till then slept in the vehicle was taken into his house. Inevitably Umesh was asked to remain with him for a few days. The next day the rites pertaining to the demise of the departed were faithfully executed and the village folk consoled Harish.

Like the road vehicles, the sorrowful days ran fast. On one of the Sundays in his chatting, Umesh began recollecting Harish the memories of those bright days passed in the elegant company of Shobha. Umesh who had already married wished his friend an early marriage. No doubt, by this he presumed the infliction of despair could be greatly reduced. No surprise, when Harish briefed the other the content of Shobha's letter, Umesh urged him to see her at once and fix up the marriage in time. However, in the mood of recent grief Harish was quite reluctant to undertake any such moves then. But due to the circumstantial pull the friends decided to go to Shobha's house. Of course, in the absence of his parents, Harish was free from any bindings now. So on account of Umesh's benevolent insistance, Harish with him went to the blueeyed belle Shobha's house firm to marry her.

Oddly enough, though a fortnight ago she had dispatched Harish a letter, Shobha had not yet found any reply. This annoyed her tender feelings. Anyway still a span of fifteen days was ahead. Occasionally Chandramma, Shobha knew, inquired her about the strength of Harish's love. Despite the fact Shobha convinced the matron, a room for a doubting lingered there in the family. Nor did Harish send a message to her either? But people who knew Harish's mother's demise could not accuse him of it either. As the disaster struck the family, how could he write anything to her? Maybe he had decided to marry Shobha, he was not in a mood to inform her either about his forebodings in regard to his marriage with her or about the saddest end of his mother at home. Indeed, the gap of communication misled the two involved in the eternal drama of suffering. No doubt, misunderstanding begets misunderstanding just to complicate matters. But here the misunderstanding as a result of information gap did not mislead either Harish or Shobha as we think of.

However, the moment the friends stepped in, neither Shobha nor any family members were outside to welcome them. Only a stubborn maid-servant as per the landlady's suggestion dared to disallow them inside. As the situation demanded Harish asked her to call forth any member of the family present.

'Hai Hari come in,' at once a melodious voice burst forth. It was indeed Shobha, the very belle.

'Hello,' the two reacted promptly stepping in.

'How d'you do?' Harish put it lovingly.

'We're fine. How d'you do?' a counterenquiry was made.

'Fine.'

From the situation it was implicit that all were fine.

'Please adore the sofa,' Karisma said them following her sister. She took no time to recognise Harish. She readily greeted the brothers-like looking friends who relaxed then. Soon Chandramma came out of her kitchen in glee and got an introduction of them who visited them for the first time. She was happy as Harish had turned up without fail. The image of her son-in-low flashed her mind and she saved no efforts in getting a deeper acquaintance with him. She asked him several questions and made an affectionate enquiry about his family. But when she learnt the demise of his mother she turned tearful.

It was not an hour afterwards Satish, Shobha's father came home. He was really all wonderstruck by the intime presence of newcomers. So far he had held a common view that Shobha's desire of wedding Harish had been just a mere streak of fancy and nothing more. But the very presence of the man-almost the wouldbe son-in-law looked to him like a cinema scene. Anyway he greeted the guests in a genteel manner. He too was touched by the event of Harish's house. Then all dined together.

Thereafter, as everything was already determined, Harish briefed the matter to Shobha when they sat down together in their home garden. Shobha became jubilant when she heard Harish had got a post of lecturer in a Jamakhandi college. Another news was that the president of a private college of Banahatti had agreed to appoint Shobha a college teacher. So the series of glad news made the tragic event effacable. Thereafter, Shobha began discussing the matters pertaining to their marriage settlement.

They began discussing of their wedding. Remedies to the unseen problems like their living together were hammered out. They undertook a decision that soon the event of their wedding was over, they should live together in Banahatti. As there was three months of summer holidays, they had no inconvenience too. After the important matters were settled down they began remembering of their campus days. They recollected the heartfelt memories of the past. Often Harish's brilliancy in studies was apprised as a singular event and it was talked of with a sense of exhilarating pride. A salient feature of the talk was that throughout the togetherness Shobha was adored a woodland nymph. But they rarely talked anything abscene or awkward as Karisma, her sister sat amid them. She too looked dazzling and behaved quite socially. It was an unforgettable moment of joy to the gathered souls. No matter, whether believable or not, the whole episode reduced Harish's despair and he returned to the esoteric world of his future mate.

It was nine o'clock the moment the elders gathered at Shobha's house for the formality of 'bride show and marriage fixation ceremony.' As everything was already decided and the hearts of the two were entwined into each other, nothing as such remained unresolvable. Nobody worried about problems. The only thing that engaged the undivided attention of them was the responsibility of wedding. However, it was implied that Satish was to bear the marriage expenses and arrange the event. The dignitaries attended the function included the heavyweights of Satish's vicinity. Soon these people of importance who were his friends and relatives declared that the two parties were ready for matrimonial alliance. They said Satish would arrange the marriage. All turned glad by this and a talkative person asked about the wedding day. Immediately the date of it was also fixed and it was duly announced. The men then discussed the prospects of the wouldbe newlyweds. No wonder, the same day, the ring ceremony was conducted. Harish was presented a nice dress and golden ring, while he presented Shobha, his dearest, a fine saree that cost him most of his savings. Truly a costly gift. A grand luncheon was hoisted without a delay. After the merrydinner, Shobha's friends talked of her fortunes in marrying Harish. Good or ill after a final exchange of heartfelt joys, the next day, the friends left for their natives.

Great is the joy of wedding in everyone's life. It was not an exception to Harish and his sweetheart. As the marriage date was fixed, the invited people of both the parties came to a huge temple which was hardly a furlong away from Satish's bungalow. The crowd had gathered outside and in the varandah, while the bride and groom sat on specially decorated chairs. Since Satish as the former MLA of Bijapur was an important person of the town, he had invited a large number of citizens. Sufficient variety of food was prepared for the occasion. Both men and womenfolk were joyous at the colourful event. Harish and Shobha sat together on dais and their close relatives and friends stood beside them rejoicing. They were extremely happy of the whole phenomenon. At the appointed time the sloka of wedlock was observed and the bride and groom garlanded each other. Harish tied a holy tali around Shobha's neck and the music band gave a sweet accompaniment to it. The things went as they were planned and expected. There was an in-depth joy and contentment in the hearts of the wedded and those who honestly attended the function. So things found their way in spite of hurdles in the way of newlyweds.

It was not long after the marriage, the newlyweds went to Bangalore for a pleasant honeymoon. Harish went there with Shobha, now his wife and stayed in her brother's house at Azadanagar, Mysore road. They were well received by the host family and for a week they travelled to notable places like Mysore, Ranganthittu, Belur, Halebid, KRS garden etc. Happy were the newlyweds whenever they were in each other's company. They also whiled away much of their time in their moods of love and flirting. Of all the places, they found parks and their bedroom pleasant and bestirring.

'How d'you find me my darling?' Harish asked his sweetheart at a moment when they were sitting together in Cubbon Park.

'Excellent my dear. I'm very lucky to have got you as my life partner. Had I been married to my distant relative, I think, I'd lose my heart,' Shobha expressed her pent up feelings.

'You're selfish dear because you say that you're alone fortunate. Don't you know that I'm also lucky in getting you as my wife in spite of some unknown force that worked against me,' he finished it mysteriously.

'What d'you mean. Did ever anyone or your mother disliked your marriage with me?' Shobha enquired him anxiously.

Then Harish explained her how his late mother insisted upon him to marry Lalita, a relative of the family. He also added her the events that quickened her unfortunate death. Similarly Shobha told him the problems that could beset her desire to get him. The two spoke vividly of the events that could nearly deprive them of each other.

'Anyway we're very happy, aren't we?' Harish refined the tone.

'Certainly Harish,' Shobha smiled upon him putting her hands on his face. Thereafter, they became more jovial moving to the moods of love. As nobody was sitting near them, they were not troubled by any outward happenings. She spoke to him as lovingly as he did to her. Now and anon each kissed and patted the other as gently as they could. They had sat body to body and talked spontaneously. No domestic worry or outward nuisance beset their moments of joys. They were happy. However, Harish kissed her more than she did and the latter responded to him with bewitching smiles.

'You look like Helen dear,' smiling upon her fair colour, Harish straightway crept his hand into her stirring her emotions. Unable to withstand the heat of her body, at once she took him into her arms and their moments of ecstasy continued quite for an hour.

Harish was an intelligent person. He also wished a luxurious life. He had an appetite for reading, enjoyment of sex and observation of nature. It is true intelligent people aspire for more gratification of sexual desires. Dark body passions haunt them. Unless they get any satisfaction of their itch, they behave like irked wild animals — impatient and unhappy. As it is lucidly reflected in much of English fiction, the people who are hardworking and hobbyless, seek solace only in women's bosom. Surprisingly to such men one woman is never sufficient. They cannot help loving more than one or living with many. No doubt, most of the intellectuals do not addict to bad habits such as drinking, smoking, gambling. But their Achilles heel lies in more craving for carnal passions. They go to women as often as they desire of them. Only a woman's body can relieve their inward hunger; abet their creative power and sharpen their sensibility. They will be arrested in bodily passions and in the absence of healthy sexual intercourse, they never feel comfortable. In matters of sexuality — healthy or not, they use their women like anything. Even a few of them do not hesitate to exploit them only for sex. No wonder, many sexual violences occur in part due to their violent fleshly ills. Sexual bout is a prerequisition to such men to keep them in good humours.

Good or ill, Harish was hardly an exception to this sexphobia. He had an inimical weakness for women. He made it clear to Shobha that her breast was his heaven. He found her thighs as his resting place, a consolation for his bodily grievances, a clear solace for his psychic agonies and agitations. But Shobha was quick to appreciate his physical illness. She had already known his pitfalls and prepared to satisfy him.

It was ten o' clock night when the supper of Harish, Shobha and their hosts was over. Shobha's brother provided them a very pleasant atmosphere in the house. So when after the meal Shobha came to his bedroom what she saw was a sex wonder, a madness for sex! Already Harish was inside lying. Seeing this she was wonderstruck to realize the fullest potentiality of her husband's virility. Now her foremost concern was to tame the bull. They were enjoying what the Lord bestowed upon man at the primal hour. No member of the house, no moods of dismay or dejection, no external hurdles, disturbed their hours of longer eroticism. They were fully sunk into each other emotionally. The intertwining was complete, meaningful and sufficient for the day. Each soul had surrendered to the other. No quarrels or skirmishes affected their mingle. Blessed were the two in the union.

When the newlyweds returned home, the colleges were reopened. Both Harish and Shobha got jobs and they were asked to join the institutions in the first week of June. So they did it. Their married life began and both were given residential quarters in their respective towns. However, Harish did not like his wife daily come to Jamakhandi. Instead he put up his family in Banahatti and he himself made up and down. The early years of their married life passed in their juvenile enjoyments and worldly festivities.

Admittedly in the beginning years Pattans led a peaceful and productive life. They were well-settled down in their jobs and they discharged their duties as faithfully as any ideal employed householders could. Harish, now a man of thirty, had bought whatever modern equipments the family required. Even, after some years, with their savings and a large contribution made by Shobha's parents, they bought a nice RCC house in an extention area. This house was in a central place, equidistant to important amenities of the town. The suburbia was posh, advanced, well developed and most of the residents were highly cultured and dignified. True the majority were in the government services.

It is in the luxurious company of VIPs of the town, the Pattans got a roster of social relations. Since the couple were lecturers in degree colleges of Jamakhandi and Banahatti, many intellectual luminaries became familiar to them. In addition, due to their literary activities, they became the venerated pair in the hierarchy of elite. They participated in cultural activities as well as socio-religious festivities together and mixed up with people-wealthy, intellectual, religious and political. During vacations they toured distant places as literary voyagers. No doubt, in the eyes of populace, Pattans were reckoned as public characters.

However, three years of Pattnas' married life passed away but without any sign of an issue in the family. When the issueless husband had been in a mood of despair, to his wonder, one day, his wife was found three months pregnant. What a happiness!

A rare chance of becoming parents! The couple became overjoyed. When Mrs. Pattan became fully ready to deliver a child, she was sent to her mother's house in Bijapur. No doubt, Harish too stayed at his father-in-law's home nearly for two months as that was his summer vacation.

The next month, Mrs. Pattan gave birth to a male child and found the kindred jubilant over the matter. The child was healthy and fair in complexion. Karisma loved the baby utmost. Chandramma's happiness was more than the happiness of any others for it was the first male issue in the second generation. Even her eldest daughter who had been in London had not yet given birth to a son.

In the subsequent winter Mrs. Pattan, a happy mother, returned to Banahatti. Karisma too accompanied her for assisting. Unfortunately soon after arriving home, they heard the news of Satish's death. This, for the time, shocked the whole family. In the inevitable absence of Shobha, everyone, daughters, sons-in-law and others attended the funeral. The local VIPs, family friends, common laity mourned over the demise of Satish, one of the former heavy-weights. As he could not attend the ceremony, the Chief Minister had simply sent his condolence message over the death of his one time political favourite. Harish too was very sorrowful about the unfortunate event which recalled him the end of his mother years ago. He worried a little more because the marriage of Karisma was yet to be done and nobody was there interested to take care of Chandramma. However, a few days later Harish and Ravindra decided to part with the other with a domestic settlement. It was decided that Chandramma should accompany her son to Bangalore, while Harish was to take Karisma to his house hoping to take care of her future. He did it for the reason Karisma had been a beloved to Shobha as well as to himself. But he rarely displayed it to anyone.

The days of sorrow about the old man's demise passed away. Already Shobha's mother had been with her son in Bangalore. But Karisma remained with Shobha because she could help her in domestic matters. Another reason, many times, Karisma herself said was that she liked her sister very much. Anyway Karisma who enjoyed Shobha's confidence lived in the family as a fourth member of the estate.

Karisma was an attractive young woman. Harish was not wrong when he said that she was prettier than his wife. This abetted the dame to love him fondly. But her loving him was not sexual yet. She looked like Damayanti, the forest princess of Indian legends. Her face was oval in shape and fair in complexion. Slender was her waist. Red as coral were her lips and her teeth shone like jasmine. Her eyes were like lotus blooms and her face was enticing. Her angelic beauty attracted Harish greatly. He could not talk to her without passing a word of appreciation. Even occasionally he praised her in the absence of her sister. Whenever he was in her company he saw her with an eye of love. No surprise, her superb beauty had made her a celestial bride.

It is because of her beauty and pleasant behaviour, Karisma a B.A. graduate found a place in Harish's adamantine heart. Everyday she assisted her sister a lot. Even when the boy Venkatesh grew up in age, she continued doing most of the domestic works, for Shobha had her college duty. Moreover, as the elderly lady trusted her sister, she did not doubt about her relationship with her husband. Similarly neither Harish nor Karisma as they preplaned showed Shobha any signs of their lovemaking or anything of that sort. Although a close relationship developed between the two nothing about it was known to the landlady.

Harish's love for Karisma was beyond the measure. No doubt, his love for his wife was equally constant. This helped him to strike a balance between the two. By this he cleverly kept his wife on tenterhooks. None either in his house or outside, knew that Harish had an affair with the young belle. Truly speaking Karisma too had been much interested in carnal passions. So she did not care for her chastity. Presently each of the two behaved like a married couple but they were careful enough to keep the elderly lady ignorant of it.

Harish loved Karisma all the way. Whenever his wife had gone away either to college or for shopping, the outlets were immediately closed. He gave up all his heart to her. Even whenever Shobha was at work engrossed in it, while passing this side and that, Harish used to touch or kiss his sweetheart. Karisma too did it but her romance with him was secretive. However, as years passed on Karisma became deftier in instigating and satisfying him. Admittedly Harish's sensuous follies were colourful and enormous. He tried his best to renew his love for Karisma. He did everything to cool her beseething heat. Harish's occasional jokes and ambiguous anecdotes regarding the matters of love and women were a clear indication of his love for the fresh maid. Although Shobha doubted it now and then she did not take them seriously as her trust in the other was firm. Only she knew it best that Harish had been sexier than herself and she tried to the best of her ability to control him. But she did not know he was beyond her control.

An added advantage to Harish in regard to his love for Karisma had been their odd college hours. His college hours had been in the early morning, while Shobha had to mind her college work at the day time. She returned home only in the evening. So during the absence of her, the moments of joys the Romeo and Juliet shared were enormous. In this way the largest disaster at home was averted.

Daily when Harish came home around twelve, his French love was ready for him. As she was not particular about her chastity, always she thought of pleasing Harish whom she called *mama* (uncle). The word *mama* to her sounded very romantic and it gave the man maximum thrill and pleasure for his lovemaking. One day when Shobha went to her college to conduct a gathering, the two had a splendid chance of blisssharing. Harish had taken every care to avoid the children from the scene. He kept the doors closed. Both then ate snacks he brought. Harish showed Karisma his perpetual love by presenting her new dress, ornaments etc which he did not do for Shobha. In fact, he made every effort to keep his dearest in cheers. But this was done in the absence of Shobha. This made Karisma give her heart to him.

'D'you really love me darling?' Karisma used to ask Harish although she knew he loved her well.

'Hundred percent. I love you more than I love your sister,' Harish used to reply. He downgraded his wife to appease her. So he was a wise fox to steal the heart of a woman.

'That's true. How far can we continue this affair without legalizing it by wedlock?' the beauteous lady put it anxiously. Her hand was on his shoulder scanning.

'Why you worry. Let's be together here until the matter requires some serious consideration. Anyway now you're twenty-five only. Besides, until Shobha trusts you, our business will flourish unabettedly. After all, I help you, don't I?' he consoled her.

'Alright,' smiling upon him, Karisma put out his shirt, while his hands took away her body into confidence. The act of kissing began. He loved her kisses more than he loved her sister's. Very amusing this was. Indeed, the forbidden fruit looked sweeter. Actually he loved both without underestimating anyone. Already the two souls were bare-bodied on a de luxe bed. Each kissed the other and their kissing prolonged. The caress made her wet, while he lipped her tight. Throughout the nightmare of carnal-emotionalization, he found himself on her and both felt ecstatic. Karisma's occasional suggestions went in making them more blissful. New things, new ideas, new ways helped them to be pleased greatly. They were regular *Kamasutra* readers too. They enjoyed the joys of flesh as and when their whims enforced them. No mental discordance persisted there. In case one of the two got any misunderstanding, the person caused it used to clarify the doubt through reconciliation. This helped them live at peace and to lead a life of pleasure in the house. During the third year of her stay Shobha gave birth to another son christened Ashok. In the following year a female child was born. More the number of children, greater was the elderly lady's faith in the younger. Consequently, Karisma grew stronger and did whatever she could without transgressing the boundary line of her commonsense. During these years of Karisma's stay, no doubt, Harish's love for her grew constant and headlong. As the bodily connections increased, he decided to marry her by persuading Shobha. He wished Shobha should accept the new situation. He could not avoid any of them. As for Shobha who had already been a mother of his three children and as for the other she had already won his commendation, he had ever been on tenterhooks. Adjustment with both was indispensable. The man, no wonder, desired a second wedding. It was not only Harish but many people of his nature toy with an idea of marrying two women. No surprise, many people in the past succeeded in doing so without losing their first wife. However, this was subject to certain conditions. Men married second time either because of the first wife's demise or barrenness. Or they remarried in case, the first wife committed adultery. Similarly in case the first wife was innocent and uncomplaining, her husband married once more. Maybe the wealthy married times and again as they were all powerful. Cases of second marriages in India because of one or the other's dislike or discordance were numerous. No matter on what ground men marry for the second time, cases in which both wives live together are very rare. However this is possible in case both wives happen to be sisters or the first bears no children or she is a weakling for that matter.

Nonetheless, today polygamy is practised on many grounds. But in most of such cases, husband's life with the first wife is unfruitful or disastrous. This has also increased the rate and tempo of divorce. But today woman's social position is strengthened due to modern education, familiarization of European culture in regard to man-woman relationship and empowerment of them. Still many reasons have placed women on equal footing with men throughout the world. In India because of empowerment, educational facilities and reservation policies women have highly been made aware of their rights. The mass media have played a vital role in reorienting them to the mainstream of modern life.

Indeed, women are quite alert today. They rarely desire to remain imprisoned in their houses. Equally, as they get education, they dare to protest against men's total domination. This is specially applicable to the highly educated women and women in service. They assert their rights and fulfil their privileges. At the same time, they declare their independence in case their husbands try to make their lives impossible.

In the light of these ideas Harish was thinking whether he could do somethig to own Karisma forever. But in the Indian context, he did not think, it could be easily materialized. Since he had been known to Shobha's imposing behaviour in case of crisis, he could not dare against her in a very significant matter that could affect his whole family. He knew Karisma had been more than twenty eight then and he had deliberately rejected some of those who wanted to marry her. The lady of his heart too did not dissent it solely on the ground Harish would give her a life. As she had already sold herself to him, naturally her idea was not unfair. But at no occasion she was envious of her sister. Her only wish was to marry Harish and lead a life in the family without disturbing it mainstream.

However, Harish was not courageous enough to take any bold steps. He simply continued the status quo. So did Karisma. Their courage in this regard was marvellous. They had lived together with illicit affairs because of modern medicare. Thus Karisma never got pregnant. Indeed this had been the strongest point for Shobha's faith in the young dame.

Years passed the way Harish and his unofficial wife expected of them. But how can the thieves be escaped? One can deceive the other at most for three times but he cannot repeat it fourth time as the other would be on his defensive. It is almost a universal law that truth has to emerge victorious ultimately. As illegal things come to light in course of time, illicit relationships are discovered or exposed to. It is what happened in Mr. Pattan's house.

One day when Shobha was cooking while her sister in bathroom, she heard her daughter's cry. At once she rushed towards the baby in order to look after it but meanwhile she saw her husband rushing into the water closet where Karisma had, a short while ago, gone for bathing. By this she was taken aback and instead of looking after the baby, she could not help peeping through a window of the bathroom. The scene was indubitably awful. One barebodied and the other clothed. Two souls together. One kissing and the other merely accepting it. Shobha saw her husband embracing Karisma who was completely nude. To be sure, as the cry of Kamala continued, Karisma asked him to rush to the cradle. But the man's love lay not in his children nor in his wife, but in the very dame, an embodiment of sex just in front of him. Karisma wished they should not be caught up as Shobha was very much in the house. So then Harish went off in response to the child's screaming. Shobha who had already been on the spot after smelling the undesirable calmed herself. She knew it best that patience saves souls. However without any suspicion or enquiry she passed the day, she thought over the issue very considerably.

Nor did she look at them with cynicism or ill-will? The strongest reason for her consolation was Karisma's neutrality to his kissing although she could do it. By this the elder excused the younger. She dismissed the idea that Karisma might have corrupted him. So, her doubt only about her husband became firm. However, she finished her work and as usual she went for her duty, a fear attached to her future frequently bothered her. Many thoughts milled her mind throughout the day. But Shobha was a woman of enquiring spirit. Therefore, she never believed in second thoughts or did she trust back-biters or gossip-mongers? She took events only after a cool and calculating enquiry and evidence. Now she determined not to accuse either her husband or her sister unless she found a clear evidence in the matter.

Yet on another day thereafter, Harish came home early and as usual he took Karisma to his bedroom in the absence of

Shobha. Both then began chatting in their mood of love and romance.

'Come on my angel,' he said.

'Wait a minute. I'll close the windows,' Karisma spoke for safety.

When she came back Harish had already become barebodied and in that very appearance he made her nude before he could take her into his arms. Kisses on Karisma's scarlet tinted body were downpoured and her body smelt his love alone.

'Shall I swim over you,' he spoke gently.

'Always welcome. Shall I tell you something more,' Smiling upon his southern parts, she eyed him with lust.

This encouraged him in the deal.

'What's it?' he asked her earnestly.

'Oh! my dear. Take it for certain that my body is an Eden Garden of various fruits and you're allowed to enjoy any of them,' she put it emotionally. Now her whole body was enthralled by his touch and breathing.

'Wonderful! Wonderful!' he thanked her passionately.

Harish controlled her elegantly; talked in a volume of voice which anybody if present in the house could hear. Surprising enough, already a person was couched beneath a huge cot right from the morning solely to catch the culprits redhanded.

It was none but Shobha who instead of going to her college, to clarify her doubt, sat under the wooden object. She did it to know whether Harish was really in love with her sister. However the emotional outbursts of the two hurt her to the core, she tolerated it all along to explore the unknown territories of human mind.

Karisma said Harish that her desire was to drink the creamy layer of his sex. Naturally as he cared more for her body he liked the bedgame heartily. Harish was also following her every suggestion. Now and then to get optimum satisfaction out of the task, she asked him to change sides or to press her straightway.

Be it as it may, she wanted to enjoy the course as much as he wanted it. So she made every effort to control his exercises, while the man exploited all his skills to satisfy her itch and to find himself emotionally benefitted.

When they came to an end fully immersed Harish took her on himself. Like a Nayar woman, Karisma began assaulting him smoothly which he whole-heartedly welcomed. As he kissed her, this time, she did it to him. Both were to be greatly benefitted in the new deal. But soon they lay exhausted. Then they began chatting about trivialities.

'D'you think this affair can be continued for the years to come?' he asked her sardonically.

'It depends upon you and her,' she said nervously.

'Anyway I wonder whether I can live without you,' he expressed his pent up feeling.

'Don't you like my sister dear?' she embarrassed him by her enquiry.

'I like her as usual. But her body is not as pleasant as yours. She has lost the charm of her body. And while she falls in my arms, she does not participate in the course as actively as any man expects. So she falls below the line. I'm cocksure comparatively she is less sexy. In fact, that much is insufficient to cool the heat of my body.'

'That may be true,' Shobha's sister nodded.

'Although she's quite healthy, her body has become cold. Besides, she does not kiss me as frequently as I do or as you do, my dear,' he laughed at her boisterously.

'But don't you enjoy her breast which are bigger than mine and more pleasant,' the sexy queen smiled upon him which roused his passions interminably. He took her into his bosom and lipped the melons of her blouse pleasantly while it greatly hurt the figure beneath the cot.

When Harish and Karisma's acme of sexuality was known, to teach them a lesson, like a Protean figure, at once, Shobha rose from the space of darkness. She stood there and saw them still cris-crossed in blissful-posture almost unaware of her derogatory presence. Suddenly an idea occurred to her that souls in love should not be disturbed. Alright but it was an illicit affair and already they had enjoyed it enough. Anyway she liked to have a good look at their acrobatics wholly naked and one. After a little longer she came near them and patted gently on Harish who like a boy afraid of snake, arose by the shocking touch. No doubt, within a moment, the brimming souls stood up in front of her, all-trembling and in dismay. Naturally as soon as she saw her sister, afraid of the situation, Karisma fell to her feet in lieu of a grand apology. So did Harish to botch up the matter.

Shobha stood still looking at their trembling. The time they dressed they sat beside her in perfect obedience. The bed had become dirty and it wore an ugly look.

'Why you did this?' Shobha asked them.

There was a long pause.

Karisma felt it difficult to answer, while Harish tried his best to work out an alignment.

'Don't worry my dear its the fruit of the same garden. It doesn't matter if I enjoy it sometimes?' he tried to mesmerise his wife.

'Shameless. Nonsense. Didn't you feel satisfied with me?' she turned angry. 'I'm also a fruit.'

'No,' he gave a word of reply.

'So does it mean that you need one more fruit?' she burst enquiringly.

'Yes, but the house fruit only. See,' he persisted, I like your sister on two grounds. The first and more important is that you're in service and we've three children. So if I marry her, it will be very convenient for all of us. We'll work and she'll look after the household,' with occasional smiles and hiccups the master gave his candid justification.

'Why you want her while I can do both,' Shobha turned singular. 'I can satisfy the itch of your banana,' she added it vulgarly causing a ripple of wild laughter in the room.

There fell a silence.

'Karisma, you're laughing. You don't know what life is. Don't you want a separate life for you?' the elderly lady asked the maid but found no reply.

'You said you've one more reason. Shall I know it?' Shobha enquired her husband desperately.

'See as I'm not satisfied by you in this matter, I want her also,' said he. There was an air of displeasure in the entire room now.

'D'you think I can't gratify your carnality,' she retorted. 'Can I challenge you,' she added it vehemently. There was a sense of fortitude in her behaviour and she turned heroic. At once, she put off her saree to prove the point. But Karisma saved the situation by consoling her. Consequently, all sat together. Harish sat her right side while Karisma adored him afar. Shobha looked like a judge but disillusioned at that in the domestic matters. No doubt, things she had till then believed had gone wrong. She had thought her husband would remain faithful to her cause. What she doubted of his constancy in love when once he saw a friend of her with an eye of lust came true today. She felt her husband was a wayward spirit. To her the whole citadel of man-woman relationship appeared slipping away. She was very sure that as a woman cannot love or live with two husbands, a man too however rich, grand and impressive, cannot love or live with two wives. She recollected a common adage 'one cannot serve two masters.' As she read widely, she thought that if a man married two, he falls short of gratifying both sexually; or he fails miserably to balance them however pleasant. In her context, she meditated, however Karisma was her sister, people could not like her to be her co-sharer. An adea of imbalance that could arise in case of difference struck her strong. Anyway she was trying invain to solve a riddle.

Days passed but the stagnant conditions continued longer than the victim of it expected. However, Shobha startled by Harish's illicit affair with her own sister imposed certain restrictions on them. She asked her husband not to repeat the event. But to her dismay, she found him thick-skinned in terms of uprightness. Harish made it clear that he could not discontinue his affair. As a result, often she could not help wrangling with him. One day when she saw him flirting with Karisma, she tried again to end up the deadlock.

'It doesn't look nice on your part my dear,' she told him with an air of uneasiness.

'D'you think it's wrong if I talk to her?' pointing at Karisma Harish exploded.

'No, but your sleeping with her together,' she spoke ironically. Possibly she did not know with him she had exchanged heat for heat. Now she recollected their bodily get-togetherness of the previous day. Although she had not eye-witnessed the event, she got this known to her by Venkatesh, her eldest son, ten years old then. This boy was of an unusual strength. He could answer most of her questions. In fact, he helped his mother while collecting any information. But he never did it on his own. Equally Shobha had not asked Venkatesh to have an eye on them. Only occasionally she used to make a mild enquiry of him. So this time, particularly in response to her questions, Venkatesh told his mother that when he came home, he saw the father and aunt together.

Shobha repeated the old question 'Why you slept together?'

But neither Karisma nor Harish made a move to reply her. Heavy silence prevailed there. Karisma glanced at Krishna's image hung on the wall, while Harish gazed at a pretty doll kept on a stool in the corner of house.

Finding her husband cold and indifferent, the elderly lady turned towards the younger. She inspected Karisma thoroughly. Then smiling upon her diffidence, she decided to ask her the following.

'Karisma you're my sister,' she put it cooly.

'Yes.'

'Then d'you have any right to sleep with my husband?' she broke the ice.

'No sister, but he wants me. Only as and when he forces me, I yield to him. Otherwise I never,' Karisma fumbled.

'Right then let me know when it started?' there was a curiosity in Shobha's enquiry.

'This's only the third time we did it,' the younger replied deftly. Though for more than hundred times, she had slept with him she did not tell her sister anything true and provocative. She was shrewd enough to be mellow when Shobha inquired her severely. Indeed, she was a practical minded woman. She knew the down-to-earth-reality very well.

'Ok! then the fault is more of your *mama's* than yours. But what's your stand about your chastity?' Shobha threw a bitter look at the ailing maid.

'I don't think about it very seriously. What can I do after all. Though already I'm thirty, none of the family is worrying about me. You know you married at 24 but I am not getting married though I am 30 already. Father died years ago, and Ravindra settled down at Bangalore as if he need not worry about my wedding. While mother can't do this. Since I'm not yet married, how can I withstand the heat? So at times, I can't help succumbing to him. Tell me sister is it wrong on my part? Sister I hope you can understand me,' Karisma fell asobbing and she was on the edge of tears now. This convinced her sister about the gravity of situation. Therefore she took not much of time to realize the importance of a husband for a well-grown up woman like her. Besides, the family position, the death of her father, negligence of her brother and her husband's lack of moral integrity, added their own mite to her dismay and dejection. Although she had tried to the best of her ability, she had not yet succeeded in striking a matrimonial alliance for Karisma. Already she had requested her friends to help her in the deal.

Under these cirumstances, Shobha could not help excusing Karisma's faults. She viewed her erring lightly while she took her husband's follies quite seriously. When she turned aside towards Harish she saw him laughing. Meanwhile he took her into his arms in the very presence of Karisma. It did not look abscene to him. In fact, now he thought, he had been the master of two. Be it as it may, the younger lady blushed it and went off to the room meant for her privacy. Cleverest was her act of closing the door of their bedroom. This coaxed Harish and he tried to take Shobha into his confidence. By this he intended to bring a reconciliation between Shobha and himself. Indeed, he tried to persuade Shobha to consent him to marry Karisma.

'Why you're so hard-cored?' he spoke to her lovingly.

'Because you're very inimical in matters of sex and women, aren't you?' she interrogated him smiling. Though she admired his robust health, she disliked his ways with women. But Harish was as much pig-skinned in this matter as Karisma. So they had a mutual understanding and they deceived the elderly lady everytime.

There was a long pauze.

'Why you want her while I'm here?' Shobha broke the silence.

'Forbidden fruit is always sweet,' Harish replied comically. But he did not know how his assertion was annoying. Indeed, it hurt her greatly.

'D'you mean you don't want me?' asked she.

'No, did I say it any time?'

'Then you shouldn'nt desire her?'

'Anyway ignore it as I love her only for sex?'

'You mean I can't gratify you?'

'You can but you're not as pleasuresome as she's,' Harish turned vulgar. Indeed, in several contexts the one lawfully married look unhappy about the other. This undoubtedly leads one or the other to turn to fresh pastures. It was what happened in Pattan's house. Ever since Mrs. Pattan could not cope with her husband sufficiently though she was sincere at that, Harish was not fully satisfied. Shobha's weakness, it was inferrable, in the matter lent a destracting tint to his carnal affairs. In fact, he hated Shobha not because she could not satisfy him, but because he wanted Karisma as she infatuated him everbefore. In fact, had he seen Karisma instead of Shobha as his girl-friend during his education, he could have married her only. This way he had turned to the other. However Shobha learnt that she should not leave him to Karisma's care and concern as it could jeopardise her as well as her sister's future. At the same time she began planning secretely to marry off Karisma, the 'interefering radical' by taking some loan or with her brother's assistance. In spite of this it was her duty to see that Karisma should not become pregnant. But she became helpless in the matter as the ant did not abstain from eating sugar at least once a week.

Thinking it futile, sometimes, Shobha conceded to the wishes of the loved ones at home. Karisma's animalistic desire stunned her. What a sexy woman! How bold she was to sleep with Harish even in her sister's presence! Everything looked awful and puzzling. She learnt Karisma's boldness in the matter of worldly issues, earthly desires and fleshly ills. Yet there was some truth. However, Shobha did not esteem Karisma highly, for the simplest reason that she was not yet aware of the right and wrong in life.

Over the years Harish's indifference towards Shobha grew alarmingly. He had become essentially a villain in her life now. He hated his wife's plan to marry off Karisma. But Shobha had been tenacious in the matter. She was right at that. To stem the situation, she had been trying hard to find out a bridegroom for her sister. One day she made a phone to her house for the sake of getting some important details regarding Karisma's biodata. But to her wonder nobody attended the phone save Venkatesh. This surprised her about Harish's business with Karisma.

When Shobha turned up home, she was furious about Karisma's waywardliness. But the moment she came home she did not find her at home. Soon she learnt that with Harish she had gone off to market. What a travel, what a pair, what a sordid affair! Shobha imagined their shopping and bodily togetherness. She knew they would enjoy the day in an unthinkable predilection. Certainly because of her absence she could not help think of this anomaly ever since it began in a mysterious way. Thereafter, she enquired the boy Venkatesh over the absence of them at the time the call came. As it had been an important matter about Karisma's matrimonial alliance, Shobha had greatly been enraged over their negligence. Presently she called her children in, while they were playing under a banyan tree.

'How are you kids?'

'Fine,' replied they.

'Papu d'you know I made a phone at three o' clock?' she put it angrily.

'Yes, I know it. What's happened? Why you're so much upset?' the eldest son spoke hotly. The boy did not like to be cowed down by his mother. Because he was round and clear in character. Certainly this reduced Shobha's acidity.

'Alright; tell me where was your aunt by then?' this time she smiled upon the boy affectionately. She was all eager to learn details.

'She'd been in bedroom,' the boy spoke frankly. He never pretended.

'May I know what she's doing there?' to find correct replies now she distributed sweets to her children Venkatesh, Ashok and Kamala. She also gave eatables to Vinaya, Ashok's friend but she sent him away as it was a sensitive matter. Then she closed the door and rested upon a sofa. The children sat beside her and were all eager about the enquiry.

'Yes, tell me,' Shobha continued, 'where the aunt was sleeping?'

'Don't you know where she sleeps. She sleeps on the cot,' the boy jeered at the mother. Wonderful was his awareness. What his mother did not know for the last eight years, he knew it. His way of speech was marked by clarity and preciseness too. He knew many things by his sheer dint of memory.

'Who else were with her then?'

'It was daddy.' This time Ashok too joined Venkatesh, while Kamala was busy in eating *ladus*.

'Why you want all this?' the eldest spoke casually without any ulterior motif.

'No I simply like to talk to you children,' Shobha pretended priding with their naughtiness.

For a while she found the playfulness of them amusing.

'Ok! I'll give you more sweets but you'd reply all of my questions,' she spoke to them like their teacher.

'Yes, Yes, I'll... I'll... We'll...' the boys turned happy and cried overjoyed. Shobha gave them more sweets and more sweets to Venkatesh in consideration of his help and cooperation. She appreciated his agency for exploring the hidden and strange.

'Right Venkatesh tell me now,' broke she.

'Ok! Ask me any questions,' he spoke remaining active.

'What daddy and aunt were doing my boy?' she asked it in low voice as she was afraid of her neighbours who could cook up any raw stuff and spread it in the colony.

'They're sleeping,' the boy equally imitative of her voice replied her in a low tone. Really he did not know why his mother spoke like that. He was innocent.

'Ah! your daddy was there?' Shobha due to a sensation put it loudly this time.

'Yes, he's with her,' the boy spoke louder than his mother just to excel her in speech habits.

'Nonsense! You'd not say it loudly,' the matron rebuked him

mildly, while she asked the other miniature adults not to make the house littered with dirty papers.

'What they're doing?'

'They're sleeping, did I not tell you just?'

'You've said it. You're a nice boy. But had they closed their eyes,' Shobha felt it very difficult to extract the nature of the unknown phonomenon. Precisely she wanted to examine whether Harish slept with her for a particular purpose. She enquired this as Harish had promised her to discontinue the affair. But she did not know how to ask the boy about it. Again for keeping him in good humours, she presented him a bit of special sweet which she had preserved for herself.

'Yes boy, I know you answered my questions cleverly. You're a wizard,' she praised him. 'Did your daddy close his eyes while sleeping?' she asked him again as if the boy did not understand it earlier.

'I think he didn't close his eyes. Like the aunt beside him, he kept his eyes open. See he kept his eyes like mine now,' the boy mimicked the countenance of his father.

'Really did they sleep on one another?' Shobha was fastidious while asking this. She, at once saw the windows and doors in a bid to confirm herself whether anybody was overhearing her conversation. She knew how such things led to disastrous happenings even leading upto murders.

'Yes, mummy,' the boy told a truth. It did not matter to him as something wonderful.

'Rascals... scoundrels...nonsense,' Shobha began hurling big words at the two absent souls. Her words looked strange to the boy. He did not understand anything of these new words which of course, occasionally he had heard from his teacher whenever he did not do his lessons at school. But Venkatesh noticed the top of her voice.

'Why you're chiding me?' frightened he burst out.

'No boy, no, no; I'm not chiding you but someone else,' Shobha consoled him despaired, while she was impressed by her son's innocence. She thought 'what guiles he knows a poor creature!'

'Then why like my teacher Miss Christ Everta, you said nonsense?'asked he.

'No, no, it's not for you but for your father. You don't have to worry about it,' said she patting him again to find out replies for her remaining queries.

'Shall I know why you abuse him?' he asked her eagerly before she could continue her cross-enquiry.

'Because... because... he slept instead of doing any works,' she managed to regale him.

'Mummy shouldn't they sleep?' the boy persisted.

'No, they can sleep,' assuaged she. Her face was melancholic in demeanour.

'But you take it seriously?'

'No, no; it's something different boy. Take this fruit. D'you know what it is? It's a fig fruit grown only in the Himalaya. Right you may go to play now,' she gave the children fruits. She did not know she had already given them much. The kids being happy of their mother's spectacular love went off to play with whatever toys available there.

Indeed, Shobha relaxed for a while. Then she inspected the household. An immaculate evidence given by the boy took her by agitation. She rushed to her bedroom eagerly. An elaborate survey helped her to see some lengthy hairs lying on bed and at close looking, she found them to be Karisma's. She picked up one of the hairs and amazed at its length and colour. In comparison, it looked longer than her's and also brighter. As Karisma grew in an affluent atmosphere than the one in which she herself grew, she felt, she had grown up healthier and more beauteous. But she never envied the dame for such trivial matters. She understood that in beauty Karisma excelled her, but in virtue and intelligence, she felt, Karisma could not match her even in the days to come. Mostly, she thought, Karisma's shapely limbs and charming look might have infatuated Harish to loose his heart to her.

Indeed, like most others she did not hate her sister. The reason was not far to seek. It was her own sister whose father did not live long to marry her off. Besides, Karisma was an innocent chap, very young in age and mental make-up.

Shobha did not forget her mission in the quagmire of these daily sexual intricacies. Already she had wasted an hour. Then she rushed to a cupboard and checked it up in search of Karisma's photos which she had wanted to send for some prosperous bridegroom. But at the first stroke, she found not the dame's photo but a photo in which she saw an image of Harish kissing Karisma on a sea-shore probably at Karwar beach. When she glanced at them she was wonderstruck. She questioned herself about Karisma's photo with him? : Where both could have romanced? What might be the background, the ulterior motif of their love-making. She had an eager look at them. She knew it clearly that her husband never took her either for a walk or for a picnic or for a sightseeing ever since the first childbirth. Alas today she found volumes of evidence of his villainy and womanizing. She amazed while looking at most of the photos in which both Harish and Karisma stood together viewing or eying each other with love. Either they had been, as photos displayed, in romance or walking together hand in hand at waysides or on hillocks or one going ahead and the other following closely at the other's heel smarting.

The innocent landlady went on observing other photos too. She did it with an added interest. The whole business seemed her worth a try. While the time passed, she saw two albums of pictures ever eager and breathtaking. At last she found some of Karisma's photos good for her immediate concern. Presently she stopped her inspection. Then Shobha came to the kitchen as she found hungry. Thoughts about thieves and their villainy flashed her mind as frequently as she recollected their ventures. The photos just seen verified the boy's witness. The whole phenomenon looked wonderful. 'What she should do? How she should find out a salvage to this riddle?' she asked to herself. It looked a hideous affair and an uncontrollable cancer. However she was eating, her mind was elsewhere. She took her food mechanically squatting on flooring. Nor did she worry about her children then? Of course, Karisma looked after them very well and for which Shobha had ever been thankful to her. As it was an odd time and as they were playing outside, she did not mind it. But she could not help worrying about the illicit episode. She thought both had been deeply in love with each other and had neglected her. Had either of the two been under her full control, she felt, she could have controlled the situation easily. Now she was sure that neither Harish nor Karisma spoke to her honestly. In fact, they conspired against her in the present matter. But in the interest of Karisma Shobha determined to marry her off at the earliest. Her misapprehension was that if she conceived, the whole family prestige would be at stake. No wonder, she fancied, in that condition nobody would select her. Certainly she was surprised about the precautions they had undertaken.

In this mood of reverie, Shobha left for her college in the middle hours of the day. The only thought recurred to her all the way was how to marry her off soon. Even she did not worry about the way she was riding her Kinetic Honda.

Not longer after shobha went off, the children were happy when they saw aunt Karisma homecoming. The dame held in her left hand a bag full of fruits, while she carried a bundle of package in her right hand. Since she looked tired of holding them, Venkatesh who loved her even more than his mother, dashed off to lend her a hand.

'Ah! Aunt's come!' screamed he.

'Hai... ai... i...!' the others cried. Their cry was hoarse and unclear as it was not articulated by one single figure.

Karisma loved the kids deeply. She was most affectionate towards them. Since she had been in the house for the last ten years or so it was she who had brought them up with maximum care and discipline. Admittedly Venkatesh loved her most. There was a very cordial affinity grew between them. Even Ashok and Kamala were very fond of her. They did not think she was not their mother. Karisma had fed and brought up them in such a way that they never disobeyed their benefactor. Whatever puddings she had she distributed them first to the children and then to her *mama* and sister. Only at the end she ate it as the last person. She was magnanimous still in many other aspects. Her impartiality won Shobha's laurals of praise always. Shobha loved her greatly because of her care and concern for her family. But she hated her sexuality. Indeed, as a member of the family Karisma had strengthened her tie with its master. On coming home Karisma kept things in selves; she gave every child some fruits or sweets. Meanwhile, the eldest boy burst forth.

'Why did you not return home soon?' he asked her without an air of enquiry.

'Why you want it, my boy?'

'Because mummy came here asking for you.'

Venkatesh said it eating an orange. Already the room floor had been littered with fruit peels and other rubbish the children made. The boy talked to her, while his juniors were at play outdoor.

'Did she really come here?' Karisma asked him as she found her sister's visit to the house rare particularly in the middle hours of day.

'Yes; she came here and gave us sweets.'

'Did she ask for me?'

'Yes; she asked where you'd been when the call came. You know, I attended it?' he said it finding fear in her face.

'May I know what you replied her?'

'I said you're sleeping.'

'Did she ask about daddy?'

'Yes, she asked about his doing then.'

'Is it? What else you told her?'

'I told her you're sleeping with him. But she enquired me many things giving us fruits,' the boy said it with an inborn sense of pride and hilarity.

'I'll also give you sweets. Come in Venkatesh. You too come indoors for sweets,' Karisma took the littlens inside and found them delighted on distribution of sweets. Soon she asked Ashok and Kamala to play outside. But she could not let the eldest of them for playing.

'Now tell me, did she ask you as to what we're doing at home?'

'I told you already?'

'Yes; but tell me once again.'

'See I told her you're sleeping together. Is it wrong for you?'

'No.'

This made Karisma burst into a scream of laughter. Since she did not worry about the misfiring, she was not afraid of it either. It had become an official unofficial event. Shobha too knew it. But no outsider. Indeed, this was in Karisma's interest.

However, presently what thrilled Karisma was as to why Shobha held an enquiry with the boy. Utmost amusement Karisma found was in the way the boy reproduced his mother's exact enquiries.

'You're wise. What did you say her then?'

'But tell me aunt is it wrong if you sleep with daddy together. We also sleep with him every night,' enquired he quite ignorant of adult relationships.

'No; absolutely no, my boy.'

'Then why she asked me these things? Once she also said 'nonsense,' '*Scondral* and something more I can't remember.'

'Oh! that's quite interesting,' laughed she.

'Yes, she said aunt.'

'Ok, it doesn't matter. Let it be. Tell me what else you said her?' Karisma looked more curious at this moment of enquiry. She was sure to know more and more funny details.

'She asked me many questions. But I don't remember most of them. Shall I tell you whatever I remember thereafter?' Venkatesh told the earnest woman in red saree ever attentive to his little expressions.

'Yes; go on telling whatever you said her,' Karisma gladly conceded to his desire of free expression.

'See aunt, I told her you were sleeping with daddy and your eyes were not closed. And like us you were playing. Many times dad was on you and you had your legs on him. Did he win the game?' the boy asked her curiously while Karisma could not help laughing at his wonderful leakage of her affair.

'No,' Karisma replied finding herself at a crossroad. She could not tell him the nature of act. But she consoled him saying that his dad won the play.

'Aunt,' he began, 'I saw you without any dress and I saw you sleeping with your eyes always open. But we don't sleep barebodied or with eyes open. Why you don't close your eyes while sleeping?' he exploded like a bomb. He was, indeed, curious.

Startled by the query Karisma sat stock still. Then smiling upon him, she decided to change the tone.

There was a grand silence.

And you sleep with him day times, while mummy sleeps with him night times. I don't know why it is so aunt. I think, because of this you can't attend to phone calls. Therefore, she might've used harsh words for you today. You know she said *scondral*? spoke he.

'That's true boy,' Karisma supported him.

Consequently Venkatesh who was patted by her, did not ask her any more either to upset her or to quench his childish curiosity. Turned happy about his wonderous vision, Karisma kissed him then. She also asked him for a kiss once or more. While the time moved she finished her domestic works. However, all this time she was grossly disturbed by one thing related to her permanent stay in the house. She was sure she could live there a long way. But her sister's attempts of marrying her off, annoyed her. Shobha's designs of avoiding her hurt her naturally. The dame was but under a wrong impression that anyway Harish slept with her sister also. She was of the theory of sharing, more precisely husband-sharing. She was aware of notions like computer-sharing, service-sharing, domestic-works sharing. Admittedly, she believed in sharing her mama. She did not know Harish was meant for Shobha only. It was out of this flawful conviction, the conflict in regard to sexual relationship in the family was arisen. As she was moved by Harish's handsomeness or his personality, she loved him greatly. His fair complexion and worldly wisdom had tempted her ever since she stepped in his house. In this dark light of thought, she did not mind to aspire for a new man. Hardly she desired an independent life. She bothered least about marrying a fresh man or setting up a separate house or getting any children. She just wanted to get the status of his mistress and desired a child as her protector. For this, her sister's liberal attitude was responsible. But even in this regard, Karisma failed to understand Shobha's genuine concern for her future. As a woman of carefree life she had just wanted to be satisfied to stay in the backwaters of life.

Presently an occasional domestic necessity led her to bedroom. A glance thrown thereby at the nearest cupboard surprised her. A photo copy of her taken with Harish at a hillside resort lay on the floor neglected. She picked it up curiously and had a nice look at it. 'I'm still very fine to look,' she said to herself as a matter of pride. Thereafter, she worried about its occurence. She felt it might have been thrown down accidently when Harish opened the cupboard. But no idea about Shobha's observation of it occurred to her fragile mind. Then keeping it in a box she moved away to relax.

An hour later, Harish who attended a function of poetry-reading in the city came back home. As he loved her the problem of owning her forever hunted him like anything. However he worried about it, he could not find out any viable solutions at the present. Also the idea that his wife would tease him irked him at times. He knew that she had been ready to inform the matter to her brother at Bangalore. Already she had threatened him by saying that the lady would be sent to her brother. However, he was grateful to her, for her withstanding of the affair. Now that alone made him cheerful. Meanwhile the clock chimed five o' clock and Shobha turned home. By the time, she returned Harish had been with Karisma chatting. Addicted to her what could he do? Both were gladly discussing about the function he had participated. Besides, he sat with her dallying. Indeed instead of stepping in the house, Shobha viewed them through a window backside. She held her breath when she saw Karisma and Harish in romance. They had closed doors while sitting together body to body. As they were aware of Shobha's bell, they prolonged the pastime until she could really come home. What a scene! Husband loving someone other than his wife? A clear betrayal of wedlock promise! All envious. She spoke to herself about the heartfelt pain thereby she got, or forced to do so.

The touching scene made its own effect upon the sensitive heart of the grieved lady. It was both pleasing and disheartening. Pleasing because it was an ideal affair man and his dame could have for a conjugal bliss. Anybody saw it could think that 'love should be like that.' It was disheartening because it was unlawful, openly carried, unnecessarily undertaken. She knew it victimised her. Surprised by this Shobha spoke 'Forbidden fruit is dangerous.' This startled the united in innermost space. Suddenly

Karisma spoke, 'See sister, *mama* has taken me though I didn't want it.' Then she escaped from his hands like a lamb fleeing away from wolf.

Having confirmed the 'theft,' in came the elderly lady. She did this to avoid the treacherous neighbours. Really the affair was disgusting. She knew in the coming days Harish had to go for a paper evaluation work for a full month. She planned that in his absence she should fix up a groom and marry Karisma off. Right was her modest calculation. Already by her a move had been undertaken. She knew one of her friend's brother was to see Karisma shortly. Natural was her awaiting of Harish's departure for a month or so then. Only with this solace, she bore the abominable.

'Venkatesh come here,' she told the boy.

'Yes, I'm coming.'

'Where're Ashok and Kamala. Ask them to get in,' said she.

The boy called the others and all of them rushed in with loud sounds and childish behaviour. Meanwhile Karisma had been in kitchen preparing tea for everyone. But Harish remained at bed just like a sick horse.

'Ah! You're resting still?' Shobha asked him with her head downcast. Her voice was ironically cast.

'Yes,' he smiled upon her coolly. Soon Shobha approached him but only to be pulled by him. The moment he held her, she protested it vigorously. In the transaction more resisting she became harsher he turned. The time, meanwhile, she walked away, he pulled the end of her saree and most of it came out in his hand suddenly.

'Hoi... oi... i...!' cried the children in alacrity. Seizing the fanciful moment, Ashok, the playful boy fell in her flying saree and the girl stood beside hugging her mother joyously. However, he did it, what he gained was only crumbs. Only he had her cloth in his hand, while slyly she stood aside in her undergarments. The scene looked quite touching to onlookers. But Shobha did not look happy by any of his playful activities. She was in an air of dismay. By now Karisma who got in with tea burst out boisterously.

'See he's not satisfied by you also. He wants me too,' Shobha chided her sister. Then the younger helped the elder to put on her saree. When Karisma was not far away from her sister, Harish got up at once and took both the ladies in his arms and stood in the middle of room wildly dallying. He kissed them making a fervent appeal to live together. While Shobha dodged him, Karisma stood still locked in his net. He held her dear. His move to bring them together was not successful. He sat between them as Krishna between Satyabhama and Rukmini. Neglecting him Shobha took the cups and distributed tea to her children, while Karisma gave it to Harish and took a cup of it for herself. All joyously sipped their tea with love and cordiality.

Months ran as days moved fast. It was April. The summer weather was very hot. There were no storms in the sky of Banahatti, a semi industrialized town. Owing to a large number of trees in the location, there was no burning sunshine. Besides, the shady trees in the garden kept Pattans cool and happy. Be it as it may, cooler was the inward sensation of all except the unhappy landlady. The mango, the guava, the custord apple, the papaya and the berries gave them necessary fruits. Next to them, lemon, vegetables and the like secured them things for cookery while palm trees yielded tender nuts in the warm days. Children played joyously in the garden. Pattans enjoyed all thing. No doubt, the garden gave ladies flowers colourful and sufficient. There was red rose, jasmine, boganville and the like. Again roses had been available in various colours and sizes which lent fragrance and adored their heads. So ladies did not go out without any garlands. Pattans' house which had been in a strategic locality was quite big. It stood on an half acre plot projecting itself as a gorgeous mansion in the surrounding. Some of its gothic structures gave the impression that it should have been built by the British years ago. Admittedly all people had a singular impression that Pattans had been rich and dignified people. None whether an outsider or an insider could deny this. People also viewed them to be good in character. But to Pattans' surprise or fortune, their neighbours did not know that lotus however impressive sprouts from dirty mud and shines thereby.

It was eight o' clock Sunday evening when Ravindra and Chandramma came to Banahatti. Now they had been on a serious mission. The mother had already been hunchbacked, while Shobha's brother had been a different person from the image she had had of him in the bygone years. This happened because of his henpeckedness. Ravindra was not a man of fortitude and individuality. He did not have his own voice in family. Though an intelligent civil engineer he had lost his previous vigour and voice. His wife was predominant. A bossing woman. Therefore, Ravindra had become passive and helpless. Even he did not like squabbling with anyone though it was fair in the deal over any matter however significant. He resolved problems only with prayer and persuation. Though due to his wife's pressures, he wanted not to help anyone of his family, he had somehow determined to see Karisma get married off. Therefore, in response to Shobha's telegram he appeared there along with his old mother.

Truly the sisters became glad by the arrival of their mother and brother. Now, after a span of many years, they could talk and enjoy the company of each other. In the presence of the mother the glorious memories of their father returned to them nostalgically. It was a chance for them to recollect their kith, kin and dear ones. The past that nourished them and the past that brought them many moments of joys and the past that made them jubilant danced barebodied in their hearts today.

Surprisingly when it was five o' clock, the talk about bride showing began. Already Shobha's friend Sangeeta had come there with her uncle Yamunamurthy to see Karisma for her brother. Presently they had been seated upon a sofa placed in a hall. The other side sat Chandramma, Ravindra and the children who were curious of the event. In the absence of Harish who had gone for exam work Shobha was busy in managing the whole affair, while Karisma unhappy about the event was dressing in her bedroom. The young lady did not expect this. Everything came to her shocking. Truly the moment she welcomed her brother and mother, she had not suspected them of this mission. The strangers who came there to see her in connection with a marriage alliance, took her by wonder. Sometimes, she clenched her teeth and cursed Harish for his long absence. She did this as she did not want anyone except Harish to swim the ocean of her heart. Indeed, he had already entered her garden. Karisma cursed her sister. She did it at times and again. But she did not dare to display anybody her displeasure and that alone saved the matter.

Undoubtedly, the auspicious occasion demanded Shobha to introduce each other. She did it faithfully. Everyone loved her sociability and her air of equality. She introduced her kindred to Sangeeta, Yamunamurthy and to her brother.

So within an hour everyone became familiar with each other. No one felt isolated at the occasion.

Soon Karisma made her difficult and unwanted appearance.

Thereafter, all became alert about the auspicious environment and felt at home.

'May I know your name,' Sangeeta's uncle asked the bride, while Mohanraj, the groom was curious.

'It's Karisma,' the bride put it politely.

This pleased one and all. Mohanraj and Yamunamuthy, Chandramma and Ravindra were optimistic about the situation, while Sangeeta and Shobha were serious about their execution of plans. Sangeeta found no unpleasantness in the bride. But how can she look into the inner details?

'Your age?' Mohanraj broke silenty.

'Twentyeight,' the bride put it briefly as her male counterpart had deliberately put it concisely.

'May I know your education?' Sangeeta shot for the first time.

'I'm a B.A. graduate.'

'Where did you have your education?' Mohanraj asked her for the second time. By this he wanted to thrill himself by talking to her.

'At S.B. Arts College, Bijapur,' the lady's reply was pleasant to everyone. She looked fine every time they saw her.

'May I know what kind of husband you like?' Sangeeta spoke to her humorously. But the lady turned shy and denied any reply. However, had Harish been at home she could have disclosed it. Now she did not do it as none was there to support her cause good or ill. Even none in Indian context preferred to reply such questions as this. This was attributed to women's timidity.

'Can you read English?' Yamunamurthy, a traditional man, asked her to read a paragraph of *The Hindu* which he suddenly placed before her.

'I wonder whether she can't read it? She is an intelligent woman,' Sangeeta supported Karisma, while she rebuked the man with a sense of dry humour.

'Alright! Doesn't matter,' the landlady chatted with alacrity. Presently everyone — man or woman turned towards the point of attraction. They looked at Karisma with an added curiosity.

"Government to withdraw Vehicles given to Ministers" Government vehicles provided to ministers and non-officials will be temporarily withdrawn from Wednesday with the scheduled issue of notification for elections to the Lok-Sabha.

The ministers cannot meet district officers for review of development work. However, the latter can meet the ministers by way of courtesy, according to the model code of conduct for the elections.

'Stop it... it's sufficient,' said one and all.

Karisma had read out a piece of information about the election code of conduct. She was amazed to hear the applause of guests present there.

'It's very good, very good!' the eldest of the group exclaimed with a sense of satisfaction.

'She's got English education uncle,' Sangeeta cut in.

'A nice reading!' Mohanraj complimented.

'Have you learnt cooking?' Sangeeta asked the lady. But her question sounded strange as every woman knows culinary art.

'Yes, I know it well,' came Karisma's prompt reply.

However, at the end of show, Karisma was asked to retire inside. By any measure the 'show' had been successful. The bridegroom party was happy both about the bride and the background of the family. They had no problems regarding her age, education, personality. Nor did they doubt the bride's character either? As per their knowledge Pattans had been cultured people and the belle had no boyfriends outside. No further enquiry in regard to her character looked essential for anyone of them. The moment luncheon was over, the parties decided to finalize the fixation of wedding business.

'Madam now we're glad to talk about the details of dowry, ornaments and the conduct of wedding,' Yamunamurthy spoke with perfect confidence.

'Well, let's do so. Are you satisfied with the bride?' Shobha enquired Sangeeta. She was, however, happy about it as she was about to end up the disgusting affair at home. No wonder, with that intention alone she had arranged this specially in the absence of Harish. She did it with a considerable degree of meticulation too.

'Yes, we're happy about the bride. That's why we want to make her our daughter-in-law,' again the leader of them spoke humorously. While her kindred looked happy about the progress in the deal.

'What's your demand. May I know it?' Shobha enquired them naturally.

'As the elders of bridegroom, we want you to arrange the marriage and bear its whole expenses,' Yamunamurthy gave his details on behalf of Sangeeta and her brother. Now Sangeeta was curious to know the response, while Mohanraj, her moody brother was looking forward.

'Alright!' Shobha broke into some silence. 'But,' she began, 'we're not able to conduct the marriage as we're not well-equipped. You know my mother and brother have settled down in Bangalore while we're in service here. Besides, my husband serves in a college away from here. Even now we don't have him here unfortunately,' she spoke it decidedly. Her brother's occasional nods strengthened her viewpoints.

'That's true sir. So you can demand a certain amount of dowry and bear the responsibility of marriage yourself,' Ravindra spoke for the first time, while Chandramma added 'it's true' during the times of her son's response. Yamunamurthy sat engrossed mostly in his crude calculations. All looked worried. For a minute or two each group of them sat thinking the pros and cons of the phenomenon. The children too sat with ease and they did not disturb the thought process of anyone.

There was a pronounced silence indicating nothing.

'Can we've a five minutes of private discussion? Yamunamurthy enquired Sangeeta as he wanted to make her aware of the marriage difficulties.

'Please do so,' Shobha encouraged them to hold a talk at her guest room. But Sangeeta took her kindred to a sofa laid in the garden outside. They sat in a corner and muttered to each other something. Their voice was low and their words did not mean anything for those who wanted to hear them from a distance. Presently the elderly man held a discussion with the elderly lady. Sangeeta was advising her uncle and he was consolidating his statistics. Mohanraj helped them in remembering the oddities of risk. Truly they discussed about the possible marriage expenses and their demand of dowry either in the form of money or kind. They did not neglect the importance of other items such as bridegroom's present to the bride. It was at this time, Venkatesh happened to observe them. His was not an inspection but a childish desire to know the mystery of their analysis. Soon outside went the meticulous Shobha. She quipped her son without any affluence. So the boy ran indoors to occupy the place gracefully allotted for him. Glad was Sangeeta about the culture that existed in the house. She appreciated the landlady when she chided the boy observing them outside. Discussion prolonged for five more minutes and then Sangeeta led her group inside and the normalcy was restored again.

Presently another round of tea was served. Yamunamurthy and Mohanraj were quick to appreciate Shobha's extensive hospitality. They were pleased by the additional curtesy in the middle hours of day. Almost a lofty view about the family culture, and magnanimity of its members entered into their heads.

'I think we're giving you troubles today,' Yamunamurthy apostrophised.

'It's a necessary evil,' Sangeeta grinned.

'Doesn't matter,' Chandramma expressed her broadmindedness smiling.

'Anyway now you're our people,' Ravindra spoke.

'Alright. Madam in case we're to undertake the responsibility of conducting the marriage, we've to present you new demands.'

'Ok. Let me know them,' replied Shobha.

'In that event, you've to present us fifty thousand rupees of dowry,' he looked at her attentively.

'What about gold and other gifts?' asked Shobha's brother. Ravindra who was worried about sundry matters wished to know their other requirments.

'You'd give us hundred grams of gold and it's left to you to give the groom what'ver else you want to present,' he stopped for clearing his throat.

A spell of silence broke there.

Now Shobha was forced to hold a closet. It was Karisma's marriage but not her son's or daughter's. She was then Harish's wife. The man who was to bear the cost of marriage was really Ravindra. Of course, as a matter of dispatching Karisma she had taken a grand initiative. Hence, she had to share a part of the cost. That was all. Therefore, she desired to seek her brother's advice.

'Let's think about it for five minutes,' she said to the august gathering.

'Alright,' said the eldest heartily.

'You can talk about it freely,' Sangeeta encouraged her friend.

'Let them discuss about it,' spoke Mohanraj though he was not expected to do.

'We come back within five minutes,' saying thus Shobha led her kindred to an anterior room wherefrom no sound could be heard outside. Meanwhile the other party continued their inward calculations.

Hardly five minutes had passed when Shobha got back to the hall. Ravindra with his mother graced his chair once again. But unlike most of the haggling persons they did not display any air of displeasure.

'Sir you've demanded fifty thousand rupees and hundred grams of gold. But as our financial condition doesn't allow us, we request you to make your demands reasonable.'

'How much is your capacity?'

'As our finance permits us we can give you twenty-five thousand rupees and fifty grams of gold,' she stopped soon expecting their kind reaction.

'Let's do a modification. Give us twenty-five thousand rupees. No problem. But give us hundred grams of gold. Yamunamurthy expressed his business tactics.

'However, if you don't mind, please restrict the gold to seventyfive grams, sir,' the helples woman made her humble plea.

'Ok! It's welcome,' both Yamunamurthy and Sangeeta yessed simultaneously.

Ravindra turned happy about the deal. After a minute of calm thinking, the elderly gentleman agreed to the other points and throughout his assertions Sangeeta was one with him. In fact, whatever he said he said it in accordance with her. So they spoke with a sense of concord, while Mohanraj sat cool and composed like a businessman which definitely he was in Hubli.

'Madam shall we know your presents to the bride?' Shobha asked her friend in a tone that was not serious.

'We'll present her fifty grams of gold,' Sangeeta told it with pride. However ever since that gold goes to the bridegroom as their exclusive property, Shobha did not think of making any additional enquiry in the matter. Nor did Ravindra and his mother desire to know more about that which would belong to groom's party. They bothered only about the things they had to part with. They knew other's property as other's property. None could claim it for oneself. Even once Karisma is married off they would have no right over her. She would belong to her husband. To be sure this was a conservative view they possessed.

'Can we fix up the date of marriage?' Shobha raised the point during the zero hour.

'Earlier the better,' Yamunamurthy suggested. He was right. He had certain reasons to justify an earliest date for the marriage. His misapprehension was that in modern times, marriages should be conducted as soon as the event of ring ceremony was initiated. Otherwise, he was sure, due to inordinate delay the bride or groom might be misled by other's charm and could change their decisions to marry someoneelse other than the one already fixed. In such a circumstance everything would go wrong. In spite of so much trust in tradition, people like him, born and brought up, say in a conservative society, bothered of harsh repurcussions. But none could deny him because such incidents were not unknown in an industrialized town like Banahatti. Karisma was also unreliable in the matter. As she looked a temptress, anyone could dismiss his conscience and seek her silken hand. Already everyone who saw her for marriage did not say 'he would not marry her.' It was only because of Harish's deftiness in the matter, she had not yet left the house. Under these conditions nobody could neglect Yamunamurthy's sound warning. Indeed, Shobha too was quick to appreciate his point though she did not discuss it openly.

'Shall I think April 10th will be convenient for you?' Shobha enquired them looking at Sangeeta.

'How will it be? Is it good for us?' Sangeeta sought Yamunamurthy's advice.

'If you don't mind, let's know his view,' the oldman could not help asking Mohanraj who was doleful about it then.

'April 10th? Mostly a Monday. Yes, Yes, it'll do,' the groom replied them after his mysterious calculations. Anyway he was joyous as April 10th would bring Karisma to him.

'Your convenience is our convenience. Let April 10th be fixed up for the wedding,' both Sangeeta and Yamunamurthy replied together.

'Where d'you like to conduct the wedding?' Ravindra asked the oldman who was noting down some points in his old diary.

'Let it be at *Kalyan Mantap* (Welfare Hall) near the busstand here,' Sangeeta told Ravindra with an air of finality.

There fell a silence.

'Now d'you mind giving the amount to us?' Sangeeta put it politely to the landlady of the house.

'You want it now itself?' Shobha asked the other worried.

'We're glad if it's given now. You know how we've to spend a lot of money these days. We've to fix up a mantap, buy gold, dress etc. Everything is costly today,' Sangeeta gave her candid reasons. 'You may present the gold at the time of wedlock ceremony. We don't mind it,' she added it as an afterthought.

'So it's inevitable?'

'Yes, it's.'

'Alright! You'll be given it now,' spoke Shobha with a sigh of relief. She went inside to the room where Karisma sat dismayed. Shobha learnt Karisma was unwilling to marry Mohanraj. She knew she loved nobody in the world save Harish. She had already decided Harish to be her husband ever since she gave up herself to him during the premiere. She was determined to live in the same house where at present she relaxed. No matter what status she could be designated, she was desirous of finding her ways to happiness in the same shelter. She had a perfect faith in the man who had already touched, kissed and won her heart. Presently she found Mohanraj a business boor. Although she loved Hubli-Dharward, she disliked the business this fellow carried out there. She knew well how the womenfolk of business families led a life of drudgery despite so much of wealth at their disposal. Probably this was not the cause of her disgust. Harish's love for her had been the real reason. Owing to this Karisma showed so much of displeasure towards the growth of her marriage issue. In fact, she never expressed her desire to marry anyone or at a time near in the future. Unless her sister created a scene in this regard, she would not highlight this anomaly. Why she should think of a marriage or a husband while a husband had already been there to keep her happy? But presently she had been in an awkward condition. Now the thought of Harish occurred to her tender mind. She decided to pull through the disaster until he turned up to rescue her at any oddities. No matter, though she should have been married, if she minded, he could still claim her. What mattered most was her decision. She knew where there was a will there was a way certainly. Gradually she learnt the reasons for which her kindred from Bangalore had come home the previous day. Anyway she was completely unhappy about her sister, for it was she who had plotted to send off her at the earliest. When Shobha came in Karisma stopped sorrowing and sat up neat and trim.

The moment she made the payment and a due inspection of kitchen, Shobha came to her. Soon the mother too joined them in the innermost chamber.

'Why you're shy and sorrowful today?' Chandramma spoke to her first.

'Because I'm not happy about this. I don't like to go away from this house which has given me so much of pleasure,' Karisma burst meekly.

'See Shobha, as I told you, how she loves you,' the oldwoman who forgot the first part of her explanation turned proud of her daughters.

'Yes, yes, she loves this house very much,' Shobha broke satirically. An air of uneasiness was explicit in her tone. But the poor oldwoman could not perceive the inner layer of her daughter's assertion. How she can? Although she felt Shobha's point, Karisma remained neutral in her outlook. Then Shobha busied in preparing a dinner for them, while Karisma persuaded her mother to undo the knot.

'I wonder whether you can remain a spinster,' Chandramma spoke surprised.

'No mummy I'll marry but not this chap. Let me see someone,' Karisma tried to explain her heartfelt feeling. Now the mother could not help convincing the dame about the futility of missing a bright chance. She said, 'Unless woman marries, she'll be looked down upon first in the family and then in society. Even she'll have no salvation.' There was sufficient truth in the mother's admonishment. She was perfectly clear about the Hindu society which never allowed women to remain spinsters. 'Since the unmarried women are sought for sex, or caught by sisters-in-law at home, or they are completely downgraded by society,' the mother viewed, 'they should marry and marry at a right moment.' The elderly lady tried to convince her daughter to the best of her ability. She reiterated the futility of avoiding marriage; and she advised the adamant maid that soon after her wedding, everything would be convenient. Besides, Karisma could have no mother-in-law, while her aged father-in-law was counting his last days.

Unlike Karisma Shobha was all but gay. Albeit she had been busy in the kitchen, now and then, she lent her ears to the hectic dialogue ongoing between Karisma and the matron. Occasional was her laughing at Karisma for her unnecessary disliking of Mohanraj. This made Karisma feel guilty. She predicted Shobha's design of teaching Harish and herself a lesson. She learnt she was undoubtedly moving towards a grand success. This was implicit in her broad smiles of relief, in her homeliest approach to the situation and in her projecting the whole phenomenon.

It was eight o' clock when the bridegroom party sat for dinner. Sangeeta sat at the right side and her brother was seated next to his uncle. The old man relaxed between them was happy especially for the reason today he fulfilled the promise he had given to Sangeeta's mother at the time of her passing away years ago. When Sangeeta's mother died, he recollected, she had requested him to take care of her two children. As his brother now an aged man had not been worldlywise, Yamunamurthy took much care in important matters of the family. So today he heaved a sigh of relief.

The pre-wedding evening dinner began. A variety of sweets, chatnis, curries, bread, chapati, coloured rice etc had been served to the newly- made acquaintances. Sangeeta took less food while his brother ate heavily. As a foodie, Mohanraj devoured food rather than he ate it. He ate in such a way while dining he saw nobody. What mattered him was good food and privacy. He ate and ate, while more and more food was supplied. The boy Ashok who sat beside them could not help pointing it to Venkatesh and Kamala. He was wonderstruck at the man's voracious eating. Ashok saw Mohanraj's style of eating only. Venkatesh too laughed at Mohanraj. Karisma too noticed this rarity. The young lady sat in her bedroom which had a tiny window and through which she beheld the external spectacle. She sat there in order to have a thorough look at Mohanraj, a business boor. When she had a glance at his dining she was awestruck. However, she did not point it to anybody as it could not look nice. Every child whether it was

Venkatesh or Ashok, or for that matter the little girl Kamala, enjoyed the typical way of Mohanraj's eating habits. He looked a demoniac figure in regard to his appetite. No surmise, when the smaller boy gaped at her brother, Sangeeta was amused at it but she dismissed it as trivial. Right within a brief span of ten to fifteen minutes, the outsiders ate enough, while with them the children too finished theirs and found their ways for playing outside.

The moment the dinner was over, Sangeeta rushed inside to see the house. But her ulterior motif was to acquaint herself with Karisma who was shortly to become her sister-in-law. The time she came to the kitchen, however, she did not find the exact figure. Thereafter, she went to the room wherein Karisma was found seeing the groom through a small hole. She was glad about it as she thought Karisma was interested in her brother. Since she had, with the maid, been familiar, she did not hesitate to chat with her for a while.

'Ah! you're resting here,' she spoke gently. Though she knew it, in order to start talking, the outside lady began smiling.

'Yeah aunt. Come in. Please be seated here,' spoke Karisma pointing the other a chair nearby.

'Will your mother return to Bangalore again?' Sangeeta enquired.

'I'm not aware of it. Even I didn't know her arrival here for this reason.'

'Which reason?' Sangeeta spoke absentmindedly.

'This... this seeing me,' Karisma laughed a laugh of shyness, while Sangeeta burst out into a peel of laughter. Both had a little commonsense in the matter.

Meanwhile Yamunamurthy had been ready outside. He knew the purpose for which he led his kith had been amply fruitful. Then he called Sangeeta. Consequently the atmosphere began to build up tensely. Immediately Shobha brought out vermillion. The womenfolk followed the old Hindu custom looking cheerful.

‘So shall we go madam?’ the male aged of them asked Shobha with a smile of gratefulness.

‘Yes, sir,’ Shobha gave them a hearty reply.

‘Ok, we’ll leave for our house. Let me see you tomorrow,’ Sangeeta glancing at her smiled upon them.

Karisma was still inside. Even she did not make a move to come outside. She sat keenly observing the spectacle. Her attention was only at the vanishing figures specially the boor. She admired Sangeeta and Yamunamurthy’s courtesy of acknowledging their thankfulness, but she reproached Mohanraj for his discourtesy. She saw him stepping out with unpleasant behaviour. She recollected his demonaic appetite for devouring rice. Really she found the business undesirable as it was dumped upon her.

The outsiders vanished while the children appeared in the front as usual. They were at play then. The absence of guests restored naturally the casual order at home. Gradually found herself hungry, Shobha asked her kindred for meals. The food was already ready. Everyone except Karisma looked satisfied over the fixation of marriage. Presently, they moved to the dinner table. But one figure of the house did not turn up at this hour. Indeed, it was Karisma. This made them wait for a while. In spite of their patience neither they saw her nor heard her sound anywhere. This worried the oldwoman and she trotted to the room wherein Karisma till then relaxed. However to her misfortune, the today’s lady of every one’s attention was not to be seen. This alarmed Shobha too. Henceforth, all the members began searching the missing figure.

‘Where’s she?’ Ravindra opened his mouth.

‘Where would she go? She must be somewhere in the house,’ Shobha pacified the feared kinfolk. All then set on an errand to see her. They were panicky. But the most afraid person was neither the mother nor the brother, but Shobha herself. She knew Karisma’s deepest love for her husband and when the day was ended up against her, Shobha meditated, she could even disappear or commit suicide. Karisma was really one of the women truly fatalistic. Since she had been grown up in an affluent environment, she had no perfect knowledge of the right and wrong. She was alarmed over the reason that Karisma out of her undersatisfaction to marry Mohanraj was even ready to die if needed. Presently everyone saw Shobha getting out of the door with a torch in her hand, children trailing behind all tension-stricken in search of the missing maid.

'Did you see the aunt?' Shobha enquired her eldest son.

'No. Where's she?'

'I'm asking you the same question. Had I known where she would've been d'you think I'd enquire you?'

Both Karisma and Venkatesh used to be together always. But he did not know her whereabouts then. Besides, other children too did not give her any clues pertaining to the dame's presence though they played outside for a long time.

Notwithstanding, Shobha went ahead towards the garden well with a torch in her hand, sound in her mouth and children behind. The group then stepped boldly. They were in despair. The present dread made her to regret about her hurry in marrying off her. She thought, she could have allowed her to marry Harish, or she should have delayed the fixation event until Karisma could agree herself. But everything had been a part of history now, unamendable. The lady was anyway keenly looking for the figure. The woman and her kids presently looked like Shiddharam who had gone panicky when he could not see Shrishail Mallikarjun the moment the latter disappeared despite his assurance of a darshana. A tree across them rose frightening. A kind of ghostly object hung across it alarmed the children. However, at a close inspection, the elderly lady found it neither Karisma in disguise nor any ghost at that early hour of the night. It was a tattered rug her sun had kept on a plant. Worried about the futility of searching, Shobha then called Karisma's name aloud. But no sound was heard in response. The mother as well as her brother who was standing stockstill on the portico looked at her eagerly. Shobha walked near the well and found nobody in its water either being soaked or struggling for life. No sound came from the water front. Failed to see the figure there she asked her children to search her elsewhere. This enerved them. Now Venkatesh cried for her at the top of his voice. This Karisma heard and this made her rush out suddenly. Immediately there stood a celestial figure peeping through a glass-window. When the landlady came near the house chastising the rude boys, she was glad to hear the voice for which till then she moved hell and heaven.

'What you're doing there? Karisma surprised the already surprised kinfolk.

'Ah! You're inside Kari?' the oldwoman spoke in her angry voice. Ravindra's heart beat reduced.

'What you're doing there nonsense?' the brother turned wild for the first time in his life.

'I'm here only.'

'Here means where?'

'At home.'

'At home?'

'Yes.'

'We've searched the home.'

Presently Karisma did not think of replying him. Yet another one was there to scold her.

'Where had you been upon the earth? What were you there upto? Didn't you hear us talk about your missing? Shouldn't you come soon from the cell you'd been? I know you're born to trouble others,' the landlady burst out ferociously. There was an air of anger, dismay and uneasiness in Shobha's voice and gestures.

'I'm here only,' Karisma who till then stood amazed at Shobha's volley of questions replied humbly. She was polite.

'We're also here. Everyone of us looked for you. But you're seen to none of us. What a mystery woman? Had you been on the floor or in the air hidden?' Shobha could not stop immediately.

Because she had made a painstaking effort to unearth her at the earliest.

'Let it be Shobha. Forget it. A poor fellow. She's a young girl,' the oldest of the group consoled her.

'Then ask her as to where she'd been?'

'Let me do it. Where're you hidden my girl,' the oldwoman put it affectionately.

'I'd been to toilet.'

'Oh! Was it?' everyone began wondering.

'Yes, very much. Didn't you notice the light burning there?' Karisma tried her best to justify her stance. This made her enquirers guilty of misunderstanding.

'Wonderfull! Isn't it grandma,' the eldest boy spoke laughing, while the other children had been still in confusion.

'Had her *mama* been here she'd have been quite ok mummy,' Shobha spoke mockingly.

'Natural, I don't think my son-in-law would treat her as harshly as you did just,' Chandramma spoke in a tone of solace. Her gestures were in favour of Karisma. This made Karisma blush up and feel happy inwardly. She felt proud of her *mama* as her mother too esteemed him highly.

'Shobha's also good, but she's not as good as *mama*,' Karisma shot her arrow with a broadsmile. She knew she could not lose her confidence in her.

'Thank God. You saved her!' Ravindra exclaimed mechanically.

'Alright let's dine now, it's already ten,' Chandramma entreated everyone of them. Now all sat together. After the storm, had come there the calm. Forgotten was the event of vain missing and futile searching. The very Karisma was sitting next to her mother, while Shobha sat in front of her. Ravindra sat a little far away crosslegged. He had already been a way ahead to them in eating. This way he resembled Mohanraj. Currently the sisters were just opposite to each other, and the mother managed the whole affair. Happy they started dining, while the children had retired to beds tired during the day time. Calm was the atmosphere.

'I'm rather unhappy today as *mama* is not with us. May I know sister when he'll come back?' Ravindra enquired Shobha.

'He'll turn up in the first week of April. Or even earlier,' Shobha replied. She was the only person there who knew Harish's return sheduled to be on April 15th. As he left Banahatti on 15th, March for Pampapati University, Pampapattan for an examination work that was to consume him a span of time not short of a month, she was quite happy and certain about it. Knowing his long absence only, she had conducted the whole affair of dispatching off her sister. Already she had given twenty-five thousand rupees from her pocket, while her brother was to give gold. In fact, the whole burden was Ravindra's. But to oust Karisma as quickly as she could, Shobha sacrificed a part of her secret earning. After all she was her sister.

'So is it certain that he'll be here on the gracious occasion of Karisma's wedding?' the mother made an enquiry. 'Anyway his presence is a must,' sopke she affectionately.

'Yes mummy, he'll attend it surely. How can he miss an important event related to Karisma, his dear,' Shobha pointed her words to Karisma who cast her face down.

'Are you happy about your future husband?' pointing at Karisma, Ravindra spoke. He was sure she would be positive about it.

There was a long pauze.

Apparently the lady remained silent over the enquiry. Even her face looked smileless though it was uncommon for such a situation. Instead, Ravindra found a kind of unpleasant demeanour of her. But he did not proceed further anticipating the eventual difficulties. Nor did Chandramma like it either? By this they learnt her displeasure due to the enforced selection. It seems the groom was simply thurst upon her. Anyway, they were glad about the fixation ceremony if not over the selection. They were not desirous of postponing the event or to marry her off to a rich man which could cost them an amount of dowry they would not afford.

When all were dining unperturbed, Karisma felt of expressing her angst at the right occasion. She wanted to point out things that disturbed her tranquil heart.

'He's nothing but boorish mother,' spoke she unhappy.

'Is it?' her brother was taken aback.

'I wonder whether there is any truth in your opinion?' Chandarmma cut in.

'I believe you've observed his typicalities. Didn't you know how, like Kumbakarna, he ate and ate. He's neither cultured nor civilized. Nor is there any charm on his hideous face. You know he went off even without expressing any marks of courtesy. In spite of this, you force me to marry him. It's totally unfair,' she stopped her say.

'Tell us then what we can do. It's your fate. So you'd bear it,' the oldwoman with her characteristic beliefs in destiny tried to console her.

'Destiny... Fate... Helplessness. It's a hellish life to live with such a man. You don't know it's we who worsen things in life,' broke she sorrowfully.

'D'you want to live in hell or heaven?' Shobha broke out hysterically.

'See sister to me ruling in hell is better than serving someone in heaven,' she explained the elder smiling. Nobody except Shobha caught the point that was hidden in her assertion. The others spoke normally while the sisters engaged in a language that was akin to a diatribe. There was irony in their statements. Undertones as well as overtones lingered in their exchange of views. Their words were pointed and emotionally charged. At times they could not help exchanging heat for heat. But throughout the discussions, the elderly sister's magnanimity prevailed to save the younger maid's foolishness. Admittedly she never disclosed what Karisma used to do there in her absence. She knew that could be harmful for the dame's future.

'D'you want to live here a maid ever after?' Chandramma spoke worried.

'Not like that. But I can wait for a better chance.'

'D'you think you can get it?' Shobha cut in.

'Why not sister? You always think that I'll not get what I want.'

'D'you mean you want a rich husband?' Ravindra interrupted.

'Someone, somehow, sometime, a better person,' Karisma spoke riddlesome, while none excepting Shobha perceived her tone.

'I think you want a man who can excel anyone in each and everything?' the mother burst comically.

'Let me think about it,' said the young sullen.

'Thinking or no thinking. Know it for sure, you'll be married off,' Shobha put it in a hard way.

Bore the belle what Shobha put it rudely. Soon she finished her meals, she went to her room, while the mother rushed after her agitated. Ravindra walked outside for fresh air. Already it was ten-thirty and they retired to bed dead tired. Each of them was of the divided opinion over the matrimonial success though it was in their favour. Karisma's outburst made her mother blame Shobha, Shobha was being made to blame her husband and none of them knew how Harish would blame Shobha for her betrayal.

Days moved. Shobha was being made to work hard with her sister always disappointed. She bought whatever gifts, items and things necessary for the upcoming wedding day. However they were not traditional, something they had to prepare grandly. So with the help of Karisma and her children, Shobha finished her preparation. Already the dowry was given and her brother was to bring gold. Ravindra had given her sufficient money to buy dress for

Karisma. Since each of the newlyweds had to buy their own dresses, Shobha did not bother about Mohanraj's attire. Indeed one day she went to a garment and as per Karisma's likings she bought enough number of sareers, blouses, and special clothes for her wedding. She also purchased some readymade clothes for her children, some for herself and some for her relatives. Both Shobha and Karisma prepared a lot of sweets and other things for the blithe occasion. By April 1st, the house was fully ready with whitewash and painting. The garden was cleaned and made fresh and fine-looking. Shobha had hired some maid-servants to help her in systematizing the house, while she managed the significant business.

On the wedding day Harish did not make his presence as everyone save Shobha direly anticipated. Shobha simply regaled those who asked for his presence. In fact, none had informed him about the catastrophe. Shobha who alone knew his address, did not intimate him deliberately, while Karisma wanted to inform him but she did not know his whereabouts. About his non-arrival, Karisma who was panicky already, cursed the elder sister. People went to the wedding hall which was located near busstand. The party of bridegroom had already gathered. But the number of people attended the ceremony had not been big as one could expect of Pattans. This was so because Pattans or Tilakawadis, Sangeeta and her people, had not been the natives of Banahatti. Yet it was not a negligible number as more than four hundred people — some from Hubli, some from Bijapur, a few others from the locality — had honoured the occasion by their gracious presence. The staff of Shobha's college was also present, while the familiar faces of the town and neighbouring villages were coming in twos and threes.

The moment the wedding rituals began, the pomp and grandeur of it started. To the tune of songs, the bride and bridegroom seated on gorgeous chairs specially prepared for them. They had been well-dressed and looked bright in the floodlights. The whole atmosphere was tense but festive. The hall was full of kindred souls, familiar or strange. Children of all types thronged there. They created enough noise to make elders' speech ununderstandable. Most of the children were playing and only a few sat calm and dignified. People sat upon chairs, while the kith of newlyweds were busy at dias in wedlock ceremony. However, all were happy on the wonderous occasion.

The moment *aksatarohan* rite was ready people hurried towards the podium. They rushed there to see the newlyweds. Meanwhile coloured rice used to shower over them as a mark of endorsing their marriage was distributed. The priest finished his rites and asked the groom to tie wedlock to the neck of his bride. Mohanraj took the object and tied it around her neck. Karisma blushed up and the people amused over it. Some people became glad, but a few others disliked the match. Thereafter, a drum beat began and the priest's sloka was lively chanted. This made people shower their rice. Immediate was the peoples' throwing it and most of which fell on the diadems of the two majestically adored the chairs. Even some of the holy rice fell upon those who stood before them.

Virtually the wedding was over. The moment *aksatarohan* was finished people hurried to the dining hall. Both the buffet and sitting systems were arranged. The educated who wore precious attire stood eating, while the less-educated or the unlettered sat down cross-legged to eat sumptously. Things moved fast. By four o' clock the majority of people who attended the ceremony had disappeared. But the kindred were held up in packing things and getting back home.

It was the happiest occasion for Mohanraj as he married Karisma. On the contrary, the sorrow of his wife was indescribable. Now she was in a quagmire of uncertainty about her future. But her husband was sure of making a happy life with her, a pretty-eyed and slender-waisted charming lady. Now they were raked by their memories of the past. They were not happy about each other. Soon a kith brought them bottles of soft drinks and each drank it separately, instead of sharing it together. This, however did not annoy Mohanraj as he was not so sensitive to such pleasures. No wonder, throughout the occasion, he made a purposive effort to see her and wanted her to look at him smiling. But to his badluck she did not look at him nor smiled. Nor did she display her deep annoyance to anyone either? In spite of this, he was unhurt. But she was more hurt than him of the whole system, her husband, the wedding, the gross non-appearance of Harish, the lord of her heart. Naturally she remained silent all the time. But her silence spoke and only the grey-headed deciphered it. To this list, Shobha was one top ranked.

The wedding was over. The bridegroom party took away the bride the same day. However unhappy, Karisma meekly followed her husband to Hubli. Similarly Ravindra and his mother left for Bangalore the next day. All were delighted over the event of marriage again except Karisma. Shobha was specially happy the moment Karisma was taken away. She had managed everything very carefully and found herself at ease and grace. In the month long absence of her husband, so many drastic incidents had occurred. Whenever people kindred or otherwise asked her about Harish, she used to say that he had been held up somewhere in Pampapattan due to some urgent examination work. Even she went on to the extent of saying that she had received a telegram from him. However, people trusting, did not doubt her. After all it did not matter them. But the absence of Harish hurt and troubled one sole woman in Pattans' family. But that woman had already been being made to go to a pasture which she had despised persistently ever since Harish loved her.

The fifteenth Monday was a fine day; and the evening sun was still fiery in the western orb. No clouds were to be seen in any part of the starry sky however. The day was gradually cooling in the evening. Many birds, pegions, crows and parrots were chirping in the aforested hillside of the southwest. A parrot that sat alone over the twigs of a nearby tree was singing a bardic song telling a sad story of a blue-eyed maid of the house. The songstress was just in the garden where Harish's house stood majestically. Some people who listened to its music burst joyous. But most others loved the song without making any sense.

It was five o' clock evening. The bird still continued its narration. Shobha was resting in the house. Indeed, she was on a move to brave up a situation. Since she knew her husband's possible protestation, these three days, she learnt some tricks to cool him down. In spite of it, she had still got some dread about Harish who, she thought, could desert her for any woman's sake. In any case, according to her, no man of any cultured family could give him his daughter in marriage. She consoled herself muttering 'none would love him too' because of his infidelity and irresponsibility. She had realised the fact that Harish of a decade ago had undergone a great metamorphosis. In her view the lover Harish had been nowhere to be found. The husband Harish, she felt, had been a rogue, a womanizer. She remembered his sadistic designs, his inconstancy in love and his illicit affair with her own sister. Even she had heard that Harish's public relations had not been cordial. His persona annoyed her. Mostly it was because of Harish's sexuality and sadism Shobha married off her sister sooner than he had never thought of. But in the deal, she learnt, she did not do full justice to Karisma. But she was helpless.

When the bird's song sounded shrill but still continuing, a gentleman absolutely tall, modestly fat and full-suited arrived there. He had been grand in appearance. The coat and suit he wore were as black as the colour of a crow, and so was his mental make up. He stood near the door. Any of those who dreaded of authority if saw him at this time of day could assess him to be a top CBI officer. Like a detective fiction hero he looked an official par excellence. There was a sense of seriousness in his broad face. His dress was neat and trim and it added much dignity to his disciplined composure. When he stood on the portico of house, he switched on the bell and wondered about the absence of any live-souls inside.

'Open the door,' after some time cried the man outside.

‘Ah! Welcome my dear,’ Shobha rushed to the door shortly. The door stood open at once and he stepped indoors magnificently.

‘How are you? Where is Karisma and where’re the children? Are they inside?’ he stopped at once in expectation of a humble and affectionate reply to all of his questions.

‘We’re okey here. I think you’ve been well,’ she tried to know his well being.

‘I’m fine,’ spoke he.

He got in, sat upon a while and in expectation of someone, he went inside. He searched for a figure who seemed apparently missing. Faithful enough the newness of the house, its colouring or decoration did not matter to him anything. What bothered him was one bewitching maid and presently he could not help enquiring for her straightway.

‘Tell me where’s Karisma?’ he turned dismay.

‘Ah! She’s left for her husband.’

‘I don’t like you teasing me Shobha. Please tell me where she’s now,’ he turned wild.

‘She has married Mohanraj, a business tycoon and he has taken her away,’ pointing to her wedding photo hung on the front wall recently, she took him by surprise as if she scored a point against him.

Suddenly looking at the photo, Harish turned wounded. However he could not believe the story, Karisma’s photo with Mohanraj stunned him. Gradually his wrath against Shobha began increasing like the summer Gulbarga temperature. He put off his bag and took her to bed for a thorough enquiry. He was beset by Shobha’s act against his will. He sat on a cot lost in inquiring even without washing his face. Nor had he put off his dress. Did he take a cup of tea his ever loving wife brought him either?

‘Does it really mean she’s married off?’ he asked scratching his head.

'Yes,' she smiled at him, a smile of victory.

'Really?'

'Yes, really. D'I lie you? I'm honest at that dear,' she spoke. This enraged him certainly.

'To whom?'

'To a certain businessman named Mohanraj Tilakwadi of Hubli.'

'When the wedding took place and where?'

'It took place on April 10th at Kalyan Mantap,' she noticed him clenching his teeth.

'Here in Banahatti?'

'Yes, here only.'

'Is it so?' he burst wildly.

'Yes, truly.'

'Just three days ago?'

'Yes,' she smiled.

'But how did you dare to conduct it without my notice or permission?' he wondered at her devilish courage.

'Since Ravindra and the mother came here urgently for this only and as I'd no address of you, I couldn't inform you of this. I was helpless dear.'

'Why it's done in haste then?'

'Because of the mother's insistance.'

'I don't want your becauses, tell me the truth,' he thundered when he found her fumbling while detailing the matter. It seems, he doubted her whole business.

'I tell you only the truth. Besides, when she saw him, Karisma too insisted for a quick marriage. She said she wanted a husband,' Shobha elaborated further.

'I wonder whether you're really honest at that,' he grinned.

There was a deep silence.

When Shobha stood yessing him, he denied the whole business and blamed her for a conspiracy against him. He stepped forth and back; showed marks of troubled heart; and became constantly restless. There was a kind of disappointment in him always. His voice grew inarticulate as he spoke more without any accent in his articulation. No doubt, he lost his senses.

'Where's she now? Tell me the truth stupid fellow,' he broke angrily.

'I told you she's been taken away by her husband.'

'Where they've gone?'

'To Hubli.'

'Hubli...? Are you telling the truth?'

'By God yes, dear.'

'What's her husband?'

'I told, he's a businessman.'

'Doesn't matter. You're a traitor to your man. Could you die if I had married her? Did she trouble you anyway? She helped you always. A good lady she had always been. Though I entertained her I was with you also. Was she not your sister after all? I think you forgot her help and cooperation to our family in our hours of difficulties? Ah! I believe, you didn't tolerate her love for me,' Harish broke madly. He was ferocious at that. 'Yes, yes, you did it deliberately,' He roared in his leonine voice. His sound was echoic. There was despair in his cries, a pain in his voice, an anger in his roaring. His voice though shrill carried its own complaint. He spoke with stress on every word that was associated with his departed beloved. There was a spark of extreme hatredness against Shobha. Though he thundered for the last forty minutes still he spoke with an intensity of heat, bitterness and remorse.

Shobha sat silent all the while. She saw the man screaming singularly. Tolerated she his verbal onslaught. She could not help avoiding it. Anyway since her purpose was largely served she did not bother about her being hated or blamed by him. She knew, afterall, he was her husband and he had every right even to manhandle her. Her awareness of scriptural saying 'Patience saves souls' and it's due practice in life saved her. Her patience was tremendous against his diatribe. Almost proverbial. But she was happy about her husband at least in one matter that, like others, he never beat her. Now she sat listening to him with prostrated face while the barking dog did not bite her.

After an hour or so, Shobha asked her husband for a cup of tea. But he responded her not. Again she persuaded him best for the supper at nine o' clock but he fell a deaf ear at her. Finding it futile, she dined with her children and went to bed. Whilest Harish who was still swimming in an ocean of dejection finished his preparation for his next journey which he did not inform any one. He was really unhappy about the development of his home matters that is too in his absence. Really he assessed Shobha's high handedness in manipulating the whole situation and marrying his sweetheart off. So he found her his pronounced enemy today. Soon readied his suitcase, he went to bed. Indeed, he did not dine.

When the children slept, Shobha came back to him hoping to mollify his swollen heart. He was then in bed halfawake. The disappearance of Karisma had beset him powerfully in the days of summer heat. He cursed the order that enforced him for an examination work. Then he cursed Shobha and then he cursed the man who married his beloved. But he did not curse Karisma as she was helpless in the game. Karisma, he thught, must have been forced for wedding. He knew she never aspired to marry any one except himself. What Shobha told about her was just a distortion of reality. Accordingly Karisma was simply victimized. He thought both were deprived of each other's life long companionship. He learnt wasted were the two souls in the quagmire of social indifference. Presently to him Shobha represented a society. However, how can he forget his Karisma, his dearest darling, her charming face, rosy cheeks, blue eyes, flapping hair, slender waist, above all her tender heart. Besides, the fruits of her garden. The word 'tender heart' sounded him loveliest. He was known to her bestirring of his heart. No wonder, he was not sure of getting or finding another Karisma in this life. Though Shobha, a greater Karisma had already been there to wipe out his memory of a dear figure, he did not think just the otherwise.

Now, after a few minutes of time, Shobha entered his room while he sat sapped of his complete vigour. Presently he looked like a wingless bird. Not only that. All bitter or deceitful qualities were his characteristic features. Indeed, she saw the fox in bed still pondering over the gone off winds. Suddenly she opened his rug and sat beside him. But Harish turned aside though she enticed him. Again he wore the coverlet and heeded her no more.

However, many years elder to Karisma in age, Shobha had not yet been an expert in wooing her husband. But by observation of the love affair that lingered long between her husband and her sister, she had succeeded in acquiring some tactics. As she remembered one of them, currently she went in and within a minute or two she came back dazzling like a witch.

Shobha came back to him. But this time she looked different. She came naked to entice him. His rug was taken aside by her as earlier. Soon Harish could not help seeing his wife fully nude. What a beautiful complexion she wore in her nudity! It seems he himself had not seen her properly. Mostly because of an apple he had neglected a good orange. The woman stood there singular. She was a Meneke in front of a rishi. She looked like a heavenly nymph came down to corrupt someone purest and unwilling. Her colour was twinkling in the orange light. She looked a golden deer. Her big brown eyes were proper and full and stood straight like cine actress's padded breasts. As during the stay and use of Karisma they were not adequately used by him, they stood challenging his indifference. Oh! they looked sweet and tender. The slender waist, hip, buttocks, the brimming downstairs and the golden triangle downward, enthrilled him. Harish sat up. He could not resist the temptation. In fact, it was his greatest limitation in his life that if any woman could kiss him he was ready to fall to her feet. Already it was a month he had no such and such meal anywhere. How can he throw away the stone thrown to him. He was such a man if anyone threw a stone to him he could use it for his building instead of throwing it back. His credo was not 'tit for tat,' but 'use and throw.' People knew he was an opportunist... ... a fortune hunter. The smiles Shobha threw and the gaze she concentrated defeated him persistently. His decision, like ice in scorching heat, melted away the moment he saw splenderous Shobha fully ready for bodily union. He saw her before him dallying. She pulled him to bedroom. Harish followed her. His heart was beating fast for an apple but when he did not get it he could not help eating an orange however unimpressive or unwanted. Certainly within a minute or two the two bereaved souls found themselves locked in each others' arms.

However, satisfied bodily, the next day Harish got up dismayed. The person who in spite of her non-appearance dwelt in his fascionate heart was searched by him in his imaginary world. He finished his morning routine and went to his college. Meanwhile, Shobha who had already taken in a maid servant did not bother much about the eternal loss of Karisma. She made her children ready for breakfast and then she dispatched them to schools. Venkatesh, Ashok and Kamala all went — Venkatesh ahead and the two trailing behind him. The eldest boy had been in his X standard, while his brother was in VIII. The only daughter was in the fourth learning her little letters. They were happy in the company of their mother. Of course, the memory of their aunt was in their hearts inaffacable. They asked their mother about the whereabouts of Karisma who had nursed them with all her love and affection. They knew she held them dear to her. The children remembered the way she stood by them in their boyhood follies. It was she who treated them more like a mother than Shobha, the real person. Shobha herself had acknowledged this many times expressing her gratefulness to her sister. Venkatesh regretted for Karisma's disappearance. To tell the truth, he had already realized the fact that it was because of Karisma aunt's going away, her father quarrelled often. He knew what kind of father he had; and he knew how he behaved belligerently. The boys' clear acquaintance with the moments of sorrows at home led him to his solitude. However he loved both of his parents, he did not find any delight in his father's company. The reasons had been clear. To begin with, Harish was very affectionate and lovable towards Shobha. But the moment Karisma entered his life, his total mode of life underwent an alteration. He became merely a chip of the old block — conservative and crooked. He fell in love with a forbidden fruit hating his own wife. Consequently the mother was hurt beyond measure. Moreover, Harish's atrocities in matters of money and sex and carelessness towards his children and domestic matters, made everyone dislike him. Naturally he became indifferent to Shobha's wishes. No wonder, the spoiled father-mother relationship had its own repurcussions on the tender minds of children. They were neglected. Loved they were not, trusted they were not and they were not respected at all. However the mother was in perfect harmony with them, the father spoke to them rarely. Or he was unpleasant. Even his college timings were contributory factors to this. He disappeared in early morning, while his wife and children went out in the middle hours of day. There was no direct communion between himself and his children. What is applicable to father-children relationship, was also applicable to father-mother's affair. Day times he was always in Karisma's fellowship. He did not entertain children with her. This anomaly affected the miniature adults' sensibility. Particularly the eldest boy who eye-witnessed many of verbal fights, closely held talks, indifference to children etc hated his father. Indeed, in course of time, this hardened the children's convictions.

However, Shobha had become vociferous in word to word fights with her husband and known for her frequent squabblings, she had been an affectionate woman. Though till Karisma's departure, she did not take care of her children's schooling, she thenon began it quite fastidiously. This enhanced the kids' love and respect towards their mother. Sooner or later it tended to have a detachment from their father who thereafter came home rarely on the pretext of his research at college.

Years passed but Shobha-Harish relationship did not improve. As existentialist thinkers Jean-Paul-Sarte and Karl Jaspers view man-woman relationship is bound to fail when man imposes his behaviour upon woman and does not remain constant in love with her.

This was what happened to these suffering lives. Therefore, Shobha regretted to have married Harish. Even she regretted to have married off Karisma, his beloved. 'Had Karisma,' she said to herself one day, 'been married to her husband, he would have not neglected her.' Besides, her sister could have looked after the domestic matters. This recurred to her mind many times. But it was already a part of history.

Harish used to come home twice a week. He did it simply to maintain his marital status. To avoid a bad image of himself he stayed with Shobha but like a detached self. He guided the children at times for education. He took them to bazaar; and to films they were led by him. He sat beside them, while they studied or played. But he had no rays of love and concern for their future. Mechanical had been his life itself. His relationship with his wife, he thought, had been normal. Although they spoke, there was no ounce of love in them flowing towards each other. Hence an outsider could think it was a marriage of misfortunes. But unlike him, Shobha worked hard and acted as a benevolent matron to the family. A great responsibility of bringing up the children was entrusted to her as a matter of disadvantages. She was systematic and well - disciplined in her activities at home and outside. Like him she could not escape difficulties. Besides, she wanted to educate her children in such a way that they should soon come up of age, get jobs and expel her burden of misfortunes. No wonder, the lady strived hard towards her family prosperity, while Harish wasted away his time in his daily extravaganza.

It was a June Monday, the same year yet. Shobha went to her

college as usual. When her first period for a BA III was over, Sangeeta, now her relative, came out upset today.

'Oh! you came late?' she asked Shobha just to start her skirmish.

Shobha nodded simply.

'Shall I ask you for a cup of tea?'

'Why not. Let's go,' spoke the younger of the two.

Indeed, the ladies went to a hotel the other side of the college garden. But the sense of immediacy urged Sangeeta to take her friend to a sofa in the garden's far end where nobody walked. Walked the ladies the little distance discussing about their classes. Soon they found themselves restive upon a stony seat.

'Shobha may I know whether Karisma has come to your house?' Sangeeta asked her companion eagerly. Her tone sounded serious.

'Why, what's happened to her?'

'She's run away from him!'

'Is it?' Shobha looked stunned.

'Can you tell me where she'd have gone?'

'Shall I first know the reason for her running away?' Shobha enquired her colleague anxiously.

'It seems she didn't find Mohanraj, a good husband. Or she'd have a lover elsewhere. Anyway, she's a spoiled child,' Sangeeta began sobbing.

'Don't worry Sangeeta. Let's discuss about the mishap. Misfortunes are bound to occur in everyone's life,' Shobha though hurt by the other's accusations, consoled her.

Sangeeta burst into tears, while her relative sat repenting over the calamity.

There prevailed a voluminous silence.

'See Sangeeta my sister,' Shobha began, 'was born and brought up in an affuent family. As she was born rich she did not learn any pains or sorrows of life. Nor did she prepare to withstand hardships? You know she is the youngest of us. Possibly due to ease and comfort, she behaves like an aristocrat. However, take it for sure she bears a good character and has none to love save her husband. But the present news has beset me as badly as it has done you,' Shobha finished her say. Although many thoughts about Karisma's evil character came to her, she kept quite because they would harm her sister's interest.

'Shall I know whether did your sister before her marriage tell you any words of dissatisfaction about Mohanraj,' Sangeeta put it gently.

'No, absolutely no. She's as happy as we're about the selection and wedding of your brother,' Shobha falsified it. It was unavoidable under the latest developments.

'D'you know Shobha it's reported to us yesterday that she did not even sleep with my brother. It's really horrible. Even she did not understand the fundamentals of man-woman relationship,' Sangeeta burst woefully. The way she said it was striking. It seemed, she was hurt by this aspect of Karisma's mischief.

'How did you find it?'

'My uncle, you know the man who came for the engagement ceremony telephonically detailed me these aweful happenings.'

'Shall I think Mohanraj could've not forced her to bed. Is he less interested in matters of love, romance and woman just like your husband?' Shobha spoke looking hedious to the other.

'No, no, my brother is not that kind of chap. Though his interest in sex is low, he's not an eunuch,' Sangeeta replied defensively. Thereafter, the two spoke about the newlyweds' habits in matters of entertainment. Even they discussed over the importance of carnal satisfaction for a happy married life, while at times they spoke of their own interests in such things. Even Sangeeta told the other how her husband did not satisfy her ever since she married him.

'What else did your uncle say? Did he say that Karisma is being searched now?'

'Ah! I've forgotten. He said she has gone off in a day time with a briefcase and hundred grams of gold. What you think about your sister's theft,' Sangeeta spoke complainingly.

'Let's enquire it,' the other turned cool.

'See Shobha I'd thought that your sister'd have been a lady. But she turned a harlot and thief at the same time even in a short run,' Sangeeta went harsh.

'What you're talking nonsense? D'you have any evidence to prove her harletry? Better you take your words back,' Shobha exchanged heat for heat.

'Tell me then why she has deserted him,' Sangeeta threw the other a fierce glance.

'How can I reply you without details? Mostly she might've left him because of his imbecility.'

'What d'you mean by this?'

'I mean your brother must be a stupid fellow unable to control his wife.'

'Couldn't control his wife? It's too much. Anyway we've decided never to accept her since she's deserted him. But at the most, you'd return us the gold,' Sangeeta asserted quickly. Finding an exchange of heat futile, she thought reconciliation to be the best thing.

'How can I give you that. In fact, you'd give us the dowry and seventy-five grams of gold back. What d'you say? Bear in mind I expect a fair reply from you,' Shobha heaved a sigh.

'Alright let's discuss the matter later,' finding it not worth a try, Sangeeta decided to close the talk.

However, both ladies were equally sorrowful over the failure of matrimonial alliance they had undertaken together in the interest of their kith. But Sangeeta's dismay was deeper than Shobha's as Karisma had fled away. She knew no woman had been in her father's house to cook and carry out domestic affairs. Besides, Mohanraj had lost Karisma, whom he loved dearly. Added to this was the loss of family prestige, a serious thing in society. On the other hand, as she knew Karisma's spoilt character, Shobha anticipated some grave consequences. She knew her sister was quite adamant and, she thought, presently she'd have gone to her brother at Bangalore.

Soon the ladies left each other even without having a cup of tea for which nominally they met today. No words of bidding adieu between them were exchanged. Sangeeta came to her chamber in complete frustration, while Shobha went to a telephone booth to apprise the matter. Both were indubitably a way ahead in search of a salvage to the newly arisen problem. Presently they were in need of authentic details to execute a final overthrow.

'Is it Ravindra?' Shobha enquired an invisible voice.

'Yes, sister, it's me,' Ravindra replied passively.

'Ravindra I heard a bad news. Is it true that Karisma has come to you. Because she has deserted Mohanraj and run away.'

'I don't know,' her brother expressed his unawareness. He was extremely surprised over the suffocating event.

Already Sangeeta, Mohanraj's sister who is my colleague here has briefed me that they exchanged 'figs for thistles.'

'Wonderful! But I wonder whether she's really done it. See whether they've killed her?' spoke Ravindra uneasy and worried.

'Indeed, you don't know how horrible she is. Even she didn't live with him a wife,' Shobha tried to convey him the astounding part of the issue but she could not do it satisfactorily.

'Has she come to you sister?' asked he over the phone.

'No, I'm asking you the same question.'

'But she's not yet turned up here. Anyway she's no place to go except to Banahatti or Bangalore. You know the eldest sister is far away in London and I don't think inspite of her money she can go there either. It's better we've to wait for her some more days and then start an immediate search. Let me talk to you later however. Meanwhile I'll initiate an enquiry.' Ravindra spoke hurridly. 'Are they searching for her now?' he asked her.

'Alas! They're dead tired of her. Even they say they don't want her back.'

'Oh! Quite surprising! Then does it mean that she's to stay with either of us?'

'Of course! But she spoiled her career and our family prestige,' Shobha turned tearful.

'Anyway let's think about it later. Now we'd get her first,' he stopped consoling the unhappy woman.

Enquiry done Shobha came to her room. Soon Sangeeta turned to her with more news from her quarters. Thereafter, another round of skirmish fiercer than the earlier started.

'I hope you've found more news about your good sister,' Sangeeta burst sardonically.

'Unfortunately, I couldn't get anything of her whereabout,' the woman in great dismay broke out.

A fiercer silence fell there then.

'She must have turned a harlot for earning and should've gone to Bombay. Your sister, what a wonderful woman! A Witch! D'you know what else she's done. Just in phone my brother told me that she's also decamped with twenty-five thousand rupees of cash. What you bad people say about it?' Sangeeta broke wild. Mostly had Karisma not runaway with money, she could have not renewed her quarrel with Shobha today.

'Why you're talking nonsense?' Shobha spoke with patience.

'No nonsense or stupidity as you misunderstand me. I'm maddened by you, the prostitute and thievish people.'

'Stupid fellow. D'you have any proofs about her harlotry? No. So then hold your tongue in control,' Shobha thundered alarmingly.

'Then give back the amount your best sister has stolen. I'll not spare you. Bear it,' Sangeeta threatened her.

'D'you have any concrete evidence about Karisma's decamping with money? Or if she's done it, until it's proven I'll not take it seriously.'

'Don't take it seriously?' like tigress the wounded woman stared.

'Yes,' what d'you do?'

'You see, what I'll do. My husband will teach you a lesson,' Sangeeta clenched her teeth.

'Have you forgotten I too have a husband stronger than your's?' the heat flowed proportionately.

'Your husband? What can he do? A fellow always in cathouse woman's sarees. First bring him from the prostitute's colony,' mocked the other mercilessly.

'It's too much of you Sangeeta,' Shobha was close to tears now.

'I know you're pretentious people,' Sangeeta did not stop. She had really annoyed the other unnecessarily just by bringing in personal matters.

Presently some of the college staff rushed there seeing Shobha weeping.

'What's the matter madam? 'the principal enquired Shobha who was more in a tragic situation than the other.

'I've found that her sister who'd married my brother recently turned a simpering woman,' Sangeeta told him in spite of the fact that he had not yet asked her. This was surely displeasing.

'Oh! anyway. It doesn't matter madam. You'd sort out your family matters only at home. You're educated people. Quarrelling either in the office or outside home doesn't look nice,' he said. The principal was all sympathy for Shobha whom he knew well. Already the staff members had begun musing themselves. But hardly anyone of them dared to enter the ladies chamber except the principal. However, everyone heard the ugliest words being exchanged, and each of them tried to catch their meanings to predict the actual situation. Even some of them had been ready for cooking up the material and living upon it for a few days.

The next day, the college people gathered sufficient news about the quarrel that occured there the previous day. One of them even dared to tell others that Karisma might have disliked her husband because she had loved Shobha's husband and heavily bent upon marrying him. On other's insistence for an evidence, the tallest of them replied he had seen them together many times in Vibhav talkies. While an elderly peon, a well-known gossip monger who stood beside them gleefully added his own mite to the wild fire. He said he had recently beholden Harish in the company of one fair woman at a film theatre in Jamakhandi. But when he was grilled further whether it was Karisma, he could not verify the fact as he had not seen her. He said the woman who walked beside Harish hand in hand was not Shobha surely. But not a single soul of these gossip-mongers had any ounce of courage to tell these things to Shobha, because they knew she was a dignified person never entertaining such gossips.

However, Shobha was totally stunned by her sister's abandonment of her husband and about her decamping with money and jewellery. Of course, in theory the things she stole belonged to her, she had no right to run away like that. Besides, Sangeeta's open verbal fighting, false accusations particularly in regard to her character, deeply hurt her. So she was not happy these days. Melancholic in demeanour she looked always. She talked less in college and minded her teaching alone. Oddly enough Sangeeta too had been made to stay or sit in the same room, where Shobha sat. But she never wished to pick up any bad air therein. She knew she could not brave that woman, horrible and quarrelsome. Nor did her staff members who knew her personal problems try to trouble her. Indeed most of them except the 'd' grade employees had been sympathetic and understanding. Unfortunately Shobha herself was mentally much troubled and she had none at home to support and console her at this unusual mental breakdown.

One day Harish came home happy. He found Shobha not at home the moment he arrived. He was amidst the children when his woman turned up at five o' clock evening from her duty.

'How're you my dear?' he talked to her first as he had made a point against her.

'Oh! you must be happy because you've spoiled other's career,' she spoke annoyed.

'What's the matter dear?' he laughed at her. 'Tell me what I've done to you.'

'Oh! You don't know the matter? I know you play mischief always,' she cut it ironically. He had sufficiently incurred her wrath.

'What's the matter?' he smiled upon her as she blushed to tell it soon.

'Karisma's marriage?'

'Yes, it's already a part of history, isn't it?'

'But that's broken now.'

'Broken now? Why?' he put it surprisingly.

'She's deserted him and run away. And only God knows where she's gone off.'

'Deserted her husband? Wonderful!' he exclaimed.

There fell a silence.

'Has she come to you?' she put it earnestly.

'See you're asking me this like Kamala, that little daughter of ours,' he eluded her carefully. There was a laugh of ridicule on his face which the woman bore patiently.

'D'you think it's fair on her part to desert Mohanraj and take away their cash and jewellery?'

'Oh! She's decamped with money and gold? If so how much my dear?'

'Twentyfive thousand rupees and hundred grams of gold. Almost more than what we gave them?'

'Good Lord?' laughed he first. 'She's taught him a lesson,' her husband seemed to be ridiculing Shobha for a hasty marriage in which his consent was not taken.

'Where she must've fled? Have you learnt anything about it?' she enquired him.

'No, why I'd?' he held the field. He began 'she'd have gone to her brother at Bangalore.' He tried to avoid her morning doubtings.

Shobha sat silent unable to guess anything.

'Let's go to an STD booth to enquire your brother,' he got up to display his gaudy faith.

'It's already accomplished,' she said assuringly.

'But you didn't tell me about it? What's the matter?'

'What's there to disclose you? She's not gone there,' expressed she her dismay. 'I hope she'd have come to you?'

'Wonderful doubting! How can she come to me?' he laughed not this time.

'D'you know how Sangeeta picked up a quarrel with me during the last two days?'

'Why she'd?' 'What she did?' he asked her smiling.

'She says we're crooks...' the wife explained him the whole tragic happening and they sat silent for five minutes. Then she sought his support in the overwhelming matter.

'Now I wonder whether you're faithful to me even after that bitch's disappearance. Is it true,' she continued 'what our neighbour Rajanna says.'

'What he says,' asked he.

'He says that you're in a woman's company at your college? Even Sangeeta accused you of this,' Shobha enquired him breathlessly.

'Yes, usually Pattar and Kulkarni madams will be there with us in the college,' he burst cryptic.

'Oh!'

'However, it's a common company,' he could not help adding it.

This convinced Shobha what Rajanna briefed her had been the college women. 'Staff' when she heard it from him, mostly in a mood of hurry she failed to enquire him more about women, their identity etc. But later she decided to get more details about it. To pay a surprise visit, if necessary, to his quarters was her idea in the forthcoming days.

Then both got up to take a cup of tea and when children came home rejoicing they passed the time in their company.

On a Sunday holiday Harish was at home. He was neither unhappy nor dismayed about his wife. Mostly the day marked a new kind of relationship with her. However, what had to happen had already happened months ago. One day Harish received a phone call from Karisma and by it she had asked him whether he would accept her as his mistress. She had also made it clear that though for a month she lived at Mohanraj's house, she did not sleep with him on one or another pretexts. Hence, Harish invited her lovingly. This was of course in mutual obligation. So the providential way was clear for them and when she received a green signal, Karisma came to him at Jamakhandi. Since then she stayed with him in perfect happiness. They also hired a good house.

The moment he got back his Kashmir queen, Harish got a fresh lease of life. Happiest was he as never before. Now everything being safe, he needed not to worry about anything. In order to be safe he changed his way of life. It was anyway his nature always to be reserved and dignified. This kind of outlook he employed for maintaining his secrets. He talked less and as an introvert, he did not prefer to be acquainted with many people. He avoided local people mixing up with him. All his efforts were channelized to be a new person to the public of Banahatti lest he feared one day anyone could brief his wife about the other side of his life. It was because of Harish's dignified social bearing, tip-top dress and introversion, nobody even a familiar person spoke to him unnecessarily. Besides, he never entertained any private persons close or otherwise in his house where his sweetheart, now his wife began her fresh life. Now her second coming was a glad thing. In fact, as he did not tell about his private house, nobody knew its existence. He had set this house in a farthest suburbia. Naturally those who were familiar to him knew that he had a family in Banahatti. A few of those particularly the staff and those who contacted him for literary activities knew that his wife was in service. But nobody was aware of his recent marriage and house-setting.

As a man of deftyness, Harish to keep his affairs close to him alone, set up a good house and had acquired all facilities — phone, TV, a two-wheeler etc. Additionally to keep a balance between the two families, he kept on staying at both families on a 40:60 time proportion. He stayed three days in Banahatti, while he lived with Karisma for the remaining four days. In his absence Karisma lived with a maid-servant. As he succeeded in getting her back, Harish retrieved his repose of mind and dignity of early life. Nonetheless, he treated both the ladies alike and tried to please Shobha thereafter. This made him happy. Gradually he began caring for his children too. The latter too were happy about their father's changed attitude. But they did not perceive the reason that lay behind it. Presently Shobha was delighted over her husband's sympathetic understanding of her difficulties and problems. Now she was cared by him in many enterprises of the household matters. Undoubtedly he took a personal care in bringing things or in educating his children. He repaired the house when it needed and he beautified the garden when he liked it. This way or that the condition of Pattans' life improved and a move was ever there on Mr. Pattan's part to abridge the family units. But he was not in a hurry.

PART II

It was a cool evening. The sky was cloudy. The colour of clouds was as black as the Sabbath night. Storms had not yet appeared to devastate the climate. The terrestrial sun was fully hidden behind the clouds that were thicker and brisker than any objects. The smell of clouds was rainy and the rain was shortly to come. When the sun disappeared from the view, people turned panicky in collecting their things-corns, grains, clothes, fuel, dung cakes, edible puddings etc kept outside for drying. They hurried hither and thither and muttering something or screaming to their fellow beings, rushed home. People who were busier in their weaving or allied activities in Banahatti, did not worry to stop their dormitory activities. They did not fear the likely rainfal or about-to-come and harass storms because theirs was indoor business. Only in the long run the disaster of rainfall could disturb them.

However, neither the players nor the lookerson were perturbed by the pitch dark sky however frightening, or about the eventual rainfall thereabout. Many boys were sportively engrossed in their war of victory and defeat. A Kabaddi game was going in the town playground. Small children as well as those either deprived of play or excluded from it were thronged on the sides of playground. All were happy while observing the play between two teams headed by Venkatesh and Ravikumar. Both teams were named after Sindhur Laxman and Sangolli Rayanna respectively. A fair selection of boys had made the teams equal in capacity, rapidity, enthusiasm and sportiveness. If one time the members of Rayanna team excelled the other, the other time, the other team was about to win the game. This kept the lookers on on a tenterhook. Followers as well as admirers of the teams were equally numbered on the ground that both the teams were equally powerful. Besides, some people kept betting thinking that they would win an amount over the success of either the parties. Children were cheerful about the sport that was earnestly going on. If Venkatesh ousted some of the members of other team, next time the strongest boys of Ravikumar's team were sure to see that their team would not be defeated.

After an hour of the play, by chance Venkatesh's team emerged victorious however marginally. This definitely betrayed some of those who bet to win a huge amount. Both the admirers and followers of him were now in an ocean of joy and mirth. The moment the school umpire declared the victory that went to Laxman team, the loudest cries of children reached the sky. Many friends greeted Venkatesh soon he came out of the ground. They were oblivious of everything.

'Hoi...oi... i...i' certain boys screamed overjoyed.

'Hei...ei..ei..i' retaliated others.

'I'm glad you've won it,' an admirer congratulated Venkatesh.

'Thank you,' the leader replied soberly. He exchanged smiles with those applauding him around.

Venkatesh had grown strong these years. He had been in his B.A. already. Five-feet and six inches tall and more than sixty kilograms of weight he had been then. In physic he was exceptional in his college. Since he had a well-built up body and a vigour he was naturally attracted by sports and other bodily activities. He looked smart and there was a radiance on his face. His sportive behaviour, jovial talk and intelligence made him a college hero. Ladies of his college and town adjudged him as the most handsome person of their age, taste and temperament. They spoke of his round face, neat nose, fresh cheeks, smart mouth as ideal-looking. A cross-section of the college admired him for his good behaviour and knowledge while his teachers loved his qualities such as honesty, sincerity, sportsmanship, regularity, sociability and the like. Even some lady lecturers wished their sons should be like him. The most appealing quality of Shobha's eldest son was his sociability and flawless character. As Shobha taught her children lovable qualities, her boys were good always. As a college hero, Venkatesh was a thing of beauty and admiration of one and all. Even, he was held dearest by his kindred.

Shobha as well as Harish had been happy about the growth, education and mental-makeup of Venkatesh and Kamala. They were proud of their eldest son who grew essentially an energetic hero though more different in outlook than themselves. As a boy or youth, Venkatesh disliked his father's prescriptive behaviour at home and outside. He thought that kind of conduct would make him mechanic in daily activities and in a long run, it could dehumanize him. However Harish who did not treat others as human tried hard to make them accept his suggestions. He did not know that children must be given certain liberties in regard to the choice of their education, job, wife etc. He held the view that traditional mode of life was still the best. According to him, the sons should follow their parents whereever possible. Hence he asked his son to learn in his own line. But the youngman hated the way the old man chose for him. Admittedly the oldman's counsel that 'parental advice was the best advice' was totally unacceptable to his son. Therefore, he regarded his father a chip of the old block — useless, outmoded and inhumane.

However, Shobha was a little bit different from her sadistic husband, she too was of the same breed in regard to man's order of life and style of working. Mostly this was a generation gap. Follower of Harish initially, she was akin to him in many ways. But one distinguishable feature that kept her distinct from him was that she was humane, democratic and of suggestive nature. She never forced anyone to follow her instead she suggested them and left them to take their own decisions according to their likings. She was a person of thought and action. Unlike Harish, she thought first and then acted benevolently. She had sufficient concern for the education of her children and she never neglected them even in times of her difficulties. However, her level of understanding in regard to higher education was not datelined. Like her husband she advised Venkatesh to do an M.A. and get a job at the earliest. She knew nothing about science or technical education. Anyway the boy too had no option and he complied to the matron's honest guidance.

In total comparison, Venkatesh emerged a different boy in thinking and action. Unlike his parents, he imbibed varied characteristics which befitted the time and space he lived. Due to the influence of clime in which he grew up a man rather than due to the impact of his family background, he became a different youth. The new values of time were in him perfectly useful. He learnt most of these things right from the environment, some of them by studies, while a few of them by his benigh mother's care. Again among the environmental factors, the strongest influence was from his schools. His college teachers influenced him substantially in their own ways. He was often loved by his teachers and he revered them for their idealhood. He liked his teacher Dr. Shyamrao as he liked his sincerity and truthfulness. Another teacher, Padnavis's humanistic outlook and sociable nature had its strongest impact upon the boy's mental-makeup. He attended classes of every one of his teachers. At school and college, Venkatesh earned a good name and a group of nice friends became his closest. Besides, wherever he participated say in debates, discussions, quiz, essay competitions etc. — he was the invincible hero to get laurels of victory. The term 'College Hero' had always been his. It is in this millieu more than of the family background, he became a mature youth. Fortunately the family quarrels did not affect him the way they affected his brother.

Certain Venkatesh loved his mother more than he loved his father. He hated Harish, for the reason, he did not remain at home the time he was expected of. Rightly because of his second marriage with Karisma years ago when she returned to him faithfully, Harish could not concentrate his fullest attention at home. Now he was a man of split-personality, while Shobha did whatever she could for the welfare of her children. Besides,

Harish's attitude towards others including his family, was characterized by 'I-It' relationship. This house-master thought as once he argued with his wife that others were less important to him. Thus Harish was callous, unurbane, inhumane and unsociable. Because of his imposing nature, prescriptive behaviour and materialistic attitude, he could not avoid earning more enemies than friends. Another lacuna of his persona was excentricity and his apparent short temperament. If anyone spoke to him particularly bitter things, he could turn indifferent. Indeed, to his domestic problems, Harish became a divided self.

On the contrary, Shobha had been gracefully endowed with nice qualities like humanness, humility, kindness, truthfulness, charity etc. She was ever a loving dame. Although she did not become a good wife to some extent, she succeeded greatly in becoming an ideal mother. Owing to her narrow-mindedness, if it can be said, she spoiled Karisma's future and her own domestic integrity. Good or ill in Harish's view had she permitted him to marry Karisma, all could have led much a happier life than the miserable one presently they were placed in. But whenever she remembered Harish-Karisma interlude, she turned annoyed and wild. The nightmare of those days, Shobha's protestation to it, and her husband's subsequent indifference had by then sapped her feminine vigour and energy. However, she could not neglect her children. Because of them alone, she lived ever fresh and strong. Harish's home-coming was just a token visit — a secondary compensation. Indeed, she doubted his fidelity but she was too innocent to decipher his love-affair with many women he had.

In between the husband and wife's conflict, the children grew their own ways. Venkatesh, the eldest one liked neither his father nor the family set-up. He started his own way of life under the sway of those who influenced him. Greatly influenced by the environment, school culture and education, he developed a good taste for life and his temperament became bearable to any persons.

Never the less, the most unfortunate being in the house had been neither Harish nor Shobha but Ashok, the second son of Harish-Shobha misfiring. This boy who disinherited his parents' virtues was fortunate to grow in an affluent atmosphere of Pattans. As Harish neglected the family altogether, Shobha could not control his misbehaviour. So Ashok grew uncultured. He cared neither for his parents nor for his teachers at school. He disobeyed all. On the ground that he was a lecturer's son, his teachers could not devise any means to chastise him. Nor did they advocate his parents about his beastie behaviour either? In an atmosphere of disorder and also of poor supervision at home he turned a broomhead — unpleasant, stupid and aggressive. Similarly his mother could not take as much care for him as she did in the case of his brother. His schooling was unplanned, his education was irregular and his tastes were erratic and by temperament he became unbearable. His unruly conduct upset all those in the house and outside. He displeased even those who advised him. Admittedly Shobha could not discipline the boy in the beginning he had to be bent. This was attributed to the frequent family disturbances. Consequently, like a wild boor or haifer, Ashok roved always and this undesirable trend continued in his later years just to destroy his career. The years Venkatesh busied himself to mould his career, Ashok misspent it. The mode of life he lived was chaotic to such an extent that nobody could alter it. No matter people advised him to go in a right direction, he continued walking on thorns. Often in shabby dress, a wastrel he wandered to places with a set of like minded friends until his pocket money exhausted. Further pocket money was given to him next day and further grew up his evil doings. He ate whatever he liked and he did whatever his whims dictated. This state of affair simply mirrored the drastic family situation.

What of the little girl Kamala? She was a good girl with all her culture and obedience. The youngest dolly bird, she followed Venkatesh instead of Ashok, her boyhood companion. Like anyone of her house, she knew Ashok's company was unhealthy. As she was not allowed to go out, she did not find a company with spoiled children either. In the docile company of her benigh mother, she read well and acquired an education and womanly behaviour that was to help her life-long.

Indeed, as the king, so the subject. The parents influenced or spoiled their children in a way every educated and humane critic could reproach. Harish and Shobha's frequently held quarrels damaged the young minds and hurt them obviously.

Venkatesh, the first boy found it very difficult to stay most of the time at home. So was Ashok, a rogue who left the house at morn and turned up only at a time when he spent all of his money or he became over-hungry. Nobody knew whether he went to school or visited brothels for B-girls. But Kamala, a donah, went to school without fail. Owing to her dejection, Shobha too kept quite and she could not guide the kids in every facet of their stormy life. But she did not neglect them grossly.

It was ever one of a bitter Sunday mornings. Harish then had just gone off after a skirmish with his wife. The children were amidst them listening frightened. Venkatesh sat silent, while Kamala minded her homework and the other boy had disappeared to places which nobody knew. Harish's disppearance had made the mother fall asobbing. This made her eldest son share her mother's sorrows. This was a common affair at least once a week.

'Why he quarrels with you every day?' Venkatesh enquired the tragic figure sorrowing beside him.

'He's a Satan son,' she spoke him her anguish. 'He is a sadist, always cunning and sly,' she cursed him. 'A crumpetman,' she mentioned something which the little man did not understand, nor did he desire to know it.

'You need not sob for that. Be courageous to brave up situations,' Venkatesh used the words his teacher had used while abetting students. Presently the mother had squatted on floor musing upon his solace. What consoled her was not the words, nor the ideas, nor his benigh presence but the boy's support of her cause.

'I'm very unhappy mother, because when we want him here, daddy does not turn up. Why he does so daily?'

'He's to mind his duty.'

'But during the years of aunt's stay he was here always?'

'True. But he says now he's some work at his office.'

'How can it be for him alone, while the parents of my friends come home daily?' The boy was right and the mother looked wrong in her assertion. In fact, she hid the truth not to corrupt his tender mind.

'That's right, but he doesn't prefer to stay with us,' she spoke helplessly.

'Mummy, I believe, you'd a squabble with him some time ago. Why?'

'I pleaded with him to save his salary.'

'Oh! Does he not give you any of it?'

'Not at all. He says he needs all of it for himself.'

'Is he honest at that?'

'Only God knows it,' the mother turned fatalistic. She looked utterly disappointed. 'Not only that he also wants some of my salary,' she added it bitterly.

'Wonderful! Wonderful!' Venkatesh burst out into a peel of laughter.

'Mummy I don't know why he's angry with us always?' he spoke candidly.

'Because he's not a good father,' the lady consoled the youngling.

'Is he good for anything then?'

There was a silence.

The mother remained mute. She was relactunt to break the silence herself. Right was her decision not to make her sons aware of her husband's whims or caprices lest they would corrupt them. It was under these considerations till then she had not yet briefed them any serious family disturbances. Like others she too opposed Harish's prescriptive behaviour and sadistic designs.

During these years of turbulence Harish had set up a house for Karisma, his dearest. After their wedding at Dharmasthala, they started leading a happier life than anyone of his relations. Luckily nobody was aware of their internal details. Now Harish was 'no more a backdoor man to Karisma.' Presently she was his rightful wife, a tendermost soul. He made her happy even though they lived in the absence of their kindred. Already Ravindra, her brother had forgotten her runaway issue, while their aged mother lived no more to see that degeneration. Besides, her one time husband made no move to get her back. In these tidings of affairs, Karisma bore a child, of course a son. No wonder, the newlyweds led a happy life with their desires few and far between.

It was an April Monday. Harish came home early. The time he reached his house at Vasant Nagar, the sun was about to settle down at the down edge of the bluest sky while his golden rays spread across the western horizon. Cuckoos were singing in the park and many other birds bound homeward chirping. The vast sky free of the rainbearing clouds was clearest and brightest. Karisma was at work in the garden when the moment her man stepped in.

'Where is the boy?' he enquired her.

'He's at bed dear,' the woman replied polite.

'What you're upto there?'

'I'm at work.'

'Did anybody come here asking me?'

'None, was anyone to see you?' she enquired him gently.

'Someone was to pass by here,' Harish scratched his head in a deep worry.

'May I know the gentleman?'

'Venkatesh, your dear son was to come this way.'

'Will he come to us?'

'I'm told Siddanna's son is his friend and classmate.'

'Good. That's nice. D'you know Siddanna's son had participated in the recent Kabaddi tournment where Venkatesh's team got victory?'

'Is it?' Harish smiled upon her big brown eyes. He knew till then nothing about his son's adventures.

'I know you want my bags only,' she glanced his chest intently.

Both kissed each other fondly.

'Tell me how is my sister and her children?' she asked him, while he began stroking her.

'They're happy as ever before.'

'I believe she's not forgotten me?'

'Certainly...'

'Mama but I didn't hate her, did I?'

'Of course not.'

'D'you know how I love her? Still fresh is my desire to live with her together.'

'It's but pointless now.'

There fell a short silence.

Though they were quizzical neither of them made a move to brake it. Each was dismayed of their hoary past. Shortly the man aspired to continue his broken conversation.

'D'you know the wonder that Shobha has not yet learnt anything about this house?' he stopped in an expectation of her reaction.

'Are you cocksure of it, Hari?' the stately queen in attractive guise enquired her David.

'Yes; d'you know that you've to appreciate me for my brilliance in keeping her always unaware of this,' Harish turned proud of his officialized den of villainy.

'Don't think I don't want to see her.' Karisma spoke slyly. Presently his hand rested around her.

'But that's unthinkable in the present circumstance.'

'Please don't touch there,' at once she threw him aside adjusting her position 'I don't think so,' she burst out.

'Wonderful! you women are always short-minded. D'you forsee the current events? I wonder whether I can be able to maintain this composure life long,' Harish shot it with an ire, while Karisma consoled him scanning his body.

'Shall I think she'll be upset the moment she learns of our marriage?'

'Hundred per cent,' he adjusted his moustache.

'Then it's useless to think of family reunion.'

'I've said it umpteen times,' he broke enerved.

'Doesn't matter.'

'You're always crazy. D'you know how I'm tired of you. If I go to her, I'm enquired bitterly and I fail to answer most of her questions. Whilest I'm here, you burn me with your emotions. Besides, some of my college chaps have spread a news that I've developed an affair with Kulkarni madam.'

'Who's that my dear? D'you go to her also?' Karisma broke stunned by this.

'Lo! nonsense, I did not say they say I sleep with her. I only said you that they've cooked up a story.'

'Is it darling?' she giggled.

'First I'm the stupid fellow,' he cursed himself.

'Why?'

'Because I told you this.'

'Alright dear.' What else do they talk of you?' she turned earnest.

'What else? They also say that I've committed the blunder of bigamy.'

'Oh! What's that my Hari?' Unaware of the new word, she turned curious again. 'Blunder ... By Game ...' she intoned the sounds.

'Not By Game, Bygamy. It means my marriage with you while still you're someone's wife.'

'Oh! sheer nonsense. Let that bloody chap go to hell. Why you worry of that dumbass with whom I didn't sleep even for a day though I'd been his wife for a month,' the biddy burst angrily. Her tone displayed her characteristic hatredness of the business 'boor' of Hubli.

'How's that man?' Harish began amusingly.

'I told you, he's a village boor only known for his eating.'

'What about mating?'

'A big ziro!'

'Wonderful!'

'I think for that reason alone you left him.'

'No, he tried for the O but I avoided him everytime in the first week of marriage. Then he stopped himself asking for it,' she spoke proudly.

'Oh! he's not an eunuch then.'

'I believe, he may not be so.'

'You said he's a villager though he lives in Hubli.'

'That's just a migration.'

'Is he a clever chap?'

'Certainly not. He's a cementhead!' There was hatredness in her voice. Every pauze of her sentences displayed her patience she had while she lived with her former husband. Even she did not like Harish call her a former wife of that bloody dog.

'So you're happy about me?' Harish asked her teasingly.

'Hari you're an anasin asking me the same question hundred times!' she spoke back injured.

'Alright! Let's be happy then,' Harish closed the talk with a sense of relief.

On a February Monday Venkatesh, the leader of a Kabaddi team came to Jamakhandi. Now he was a sportive youth with impressive moustache. He also had some tender beards which looked like newly born sheep wool. Now he looked a big man with a height that was more than his father's. He looked impressive to everyone of his kindred. The charm and vigour he possessed was stronger than his father's. His short but attractive hairs black in tint looked handsome. His fair complexion, good health and pleasant outlook made him a hero of his class. Every studentfolk respected him alike — juniors liked him as a model and inspirative, and seniors admired him. Besides, his relatives and well-wishers abetted him everytime he showed a mark of growth. In an atmosphere of love, support and admiration, the young man became a jem to every adoring figure.

The moment he came to Jamakhandi he decided to see one of his important friends. He went to Shivakumar's house which was near the government quarters where Harish, Venkatesh's father lived temporarily. As he had no scootar though he wanted one urgently he could not avoid walking. Although he urged his parents for a two-wheeler, nobody minded him. So he walked to Shivakumar's house. Occasionally he also had certain worries. However, his immediate concern was to obtain an M.A. and, like his parents, to become a lecturer. He liked this job as it was easy and gracious. He knew how his parents as lecturers led a life of ease. But the way he had to traverse for getting it was not as easy as his doting mother often thought of.

Now Venkatesh came to his friend's house near his father's quarters. He saw the house. But to his surprise he found none there. The house was locked. Some labours were working outside at it. Thence he could not help enquiring the supervisor of the hands and on enquiry he learnt the family of Siddanna, Shivakumar's father had been shifted to their own house newly constructed in Vasant Nagar.

Now Venkatesh turned to Vasant Nagar. Presently he came somewhere near Siddanna's house, but he was lost in the way. An urgent enquiry gave him some correct idea of the location. Admittedly now he came very near a house where he had never been supposed to go in accordance with his father's wish. Trotted he to a bylane where he had been shortly to be taken aback by a rare sound and sight in his life. No wonder he had not yet passed a short-cut road a voice so melodious, so familiar, so touching like a nightingale's, reached his sensitive ears. At once, he saw the figure. The sight looked hearty and the sound pleased him. It was the sound of a woman who had brought him up withal her love and affection. It was also the woman who brought so much of sorrow to every member of the Pattans. It was the person who had loved him more than his own mother. How was Venkatesh to forget Karisma, his beloved aunt, motherely aunt and sweet aunt? It was Karisma, the mother like figure at once asked him to get indoors. The moment she called him, he could not help recollecting his inward thoughts-her love, affection, adamancy, help, protection, so on and so forth. He also recollected the demerits of her in spoiling his father-mother relationship. Indeed, to him Karisma looked none other than a forbidden fruit, an Eve of the Eden as he heard it of in an English lesson. But he knew how his father accepted such a 'Sweet Poison' without any introspection.

Wonderous things are pleasant. No sooner he heard the voice of the blue-eyed belle, than he was patted by her fruity hands. Presently he was happy beside her. Nor was Karisma less glad to see, hear and love him with her whole heart.

'How are you?' the aunt spoke to him first with an unknown pleasure.

'Fine, how are you aunt?' he spoke back to her with cheers. 'Why you're here?' asked he earnestly. Presently each held the other very dear.

'Don't you know I'm here only,' she smiled upon him.

'No, we don't know anything about you since wedding.'

'Of course!' she spoke cautiously. Like her sister she too was afraid of her cruel neighbours' gossiping. Immediately the little man dearest to the dame was asked to get indoors. Great was Venkatesh's joy about the building. It looked very gorgeous and exotic. It was a mini bungalow. Though only a two bed-roomed house, it possessed all facilities promised by modern science including a garden. It was a newly built up RCC building. Modern facilities like TV, washing machine, refrigerator, nice dining table, a set of sofa and several other things he knew not all made of teakwood adored the rich residence. The flooring was made of Shahbad marble. It shone like mirror. The roof was richly decorated with designs made in Plastar of Paris. Additionally the house was sufficiently sunlighted, ventilated and spacious. The newly-brought up electric devices kept it cool and comfortable.

The moment Venkatesh stepped into Karisma's house, he glanced at TV whereon he found some glamorous and exotic scenes. It seemed to be a movie. The scenes looked fascinating and sensuous. Certain abscene pictures did not take much time to engage Venkatesh's emotions. His attention was wholly diverted to it now. Meanwhile, Karisma shut the windows. Venkatesh was engrossed in gazing the scenes. Anyway it was nothing but a film. True but the nature of it was unknown to him or he was new to such exotic scenes. Therefore, he took much time to learn it to be a blue film. The pictures he saw were about an Englishman dallying with a woman of his own breed. The two sensuous couple married or not, flirted on a sandbank by a riverside. They were not disturbed by anyone. The sight of sea waves incessantly coming to them witnessed their ecstatic moments. He saw them to be in bollock-naked. The man's act of giving her a French kiss and getting his leg across her was shown. Venkatesh's heart was enthralled by this. He kept on looking at it. The episode was hearty. The next scene in which the Anglo woman fell in Anglo man's arms made him totally unaware of the external disturbance. This spectacle simply confirmed his raw beliefs in matters of love and woman.

Venkatesh was still looking at the TV when he heard a more familiar voice. Admittedly he did not know Karisma had called him twice. But his mind was elsewhere still. Amused by this, Karisma made no move to awaken him. In fact, she saw Venkatesh's charming body and made no hesitation to think of him in terms of something. She was sure of his sexual maturity by his interest in such scenes as just evidenced. She was busy in designing a seduction. However, the execution of it urgently looked absurd. Only after an eight years of gap they had met each other and to her tasting him today looked odd. Therefore, she gave up the idea for the time being. But she could not help seeing him with an eye of lust. A poor fellow. She could not understand the little man's strong moral fibre or his singular mind.

'You're happy to watch the film?' kissing the youth the aunt spoke in an erotic mood.

'No, no,' surprised by her caress, Venkatesh replied shyly. But he did not mistake her kissing, which he thought, had been a symbol of her affection. In fact, it was the continuation of her old motherly love after a gap of eight years.

'I think you love such films,' she spoke.

'Usually I don't. But this time I can't help seeing it in your company. You know had it been in mother's company, she'd have scolded me like anything.' Amused by the scenes, he spoke to her freely. 'Is it a blue film aunt?'.

'Yes, it's a blue film very special,' she smiled upon him with a loving eye.

'Blue film means ...?' he broke in wonder.

'Blue film means... kissing,' she embrassed him again in the manner she did it to him years ago. This thrilled the boy. 'Come here next time, I'll tell you what it's and also you can see one more blue film,' she told him pleasingly. Soon the film was over and Venkatesh who sat next to her, body to body, glanced at the snacks placed by her in front of him.

'Take the *ladu* and *kara*,' she told him affectionately.

'It's too much. I can't eat it unless you share,' he told her happy of it. This coaxed her and she began sharing it. Now they were talking about the matters that concerned them most.

'Aunt I know you married a Hubli business man.'

'Yes.'

'Aunt I also know you left him to his misfortunes,' broke he complainingly.

'Of course.'

'Aunt thereafter where have you been?' he looked at her earnestly.

'I've been here only.'

'Shall I think you're in service here?'

'Something is being done,' she eluded a direct reply.

'D' you mind if I want to know it?'

'Let me tell it to you later.'

'Can you kindly tell it now itself?' he implored. He was curious. But greater his insistence, more stubborn she became. Of course she had been right in withholding an immediate reply in the interest of her future or of the whole family. Thereafter seeing the youngster's amazing, she kissed him once more. Or it could be said, she kept him awaiting for a reply in a bid to entice him passionately.

'I'm living here.'

'I know it, but who else lives with you?' he stopped eating now making her more joyous.

'I tell you next time,' she held the field.

'Why aunt?'

'Because I want you come here.'

'Don't worry I'll come here often.'

'Are you cocksure of it?'

'Hundred per cent,' he assured her.

'Promise me then.'

'Alright,' he promised her at once. As he put his little hard hand upon her silken, she took it tightly to her big brown eyes. At times she kissed them. No matter he turned shy of her frequent kisses, she enjoyed his hands and held them dear to her heart. Now he was conscious of his adulthood and he knew that he should not kiss her or fall upon her as he did it during his childhood years, whereas Karisma had learnt nothing in the matter. She kissed him as she did it last decade. Possibly she was heavily bent upon enjoying him.

'Tell me aunt,' he persisted.

'I've one more condition,' she broke dallying.

'Damn your conditions. Let me know it soon,' said he.

'You'd visit me frequently and shouldn't disclose the matter to any one,' Karisma stopped in lieu of his yessing.

'Agreed aunt,' he looked all assuring.

'Promise me again.'

'Take it for granted,' Venkatesh threw his hand again and he did not worry about it's misappropriation. She shook it to her bosom. Now Karisma came close to him than ever before. She put her hand around his body. Both felt a kind of sensation. She enjoyed the tenderness of him while he tolerated her motherly embrace. He recollected the film a short while ago he enjoyed. He could not help it anyway. Indeed, Karisma's touchings gave the youth a kind of message but he failed to understand it. Mostly his strong morale hindered his perception of unlawful sex.

'What you learn by this?' she asked him tenderly as he was looking at her uncovered breasts. She did it deliberately.

'I don't find anything new aunt,' the other made a move towards her. Shortly he turned his body down. He was resting in sleeping position his head on her laps. He pulled her as he did it in the past. Karisma loved him doing so. He cought hold of her hands and at close insistence found her ready to disclose the matter. Really she was enjoying him, keeping him curious of the matter.

I'm living with *mama* together,' she burst out cheerfully. By now the lustrous woman took the little man in her silken arms intermittently allowing him for a separation.

'With daddy you mean?' he was surprised . In the mood of wonder he forgot his body which she had taken.

'Yes with him! why?'

'No I mistook the word *mama* for Mohanraj,' he turned eager.

'Stupid chap,' she cut it jovially.

'Then?'

'Harish *mama*,' she held his hands again. In fact, they slept like two friends, while only the woman being intentionally sexual in her touchings.

'It's wonderful! Are you here aunt ever since you left Hubli?'

'Yes.'

'Then who is that boy crying in cradle?' Vankatesh who heard the child's cry could not help asking her about other matters. He was earnest in exploring mysteries.

'He's your little brother,' spoke she lively.

'My little brother? Very nice to know it.'

'Yea don't you want him?'

'Certainly I want him. But now I'm at a loss to understand. Is it born to daddy or...?

'Yes it's your daddy's, not Mohanraj's. I know now you are mature enough to know the deeper truths,' she spoke like a woman who interacted with an elderly person.

'So this means you and daddy are living here together. You've a child also,' he saw her with smiles and she loved his understanding of the situation. Her hand was on his shoulder, and some portion of her saree flapped down. Karisma did not sit properly and the other looked at her curious. Good or ill, he thought about her bad qualities — diserting her husband, marrying his father much against the wish of his mother, house setting, a child — all mind boggling. Indeed, he looked at her with a questioning smile.

'I'm happy that I've a brother,' he said coolly.

'Not only a child, but also a happy life,' she giggled.

'Shall I think you hated the uncle as you couldn't live with him?'

'I found him unbearable.'

'Really?'

'Hundred per cent.'

'Or did you love daddy more than you loved him?' the other put it smiling. He looked charming to her if not emotionally.

'Yes, I loved *mama* most,' she grinned.

There fell a heavy silence. But soon it was broken by the elderly lady.

'Are you sure of seeing me here again and again?' She put a piece of sweet in his mouth which he ate gladly.

'Oh! Yes aunt don't you know that I'm as good as my words?'

'Anyway I believe you,' she put another piece of sweet in his mouth. 'Did you come here to meet anyone?' Now the tone of her interest sidelined.

'Oh! That's a story of wonder,' he explained her the reasons of his dropping there. Then she heard about his achievements with a genuine concern. But she did not ask him anything of others. Nor did she try to know about Shobha during his stay there almost for an hour. In fact, she had an upto date knowledge of Shobha's family by her man.

'Shall I know as to when you'll turn up here?' she looked at him with a broad smile.

'I can't say the date. But I'll come.'

'Please do come. Next time I'll show you a 'Raja and Rani' film. That's very nice,' said she.

'Ok, aunt good bye,' he smiled.

'Good bye,' she spòke with affection.

The infatuation started in the woman on seeing him visiting her for the first time. No matter, he was her own sister's son, or more interestingly a son to her husband, Karisma felt it worth a try. Presently she stood at the gate gazing at the vanishing figure. Already he had entered her passionate heart, and her desire for him increased as she thought of him. She was sure he would come to her again and would touch her bosom. She had made her efforts to woo him sexually. The moment he went off, she had also given him some pocket money and found him jolly. The talk and treatment she gave him was warm. Karisma still stood at the gate looking at the direction of vanishing figure. She regretted for his quick disappearance. Both were equally happy about each other's visit and in theory they desired it often.

Thereafter, Venkatesh met his friend and the same day he left for his house. He was happy about his journey. When he came home, he could not avoid a guest who wanted him utmost. Like a constable who catches criminals, the newcomer, cought hold of his friend. As he had come from a far off place, Venkatesh too could not avoid the situation. As there was some urgent decision to be taken up in regard to the finalization of Kabaddi team, Venkatesh followed him. However, before he went off he left his mother in a state of scuffle.

'Where're you upto so long?' the perturbed mother enquired her son.

'I'd been to Jamakhandi in connection with sports activity.'

'Of course, why you did not turn up soon?' she retorted him. 'D'you know, how the guest is waiting for you since the moment you left the house?' she spoke of the situation.

'That's a great story *ma*,' burst he.

'Great story? What's that? Can't you tell me.'

‘I went to daddy’s quarters and found someone there,’ he laughed at her. No sooner he said it to her than he recollected the promise he had given to Karisma aunt. So on further enquiry, he did not disclose her any inner details. Partly he had been in a hurry too. Fortunately, he had mentioned her ‘quarters’ instead of ‘house.’ Moreover, he told her he found ‘someone,’ but not ‘any woman.’ This protected the interests of Karisma. Since he was going out, the mother too did not persist on it further. She knew in the presence of an outsider, it was not fair for her to talk of family matters. No doubt, within a few minutes, he disappeared much to her dismay.

Indeed, in the presence of some clues, it could be said, doubts of women particularly in matters of sex are strengthened. This was greatly true in case of Shobha. She took her son’s words as real and started to think of her husband’s affairs secretely carried on. She thought Harish should have a woman in his quarters. Then the view that Karisma should be living with him came to her mind. Since she was known to Harish’s vagaries, Shobha did not take much time to predict the unthinkable. No wonder, ever since she found her husband visiting her only twice a week, she found something wrong with his sex habits. Unfortunately her doubtings were not yet corroborated by any proofs. But Venkatesh’s jocular comment strengthened her suspicion. Perturbed at once she left for Jamakhandi mentally. Soon she found the house of her husband, a woman with him very fair, fairer than her sitting skin to skin and dallying with him. She amazed at her beauty, shapely limbs and celestial features. At once she turned envious of her, indifferent to them and began hating their business. The upset woman could not control herself. So she hit the woman and when she found her husband angry, she saw him coming to her with a cane. The scene turned horrible. ‘Nonsense,’ cried Shobha at once. Quickly she saw outside and turned reticent of her imaginary search. She found unhappy about the mad recallings. Now she forgot what she dreamed. But she was still thinking of scolding them harshly if found there. But Ashok and Kamala had not yet returned home. As the food for them was ready, she had sufficient time to sit whiling away her time. Shobha recollected Harish again, his gross negligence of the family and his probable frequenting of cathouses. Sufficient doubts about his habits entered her sensibility. How can she forget Sangeeta's accusation that 'Harish lies in brothel women's sarees?' She recalled her colleague's quarrel with her and her tabernacle groan thereby. Incident after incident came to her in reels. Presently she remembered how Sharada, her friend found her husband frequenting a woman at Shetter Colony. One day, as Shobha learnt, Sharada found a clue of his affair and suddenly she followed it. No doubt, she found her husband with a woman and caught him in red hand and taught her a lesson by dragging her out when she had still been naked. This had, in fact, been reported in massmedia. No matter though her husband was rich, Sharada divorced him on the ground of infidelity.

Be it as it may, Shobha was still musing over the course of action to be pursued if Harish was seen with anywoman, anywhere, anytime. She was disturbed by legal actions against them. Quickly an idea came to her as to why she should not pay a surprise visit to him immediately. Indeed, the disturbed dame left for Jamakhandi at once.

Exactly within half an hour, the woman had been very much in front of Harish's quarters near the Government bus stand. She found his quarters open and within no time, like a cat, she got indoors. Things of surmise awaited her. She found a bedroom bolted inside. This strengthened her doubt greatly. She made no noise. Nor did she call for him either? None stood outside and the varandah, sit out and hall looked empty and desolate. The flooring was unswept. The woman saw all rooms except a bedroom which she thought to be closed inside. Apparently she did not notice the toilet. The closure of bedroom and hissing sounds coming thereby made her an extremely curious figure. Due to her shortness she could not see anything through the window. Very eager, as she was to catch him, she knocked on the door amazingly. Could she get any response? No, nothing came in turn. Enraged by this she knocked the door violently. As a result, a hoarse sound gushed out suddenly and within a minute like a protean figure, a huge body appeared there out of a cell of nothingness.

'Who's it?' the man asked her. But she was immediately identified. Her very presence surprised him and he did not expect a reply to his question.

'What you're upto there with hissing sounds?' Shobha cried but with a guilty consciousness as she found her act awkward.

'I was in the bathroom, is it wrong?' He spoke calmly. There was a smile of worldly wisdom on his face.

'I think there is someone inside?'

'Where in this room? None is there,' he spoke.

'Then why it's closed inside?'

'No, it's not bolted inside. It's kept close because of bad hinges,' he explained.

'Is it? But I found some sound coming from there?' She remained-doubting.

'I know women are cynical and sufficiently impractical. You've nothing but doubts about me in your cementhead. Nonsense,' he started reproaching her.

'Stop your verbosity,' she quipped him.

Presently she was sitting upon a sofa. He came to her teasing. They chatted for a while. The theme of their discussion was children's education and handloans.

'I'm surprised over your coming here,' he spoke coolly.

'I came here as I got a news that some lady had come here. Just I wanted to befriend her,' Shobha voiced her heartfelt apprehension which already he had anticipated at the very moment she rushed in.

'Wonderful! You doubt me always,' he sat criticising her. 'Who told you this?'

'Your son.'

'My son?'

'Yes, Venkatesh, the hero.'

'I wonder whether he saw me here.'

'It's what he told me darling.'

'Stupid fellow, idiot. What he knows of me here. He knows only how to fish in troubled waters,' Harish turned angry.

There was a pauze.

'Then you, the shrewdest woman came here to catch me, didn't you?' he giggled.

'Mistake me not. I simply came here to know whether you are happy or not. That's all,' Shobha improved her tone. 'However,' she continued, 'I don't find you loving me these days.'

'Is it the first time you're accusing me this? In spite of the fact that I do love you, you say I don't. When will you say I'll?' he asked her musingly. 'Mostly you tell this only when I die. Whom else I love, if I don't you? Forgotten you're about my love. Besides my genuine concern for the children is always there,' he spoke imposingly.

'Then why you don't turn up home everyday as you did it earlier. I mean you came home daily when Karisma stayed with us,' she looked complaining.

'Let me convince you. See these days as I've undertaken a UGC project, I'm very busy here. That's why it's become difficult for me to come there daily,' Harish falsfied things reliably.

'I know you're a perfect liar,' Shobha touched him in a manner that stirred his heart. Soon he bent upon her heavily. He was shrewd enough to entice women and to keep them under an impression. Although he was with Karisma almost for a decade he did not yet make his wife aware of it. He was marvellous at mischief. The art of hiding came to him naturally. He played every gimmick to keep women obedient. Harish had embraced many more beside these sisters. He had an affair with a woman at Pampapattan when he had been there for examination works. However, his liking of that gross-widow was just for a bait. This affair of him took place accidently. The time he first went to Kamalamma's house as a familiar person, he saw her door open. As he was very close to her, he rushed in while after a fresh bath she was just dressing then. He stepped into her room even without making any sounds. Then he saw Kamalamma and kissed her. The woman's submission turned the two to love-romance-lust. No wonder, his frequent visits to Pampapattan made each other closest and the affair flourished. The poor woman deprived of her husband's love gave herself to this sundry star. She could not help it since she had none for her bodily relief. In fact, Harish named his daughter just after this kept.

Venkatesh's education progress was rapid. As a sportstar too he made a name. As a student leader, he was much heard. People liked his leadership in sports and intellectual brilliance. The hero's perfect sociability, friendship and concern for fellow beings contributed a great deal towards his coming up. During the months of January and February, his team had won inter-university as well as zonal Kabaddi competitions. The principal of college, the staff, his friends and a cross section of sports lovers had a special love and admiration for him. His parents as well as Karisma apprised his talent and encouraged his enterprises. All loved him as their hero of the days to come. In turn, Venkatesh too had been a nice person. He respected all alike and never tried to find fault with others. He had warmth and concern for others who did anything towards his career either in words or deeds. Nor did he show any sense of ungratefulness to those who lent their hands to him in his hours of crisis. He had a perfect confidence in others and trusted people. His behaviour and relations with others were always in the boundary of commonsense. He was modest, he never did anything in excess. In this way he became a gentleman, a rising star, a hero to everyone including his college girls.

Ashok had been an exception to the above character sketch of his brother. Already he was a youth of more than twenty. But to those who saw him closely, he looked more a spoilt child. A genuine observer could say he was an unboiled egg, only chaff yet. People's apprisal of him differed as the assessment of him by his own parents. Harish thought his younger son was a spendthrift. He did not respect the rogue. His hatredness stemmed out because of Ashok's wrong code of conduct. Ashok hated his father on the ground that he did not care him. Never during the years of his growth, Ashok found Harish loving him. The man rarely complimented his son. However, Shobha loved him on the ground she was his mother. But her mistake was unpardonable in so far as she gave him pocket money liberally. This made the prodigal fall into a bad company. He took money; spent it on anything he liked; and turned a wastrel. Needless to say his addiction to drinks and his accompaning of squanderers spoiled him. Nor did he care for his brother's advice 'a wrong move in life will spoil one's career.' As entertainment mattered him most, Ashok loved luxuary. Besides, the dearth of proper parental care gave a death knell to his future. However he went to college, he did not study. Consequently he was a pass class always. Additionally his love for women added its own mite to his failures and frustrations.

However, Kamala was an exception. A girl of rare beauty, docile character, she attended her classes regularly and found her studies useful. She was like her eldest brother in matters of study, hobbies and attitude. She too found Ashok a gross villain. She did not like him. Consequently none could chastise the degenerated boy.

Shobha returned home. Her investigation was an utter failure. Though the man committed blunders she could not detect him as he excelled her in everything. Her eldest son too came home. But the matron could not get any clues for an exploration of the mystery. In this light, Venkatesh's exposition did not matter her. Nor did she make an honest effort to trace the truth? While

Venkatesh sat silent over the matter, she did not ask him about Karisma's exile. Besides, he was busy elsewhere. So the truth found no outlet. How can it? Things only moved. However Shobha asked Venkatesh whether he really saw any woman staying with his father, the boy spoke nothing. He merely laughed at her. So his reel of laughter did not strengthen her doubting. Later the woman herself dismissed it as a matter of joke. Her inspection of Harish did not convince her anything. Thus, the mystery remained a balloon of the air.

Venkatesh passed his BA with first class distinction. Happiest and much loved he was when he stood first to his college and got gold medals. He also received a letter from his principal about his academic excellences. People familiar or not, good or ill, spoke of him in high terms. But Venkatesh was least proud of his achievements. However, good results brought him good satisfaction. Since he knew both defeat and victory, he did not boast of his credentials. He had his own set of standards and as per them only he judged himself and others. He was not emotionally charged by any external laurels however impressive. Nonetheless, the results gave him an elation and a sort of proven confidence. It increased the list of his friends as he was social and pleasant. Thus, he found himself an acknowledged hero in society.

Wonderful enough, Venkatesh's spheres of activities expanded by many folds then. People called on him for social, literary and even for political activities. As an NSS leader, he had actively participated in social welfare programmes. His team had successfully built up many shelters, repaired public buildings, had donated blood. It had cleaned the silt of tanks and skirted playgrounds. It did much service to his college in a variety of construction activities. Those people who were in touch with college activities knew his social works. His concern for others had by then indubitably been recognised by local leaders. Similarly Venkatesh's interests for literature had been sufficiently nurtured. Manytimes he had participated in debates, discussions, essay and poetry competitions. His grip over English had been modest and he spoke it fluently. He conducted many functions as efficiently as he spoke with townlet gentry. His literary taste, cultural awareness and new ideas went in making him a promising figure. There was melody in his speech and vigour and freshness in his linguistic competence. As a brilliant student on several occasions he had given Radio talks too. Venkatesh had been interested in religious activities as well. It was because of religious impact, he had become a disciplined and virtuous individual. Even he had attended many religious celebrations.

The greatest man of religion who influenced him was Swami Vivekananda. There were other influences too. Once when he attended a lecture of Kashi Swamiji at RLS College Pampapattan, he underwent a benigh change.

The great event for him ran thus. On one fine day, Venkatesh went to Pampapattan. On his friend's persuation, he attended a religious serman. It was a Monday evening. The atmosphere was religious and pleasant. The whole college ground was filled with thousands of people. There had been a huge pendalin on the western side of the ground. Adjoining to this extended a mass of chairs and carpets. On all sides brightly burned tubelights like the lights of heavenly wisdom. In fact, the ground looked like a stary sky. Amidst this arrangement erected was the huge podium for the Swamiji and his retinue. The floor was fully covered by devotees. Everything was full of human activities.

Upon the other side of ground stood the Town Hall. The opposite area was occupied by a college building. This edifice of education was bigger than one thinks of it. It had its own porch very wide and it spread throughout the length of the huge structure. The vehicles of people as well as of the institution were grandly parked along the walls of buildings. The rich men came in vehicles, while the poor attended it on bicycles or they came by walk. All kinds of townfolk of Hindu faith, men and women, rich and poor, educated or not, good or evil, had thronged there. Both sexes were in equal numbers. Even the population of children was not marginal. It was seven o' clock when the Swamiji stepped up podium to enjoy a classical music recited by Dr. Nanda M. Patil, a well-known Hindustani vocalist. First the artist sang some prayer songs followed by several hymns. But her devotional songs that gave the meaning 'life is a futile doing' appealed to many a heart. No sooner the Swamiji had come there than the artist finished her music which soothed many souls. The Swamiji sat on an elevated silver chair and his presence drew the attention of the august gathering.

No people even the children talked while Dr. Nanda sang her melodies. No matter how large was the crowd, it was calm and engrossed by the divine insights flowing in the air.

Shri shri shri Gangadharayya, the Swamiji of Kashi Peeth first had a look at the audience which submitted to him in all humbleness and devotion. The body of spectators was eager to receive the advice unaware of their home activities. Children were being made to sit dumb while beggers were scolded off. Swamiji began his virbosity with a casual sloka and his voice sounded serene and dignified and inspiring. There was nobility in his personage and an air of religiosity flowed around him. The whole atmosphere looked mesmerizing.

'Life,' the Swamiji began, 'is an illusion as just the vocalist voiced it in her lyric 'Sangharsh.' The world is a hugeboat wherein we're set asail while fate issues its orders for us every day. In this universe everything is mysterious. In fact, life itself is a big accident. The Almighty God is our Saviour and it is He who alone can save us. Therefore, our primal aim and objective in leading a life here should be to live and let others live. Admittedly we'd live to attain happiness as well as to attain salvation. In order to achieve this two-fold object we're supposed to be good in character, elevated and social in our behaviour, hard-working, sympathetic and helpful to others. What should matter to us is our uprightness. There'd not be any dechotomy between our words and deeds. D'you know, what our liberator Gandhi said us. He said that our words must be sisters to our deeds. He advocated the view that

Truthfullness is Godliness. Don't think Gandhi had been a theorist alone. He was also a practitioner of his creed. Let there be alikeness between our faith and practice. Let us be in perfect harmony with our fellow beings. In this regard, the point I'd like to hammer out is that let there be co-existence based on the tenets of love, equality, trust, respect, mutual understanding. Co-operation should be our supreme creed. What's religion? Religion is just a book of right guidelines to the flock of followers. Also bear it in mind that as there is only one God, there is only one religion. Then you might ask me a question as to why there're many religions — Hinduism, Islam, Christianity, Buddhism, Jainism, Jorastrianism, Judaism etc. But they are nothing but different versions of one single universal religion. However, each of these versions has differences but only to be overlooked. These differences are truly created by us simply to protect our vested interests.'

Swamiji continued his lecture for an hour or so. Then he desired to give some anology to make his audience better understood of his viewpoints. As a part of this measure, he used some folktales. There were a variety of literary anecdotes used in his lecturing for spicing his message. But no tale of him enthused the audience better than the tale of a buffalo. As soon as he began to narrate it a kind of interest in audience appeared overflowing. All the young and old, the curious and cold, threw their glance at him beside the floodlights. The tale drew people's attention like a wild fire.

'There was,' the Swamiji began, 'a man by the name Narasappa. He led a happy life in his early years. But gradually he became corrupt as he fell in a bad company. Over the years, he turned an unwanted fellow. He began smoking, drinking and frequenting brothels. This made him fall short of money. Thereafter, what he'd do? No wonder, he began stealing. One day, he entered a poor mason's house. Narasappa found the house but empty. None lived there nor seemed to take care of it. Nor were there any precious articles either? What a pauper can have after all? Just some earthen pots, old rags, tattered beds were lying. Curious about these things Narasappa looked around the dilapidated building. In his search of things he found a small earthen pot with butter milk. He knew that he could steal nothing from the house. Then an idea struck him. Since, he had come to steal why should he go back empty-handed? Going empty, he felt, was shameful. So he decided to take the pot. But when it looked awkward he simply drank the buttermilk before he went off.'

'God's punishment,' Swamiji continued, 'for man's sins was there ever ready. D'you know what happened to Narasappa who passed away soon in an accident? I tell you Narasappa was reborn a buffallo. So this buffallo came agrazing one day towards the house of a wealthy man. The time was midnight. Soon this Narasappa buffallo saw a thief stealing the house of a baronet. The moment Narasappa buffallo noticed the thief d'you know what it thought of.

It questioned itself as to what'll be the punishment for this man who's robbing the goods worth a million, while it was reborn a buffallo just to have drunk some buttermilk of others? Yes it felt that this thief might be reborn a pig or a dirty animal that perpetually wanders and suffers.'

The audience listened to the tale eagerly. They enjoyed Swamiji's lecture. Soon the programme ended with mangalarthi and the gathering melted away.

People liked the Swamiji's lecture. So did Mr. Venkatesh and his friends. Since he had been sensitive Venkatesh learnt things very meticulously. His respect for savants, his desire to acquire knowledge and his interest in knowing unfamiliar things was admirable. Venkatesh was quick enough to appreciate nobilily but was not credulous. Whatever he learnt, he accepted it with a due enquiry. No matter, how much he learnt, he learnt it with enquiring spirit. He found most of the people short of worldly wisdom. He knew human nature to be universal. Like most others Venkatesh knew men aspire for recognition. This he thought to be Aristotle's *hamartia* or a human flaw. Whatever might be his observation of life, he acquired a balanced order of it. He was a man of understanding, clear vision and mental balance. Most of the times he saw things as a detached observer. This made him impartial. He was cool and calculative moreover. He acted without any fear. People appreciated him for his tastes and genial nature. No one was a man of more adjusting nature than Venkatesh. Nor did he hurt others whenever they annoyed him? The true Christian qualities were the marks of his originality. Venkatesh had already read all sorts of books of other religions. As he was a voracious but diligent reader he learnt things by self-study.

It was a summer vacation. The climate was dry but humid. No rain was to downpour over the Banahatti sky. All around there were hills and dales. An external observer could say these mountainous regions were unfit for human habitation. No trees or shrubs of tropical climate of Pampapattan grew over there. But one could notice trees like neem, acacia, thorny bushes, wild grass, tammarind and patches of new afforestation. Lack of woodland resulted in lack of rain. But everyone could see vales and dales, rocky uplands and stony soils. In fact, this was the characteristic feature of the land. The whole northern part of Karnataka was similar everywhere. Nonetheless rainfall was short and winter severe, people lived there as they were accustomed to this.

Venkatesh was free during these months of holidays. However, he did some sort of activities which contributed to the growth of his life. He got his house repaired and painted; gave lessons to his sister; and tried to improve Ashok. Of course, he could not improve his brother sufficiently. He passed his time in his mother's company. Occasional was his visiting of Harish. Like most others, he left the house for pastime activities. The list of his friends was quite big. Everyone knew he loved friends for fragrance of life. In all possibilities Venkatesh had a good social bearing.

On a fine morning Venkatesh found his way to Jamakhandi. A photo of his aunt that he saw while doing some domestic work forced him there. Immediately recollecting her he decided to pay her a visit. Had he lived in Jamakhandi, he would have seen her times and again. As he was in Banahatti many miles away, because of responsibility at home he was not able to see her often. Presently Karisma's memories took him to her like a lover visiting his sweetheart. He had not yet forgotten her affection and concern for him specially in his bygone days.

Venkatesh arrived at Karisma's house in Vasant Nagar. It was three o'clock afternoon. There was no decrease yet in the fierceness of sun, while the dry clouds bore no rain. Men were scarse outside. The sun had forced them either for siesta or for indoor works. The absence of human activities outside made the surrounding tranquil. Even trees stood still and there was no wind moving.

This time Venkatesh wanted to see Karisma and his father together. Although he had seen him thousand times, he wanted to see him in his aunt's company now. Even he did not know the perfect reason for this. Mostly to see whether his father feels guilty of his second marriage would have been his predilection.

Venkatesh stepped into the gate of his aunt's house, 222, Mohan Ville, Vasant Nagar. He was glad of his visit. But the aunt was not outside. He did not feel uneasy anyway. He switched on the door bell. But no response came or sound heard. Then he thought she must be with his father. He knew it best that Karisma would turn wild if her companionship with him was disturbed. It was also true before she was not his wife. Moreover, Venkatesh could not forget his father's anger on disturbance while he was with her. Now he was rather reluctant. Be it as it may, he had not yet seen the charming face that inspected the outsider through a tiny whole made in the door frame. The time Karisma saw Venkatesh she turned glad. Consequently to trap the bull, she asked him to wait for a minute. Contrarily this strengthened Venkatesh's doubts. He took it for certain that his father must be in the residence. However afraid, he was not to go back. He fell in a deep sigh. He was already a youth of not less than twenty two. Now he wore moustache and little beards which were enough to his maturity. Every sexy woman who looked at him never went without dreaming him. In fact, he had become a hero to most of the girls familiar. But he had his own dreams about his life partner, while his mother had her own ideas about his marriage. Nor did Harish not think of his son's future? Even Karisma too had her own right to say something in this. So Venkatesh had been a loved one to everyone.

The time the door was opened, a woman's flowery hand pulled the man inside as he stood in deep waters of life. It was the same house, the same aunt, the same feminine grace. But the same aunt was not in the same dress he had seen her earlier. She had come out in a blue nighty which had been of such a texture that every part of her body looked as clear as a naked object. For a moment, Venkatesh stood amazed. He failed to know the reason why the dame came in such dress which he never saw. What a marvellous nighty it was! It looked splenderous and the fair body of Karisma looked fairest. Presently Venkatesh hesitated to follow her while his aunt led him to her room. Actually she stood before him with a view he knew not while he was being made to sit on a soft cot. But he did not lose his hart and he could not help seeing her. Karisma looked fairer in the glow and her body attracted the enthused youth. Red as coral were her lips and her teeth shone like jasmine. The oval face she reflected was Helen's. Karisma's eyes seemed like lotus blooms and her heart was enticing. Any youth who saw her now could say, love dwelt in her eyes so soft and lustrous. She looked a fairy queen. Indeed, she was a sort of fairy queen — bewitching. Though slender in waist she was tall enough looking with shapely limbs. An angelic beauty she was. Indeed Karisma looked celestial in the nullity of attire.

'Why aunt you have worn such a dress?' Venkatesh asked her childishly.

'Just to see how you feel about it,' Karisma smiled, a bewildering smile upon him.

'But I don't like it.'

'Why?'

'Because you look naked in it,' Venkatesh turned his eyes aside yet smiling. This encourged the lady to hold a romance with him. She loved his smiles and she loved his face. The shape of his body had been a piece of her adoration. His chest, his arms radiating. He looked handy. Karisma then sat beside him her hands on his shoulder either patting or rubbing — doing something. She was sure that he couldn't disobey her.

'Why you came here many days later?' she asked him a bit angrily.

'No aunt I visited you just a month ago,' he replied her humbly.

'But I expected you soon within that.'

'But I could not come,' he expressed his helplessness.

'Anyway you've come now,' she threw a glance at him. She thought a bird in hand is worth two in bush.'

'Yea, I'm amidst you now. You can enjoy my company,' he said comically.

Now they took a luncheon and wished to take some rest. Karisma sat down beside him. She managed to see that he was beside her like his father. Already the windows were shut. She was sure her husband was out of station. Nor did she worry about any neighbours? She was free there to do anything.

Now Karisma and Venkatesh rested on the silken squaire bed. They sat like a married couple. Gradually Karisma displayed her beastial emotions. She told him a story or cut a joke to rouse his sex. But Venkatesh who knew his position well rested with her fearlessly. He had not yet understood her desires. He took her for his aunt and as an aunt alone her image got imprinted in his mind and heart. On the other hand, mistaking his cooperation, Karisma started to enjoy him. However, Venkatesh was not surmised by this. As it was common of a mother to kiss or touch her son he allowed her certain freedom. Presently her outward touchings extended to keeping her legs on him. Enforced by the emotions, Karisma took his hands on her. But unaware of sexual pleasures he yielded to her externally. A gender fixation. Even he tolerated her embraces. But revulsion started in him. So no sooner when she came to him again nude than suddenly he went off understanding her caprices, and then he never met her in the near future.

Venkatesh was back home now — thunderstruck. He looked unhappy. Aunt's sedition was still grilling him. Illicit sex, he knew, was more dangerous than any type of black money. Although he had, due to his youthhood, been exceedingly desirous of sexual pleasures, he considered illicit love affairs as outright evils. He recollected Valmiki's saying '*Kama*' stands for lust and greed and every kind of desire. He knew he had heard the Swamiji of Kasimath saying 'sex is man's internal foe which he has to vanquish.' Admittedly this was the lesson taught in the last seven slokas of the third chapter of *Geeta*. He read Shri Krishna's exhortation *Jahi satrum kamaroopam durrasadam* meaning lust and cruelty are the ultimate causes of sin. However, Venkatesh did not stand against sex, but against the misuse of it. He was of the view that man must enjoy sex but his enjoyment should not make him a sinner. He stood for harmonious fidelity. Nor did he admire the theories of charwakas who were Indian counterparts of Epicurians. He hated polygamy, polyandry, bygamy, illicit affairs, homosexuality and everything that corrupted human mind.

The month of June came amidst the flow of life — its joys and sorrows, events loved and hated, people good or ill. Shobha had already been a middle aged woman mature, learned, more patient now. She knew how patience saves life. In spite of Harish's unruliness towards her family, she ceased hating him. Nor did she blame him either for his indifference.

Venkatesh had already finished his graduation. Postgraduation was the degree he was then in need of. Many ideas about his future crossed his sober mind. In the quagmire of idealism, none of them, save his aspiration for higher education, stayed in him for long. Found happy about educating himself, he decided to go to Pampapati University for an M.A. He was cocksure that after an M.A. with good score, like his parents, he could get a job. This confidence had been in him ever since he got succeeded in graduation.

Ashok had been turned out from school. Owing to bad company to whom he gave up he had spoiled his golden career. Already he was in his twenties, quite optimistic of living on his mother's salary and on her pension thereafter. But he did not know he could get nothing after her end. He was overtly misguided. Any of those who talked to him for five minutes, were certain of acknowledging this. He inherited his father's habits of drinking, smoking, rude behaviour, short temperament, wrong tastes etc. What Venkatesh and Shobha were not he was, what they thought bad, he esteemed good. He mistook chaff for wheat, and wrong for right. Besides, he was eccentric. He heeded none. If anyone guided him, he would say they were not his benefactors. This 'anyone' also included his father and brother, if not his mother.

Ashok was a man of vice and excesses. He loved those people who never disapproved his acts. Knowing this most of the parishioners had a smooth way with him. If he said 'he wants drinks,' they would say 'you can have it, sir' and if he said' he would like dice,' others plainly nodded. Others did not bother of him as it did not affect them. Mere yessing, or consent, after all, did not cost them anything. Nor did he introspect about his mode of life whether good or ill. No... nothing perturbed him. He ate, he slept and he roved around. Those who had a concern for Shobha, tried to convince him but in vain. Whenever any neighbours tried to guide him, he could tell them 'I'm a teacher's son. Hence, no need of guidance.' The mother knew he was wrong, the father knew he was wrong, the brother and sister knew he was wrong and the whole world knew he was wrong. It was futile to tame him any further.

No act of Ashok was distinct in his life than his visiting a brothel. When one day he was near a Monday Market at a lane, he noticed a pretty dame calling him. He did not know it was a brothel and the woman a prostitute. This happened plainly. The woman called him and mistaking her for a good chap he went to her house. Seeing him very robust, charming and rich the biddie led him to her indoor cell. The hut was small, ill ventilated and poorly sunlighted. There were two rooms — one a kitchen and the other a bedroom. Finding it enchanting he sat down flirting.

'What's your name?' Gauri asked him smiling.

'Ashok,' burst he.

'A very good name,' she complimented.

'What you're?' Gauri enquired him with an air of concern.

He said he was a businessman which though he was not yet. Simply he had an idea to make his career so when he had no avenue to follow. Presently some of her co-workers saw Gauri with an eye of envy. They were sure she got a good feller to exploit. Some neighbours who were not connected with cathouse ethics noticed the guy being duped there. They sat outside distantly seeing the goingson at Gauri's Eden Garden.

'These days doing a business is good Ashok,' she supported his whim.

'Yea, it's what I feel,' the man happy over his envisioned idea replied her promptly. Gauri had been known for her bewitching appeal and, it could be said, she had been a tactician in seducing youngsters both for delight and money. She knew best to entice and trap such customers. As she had a very good experience due to her lifting her legs business, she had gained a notoriety in the town. Whenever customers came there though they saw other women, they could not help going to her. There was magic in her eyes and music in her voice. It was why already she had slept with hundreds of persons — two or three a day. The property she had made out of her filth was enormous.

But her motto had been to supersede even the rich of the town. So, she did not save any efforts. Now after a few minutes Ashok sat with her body to body cross-legged on her rosy bed, she began praising him for his plans.

'D'you have any backing for your business?'

'Oh! yes,' Ashok nodded.

'How much would you like to invest?'

'Fifty thousand rupees,' he broke though he knew nothing about it. He spoke to her untruly. Gauri's homeliness fascinated him like anything. Now he began eating the fruits which she used to arouse the customers' carnality. He felt at home in her pleasant company. Already the door was closed and the hut had no windows. They had been on a bed engrossed in their exchanging joys business. Gradually Gauri gained control over him and touched him freely. He had already let her know his weakness. When Gauri showed him the heart of her sex, he could not help succumbing to it. She was certain that he would liberally pay her. Therefore, the next moment she brought him a bottle of beer and both shared it cheerfully. Ashok turned moody falling in her arms. Needless to say the two souls lost themselves in the passion.

The time the play was over, he sat with her exhausted. Hardly after an hour, a woman who saw Ashok screamed over his non-payment. It was Kenchi of Shetter Colony who had given him her body last week. In spite of so much enjoyment, Kenchi said, Ashok had paid her nothing. In fact, he had cheated her. Now after many days, she found the culprit and decided to avenge for the annoyance.

'Lo *neech* (bad fellow) give my fee,' the vulgar woman pulled him by his collar.

'I'll give you,' he replied embarrassed.

'When?' she pulled him indoors of her sister's brothel sideby.

'I'll give you,' he repeated her trembling.

‘I know you never give it, scoundrel. You drink the juice of our melons but pay nothing.’

When the people heard hustle-hustle, they rushed out. The sound increased. Soon children gathered all around. Brothel women except Gauri stood by Kenchi to support her. The bystanders gradually came in more numbers and the children began crying. The sound multiplied as many mouths spoke about the trifle. Found it the best occasion, Kenchi who was stronger than Ashok physically, dragged him violently. Soon she snatched his watch and tore his dress. Not occasional was her enlistment of Ashok’s cheatings. Although he had not cheated her the way she spoke of, her design was to exploit the situation. She had already taken his wrist watch and tore his dress. She said he drank her wine and deceived her times and again. However Ashok said he visited her only once, she outwitted him and declared that she was right and he was wrong. Indeed, there was much truth in her cries.

Venkatesh had been in the campus of Pampapattan University for an M.A. degree. By this time his mother had learnt the cruellest fact that Karisma, her sister had become her husband’s second wife. One day in the absence of her eldest son, while searching a book from his cupboard, she found his diary. She saw it eagerly. She opened it curiously but closed it in dispair. The little book gave her the hint that ‘man proposes but God disposes.’ Right from the time of her catching Harish red-handed with Karisma, she had moved hell and heaven to dispatch the bitch. She recollected the move she undertook to arrange Karisma’s marriage, the way she had adjusted twenty-five thousand rupees for Mohanraj, and the very phenomenon of her wedding. But after all everything went awry. Karisma’s very desertion of her husband, Sangeeta’s humiliating quarrels with her and heartfelt feelings thereby swept her mind. But Karisma’s running away with gold and money in retaliation of her wedding, annoyed Shobha deeply. First she was happy over Karisma’s wedding because she had succeeded in separating the ant from sugar. But to her awe, she did not know that the adroit ant had already found its sugar again. Shobha fell in deep sigh. She sat down worrying on an arms-chair. She was hurt by the riddle. Still cancerous had been her doubts. She sipped tea thinking about the worst happenings. 'Things,' she said to herself 'went wrong.' She knew how life had been tragic and how she landed herself in problems by marrying Harish or in having a bad sister who troubled her in spite of her benefaction. 'She is a bloody woman, he's a bloody man,' said Shobha to herself adding 'bloody bitches.'

Still worse was her hideous grief when in an effort to see the diary again, she turned the next pages of the one she had seen earlier. Alas! she found a page in which Venkatesh had noted down the following...

> Today I visited aunt Karisma, the second time. But found myself seduced by her. God save my soul and forgive Karisma, my dear aunt.

On reading this sin fell down Shobha deeply shocked. Her eyes displayed the extent of her mental agitation. Her body had been on the same arm chair; she had been the same Shobha and it had been the same news, but like cancer or aids, it had been outrageous, unretrievable and unpardonable. The house looked revolving, the surrounding objects, enemies, the very existence of hers futile. Shobha fell in deep thoughts of good and evil, evil and good, and evils mixed with good. The very existence looked a futile doing, a vain effort, a purposeless mission. After a little longer, she regained her former conscience. Now her vision became clearer but her heart became more troubled and her mind a grinding millstone. Ideas came and ideas went. Emotions were born and burnt. Feelings had their own sway over the finite. She turned whimsical and hysterical. The questions that astounded her were 'how daring is my sister? Has she slept with many others also? Why did she seduce Venkatesh, almost her son? What is the reason for it? How long it had been? Why she is so sensuous?' The same questions found repeated and reversed.

There was recurrence of bad feelings about bad women, about unlawful sex and about human filth and failings. Shobha turned normal gradually. Her vision became nobler. She began seeing the external objects as objects instead of enemies. Now she found in her senses.

However, perturbed in mind and cursing herself, she realized that she would get nothing in quarrelling with her fate however malignant. 'The thing,' she thought, 'she desired was denied to her.' She wanted a good husband who would remain faithful to her cause. But the desired was denied; and the past looked past. None could alter it. Already what had not to be taken place, had taken place. She heaved a sigh of relief and got up to open the door just knocked upon twice.

Venkatesh knew the rare occurrence that had already taken place at home. One day when he had been just out of his class, he saw a postman calling his name. After a due enquiry, he was handed over a letter. Venkatesh while he had been in the company of his classmates hesitated to open it. He decided not to read it then. But he learnt that the letter came from Banahatti just within the past three days. He had also received another post in the last week. However, he had been amidst his friends he could not help questioning himself — 'why this is a big letter? What might be its content? What made my mother write it urgently? Who might've caused her this? Why it's a costly registered post instead of an ordinary one which he got always? Would it be something about someone's death? In that eventuality who might be dead? Where? When? Why?' In the turbulence of thoughts, Venkatesh simply nodded his friends whenever they put him questions about the excentric behaviour of their prosody teacher Dr. Ramayya. But finding him more engrossed in some other business, they thought it unfair on their part to disturb him. The easy avoidance of his friends who were all but love and admiration for him on account that he had been the wisest wizard helped him to meditate over his domestic problems. Venkatesh meekly trode towards a garden mostly near the gigantic one in which his father and mother in their university days had fallen in love with each other.

Venkatesh sat calm and opened the letter. Presently he glanced the surrounding to confirm whether anybody was spying him. When he found no such detection, he began reading its content. The letter was about his mother and his mother's decision to divorce her husband on the ground of his lack of fidelity to her. Shobha had made it clear that since Harish did not live with her, she could not continue her relationship with him. Besides, Karisma's misbehaviour, her seduction of Venkatesh etc. had deeply convinced her the futility of relationship. But Venkatesh did not appreciate his mother's move to complicate matters. He knew the harsh fact that separated woman would incur social wrath, hostile attitude and numerous other socio-religious crisis. Moreover, Harish had not yet lost his link with Shobha. Admittedly Karisma's seduction of the boy had disillusioned the matron. As he understood the letter, he felt Shobha's misapprehension about Karisma's misbehaviour. Besides, Shobha's dissatisfaction about Harish's unsupport to the family was implicit in the note. Although Harish had gone against Shobha's desires in marrying her sister, he had not given her any moral or mental backing. That was sure. So it seems when Shobha found her husband belligerent to her, she determined to alienate herself from him.

Venkatesh read the letter many times. First he read it forward and then he glanced at it backward. He saw the reasons his mother had enlisted for her crucial determination. He counted and committed them to his memory. All this time, he was engrossed in his family disturbances. He could not help thinking of this seriously as it had to bring the family some grave consequences. Every member of the family had to suffer due to this disaster. Nor could the mother, he thought, who was to divorce Harish be happy ever after? But he remembered the point that his mother had not divorced him in a court of law. She had simply expressed her decision and dropped a letter to Harish for his moral backing.

Days moved while Venkatesh adjusted with the system of campus studies. He attended classes regularly. He learnt things. In no way or circumstance he misbehaved or acted in a way forbidden. Exactly like his father, he passed the first year of M.A. with first class distinction. This excellence brought him recognition in and outside the department. No wonder, his classmates and teachers began respecting him. By then Venkatesh developed good public relations through interaction, by participating in departmental programmes, by helping his teachers, by doing cultural activities. He displayed an aptitude for research. Besides, he had developed a taste for journalism. Already he had contributed three papers to local dailies which had a good network. These papers had brought him a laurel in the teaching community. Side by side, like his mother, he wrote short stories and some of them brought him fine comments. His enquiring spirit, truthfulness, religiocity, good taste and temperament were pleasant to any person with whom he came into contact. He was dutious, responsive and responsible to his actions good or ill. As a hostelite he took a lead in everything that happened over there. No doubt, Venkatesh's docility, humbleness, brilliance pleased all alike in the happy environ.

Soon after his post-graduation with a rank Venkatesh got many job opportunities. But with an end in view to become a University teacher he decided to do research. Shobha, his mother abetted his idea to join a university where he will flourish like a morning star. She supported him in terms of finance and aptitude, while his father admired his stance whenever he came over to Pampapattan University for examination work or for seeing his old woman in her parlour. He also encouraged his son to work in the field of creative activities. Whatever might be the opportunities he was to find in future Venkatesh registered for a Ph.D. He decided to do his research on the life and works of Basaveshwar, a noted religious seer of twelveth century Karnataka. Basaveshwar, also known as Basavanna the greatest devotee of Kalyan and Kudal Sangam made a socio-religious revolution in the beginning of medieval age in India. However he had been the prime minister of Bijjal, he led a team of Sharanas, religious people in framing a new socio-religious order. These seers of the time were large in number and most of them like Allamprabhu, Siddharam, Akkamahadevi, Dasimayya, Marayya, Machayya, Neelayya, Haralayya actively participated in heralding a new age. The way they struggled enthused him. He found their ideas very simple but quite practical. Sharanas, he learnt, found the world not a day dream. Nor did they consider human life an accident as Jean-Paul-Sarte was to find it many centuries later? To them life looked quite purposive. The desires like sex, love, wants etc., sounded essential for human co-existence. Unlike the Vedantists, these Sharanas found the body not useless or easily decayable. Their particular idea that 'truth is godliness' enlightened Venkatesh. The ideas 'lie is hellish,' 'virtue is its own reward,' 'civility costs nothing,' 'ripeness is all' appeared as endurable gems of human virtues. Besides, what Venkatesh loved was Sharana's ideas of liberty, equality and brotherhood as expressed in their vacanas. Sharanas knew the distinctions of caste, creed, colour, race were foolish. According to Basavanna, it might be a king or slave, the rich or poor, the educated or unlettered, all were equal and each of them had his own right to live freely and to love the good.

Stay not with an impious person for lucre
Even if he proffers you a fertile land
Stay with a Shiva-devotee even though he is a cobbler
Better to serve under him better to serve the Kudala
Sangam's devotees
Though one has to live on wild leaves fried in pan?

Similarly Marrayya's views about concentration or dedication to work looked useful to Venkatesh as they are expressed in the following vacana :

Engrossed in working
One should forget his God
Even one should forget the presence
Of priests, presents and parties.

What a beautiful idea! A noble thought! An elevating clue! Venkatesh wondered whether such ideas were expressed in the literatures of other languages — didactic, aesthetic or otherwise. 'Engrossed in working/one should forget even his god' looked to the young aspirant an idea that can purify a grieved soul. Venkatesh read the vacanas of Allamprabhu, Siddaram and Akkamahadevi — all great seer-philosophers of Basavanna's time. They were socio-religious reformers and their chief contribution was emancipation of women and the uplift of down-trodden. Apart from attempting to translate their ideas into actions, they expressed them in writing in the form of vacanas, a unique form of Kannada literature. The nearest approximation of which, Venkatesh searched, is found in the form of Rabindranath Tagore's *Geetanjali* in India and in the form of meditations of Marcus Aurelius Antonius and the sayings of Confucious abroad.

However Venkatesh had already registered for a Ph.D. study, because of some technical anomalies, many departments of Pamapapati University restricted chances of doing research. The prime reason for this was the Vice-Chancellor's desire to curtail research guides' design to take more students for research. As someone had misguided the authority he had thought that many guides took more students of research only for the sake of economic exploitation. He heard the news that a few of the guides took ten to fifty thousand rupees from their wealthy students and gave them Ph.D. One day the Vice-Chancellor found that a senior professor of the Dept. of Economics had guided a Ph.D. student, an IAS officer and had extracted fiftythousand rupees from him. Under these impressions, the VC issued an order that each department should take only two Ph.D. students but exclusively on merit basis.

The order "Research facilities for only two students on merit basis" enraged both the teaching and student communities. The research aspirants who had been deprived of facilities gave much thought to the vexing issue. As they were capable, meritorious, hard-working and desirous of making a career, they were grossly upset by the malefic notification. They disliked the university set-up which instead of facilitating the learner aspirants to whet their knowledge and sharpen their sensibilities, tried the contrary to thwart their very aspirations. In fact, they thought, it made a move to make them handicapped. This outraged a cross-section of the teaching community too as it had its own parochial interest in the venture. Consequent upon this the students mobilized their unity. "If we unite, we stand, if we divide, we fall" said a voice rebellious. There was greater emphasis laid on the word unity. Soon Venkatesh who delivered his maiden speech at a gathering stressed the same point but gave a war cry to all attended. He said 'Unity is strength.' The other student leaders, thereafter, requested the studentfolk to line up and guided the unruly to move in right way. So within half an hour students' procession started to move towards the castle of vice-chancellor's office which had been a huge building very rare in the whole town of Pampapattan.

On the way to the Administration Building most of the students cried aloud the slogans 'Unity is strength,' 'Education is All,' 'Students must be helped,' 'Discouraging university bad University,' 'Inquilab Zindabad,' 'Do or Die,' 'Step Down the Vice-Chancellor.' The last slogan was uttered with a diabatric tenor and it was often drilled out. Students looked happy in uttering slogans for the sake of redressing their grievances. Some of them criticised the authority's designs to slacken the standards. While others reproached the VC to have sided with some professors who worked for their vested interests. A few others suspected the high-handedness of campus people in perverting the VC's mind. This way or that students who had learnt most about vice-chancellor's nepotism, bribery, self-centred designs saved no efforts in censuring him. When most of the students were busy in shouting and responding to their leaders' slogans, some of them even gossiped and idled away their time in just walkmarch. Around 11-30 a.m. the crowd came near the VC's building and on a Police Sub-Inspector's stern warning, stayed for a while near the structure. But a cross-section of the aggressive students soon incurred the wrath of a police officer which resulted in lathi-charging. Soon a platoon of constables alighted to subdue students. But the police were soon outnumbered and overcome by the student crowd. A policeman's lathi enraged many a young student who beat a few of the security personnel before they could rush to the Vice-Chancellor's Building. Mr. Kalpanatha Rao and Mr. Venkatesh Pattan, the two ablest student leaders then visited the VC and presented him their just demands. Needless to say a deadline was given. But to their utter surmise, the authority who had already ordered for more police forces did not yield to their demands which, after all, had been very modest. This outraged the students who then collected stones and stoned the glassed window-panes. No wonder, within an hour or two when the VC displayed no move to make a reconciliation, almost all the windowpanes of the majestic building were destroyed. Meanwhile the VC's secretaries, defenders and supporters made a vain effort to cool the mob. Did they find the VC convincible either? Of course, one more vehicle of force rushed to the spot, it did not make any move to beat anyone as it did not find the condition worthwhile.

It was true students destroyed a large number of glasses and the VC's car was broken by the time Mr. Shivprakash, the eldest Syndicate Member of the University arrived to the spot.

'Stop! Stop! Stop! Please stop,' the man clad in safari spoke in a mellow voice. This tone sounded to the next generation scholars mellifluous and optimistic. The breakng process was then discontinued and the crowd gathered around him. Dr. Shivprakash had been a professor of Chemistry, almost a par gentleman known for his diplomatic measures. He had just come from his house in obedience to the VC's call. No wonder, his immediate concern was to find out amicable solutions.

'What's your problem?' he asked the student leaders as if he knew nothing of it.

'Research facilities are restricted,' a senior student explained the anomaly.

'That's true. But why you've resorted to violence even without consulting the body of Syndicate or Senate?' he put it authoritatively.

'We've already held discussions with the VC but he tells that he can't help us in this regard.'

'He wants to spoil our career, sir,' cried a student.

'He's a bad Vice-Chancellor, sir,' the third uttered the truth vehemently.

'Wait, wait. Talk one by one. You're all students. You'd be disciplined. You'd have manners,' the man big in size pacified the hundred angry voices.

'But too much is too bad, sir,' they cried in large anger.

'True. But a discussion with authority must be held soon,' Shivprakash responded cooly.

There was a silence.

'Alright,' the Syndicate Member began, 'now I'll talk to the VC and see that something is done in this regard. The professor went towards the VC who had come out to see the startling crowd which had already damaged the adored building. The way the students behaved and stoned the glasses took him aback at once. Presently he had been amid the superior police force, while students were frenzy outside-crying, screaming, abusing, joking and doing anything dictated by their whims. They were merrysome, for they brought down all the building glasses in response to the VC's belligerent attitude.

The next day surprising enough the grieved students saw two important news one in the English daily *The Hindu* in its caption saying, "Indifferent Vice-Chancellor and Adamant Students." However, the first part of the headline had been correct, the second had been a slandered opinion. Student's adamancy irrupted because of the VC's malevolent attitude but not because of their own aggressive conduct whatever might be the linguistic interpretation. True due to press criticism and Syndicate member Shivprakash's sincerest efforts, the VC had agreed to the cause of student community. This, in fact, had got a closer appreciation in the teachers' community. But most of the teachers and students thought that, had the VC agreed to the students' demands prior to the *dharana* (demonstration), so much damage to his prestige could have not been done. But only God knows why the VC due to his pride of power acted unreasonably even at the eleventh hour. This is what history says angels too 'fell because of their pride.'

Not many hours later, the Vice-Chancellor of Pampapati Univeristy, in consultation with the administrative body issued a circular stating that all eligible students may do research. Likewise, the last date, new restrictions and procedures were laid therein. So like a wild fire, the irrupted lava was cooled down due to a heavy shower. But the minds that worried all these days chattered about nepotism, excentricity and indifference of men in power. A particular point bothered them was intellectual arrogance and hostile environment. These factors contributed towards the downfall of education standards in the set up. No doubt these and many other reasons including students' lack of aptitude, hard-work, ambition paved a way for the successive sub-standards in R and D activities of every department of Pampapati University as elsewhere.

Venkatesh adjusted to the research community. He consulted his guide regularly. He made much progress in acquiring knowledge. During his second year, he began even drafting of his thesis. While he studied, he had a research room where Mohini a newly joined guest lecturer also studied with him. It was a research room where hardly more than five members sat together. The room was well spaced. It housed a departmental library, a set of furniture and other necessitous objects. Miss Mohini, a year senior to Venkatesh met him there daily for two reasons. Firstly, like him, she had been doing a Ph.D. and secondly, she was attracted by his magnetic personality. They talked daily on workaday life and they chatted at leisure freely. Mohini loved Venkatesh so deeply as he did her. But the nature of their love was polemical. Venkatesh loved her for her knowledge in classical Samskrit literature, and Mohini loved him for his handsomeness and well-marked bodily features. No doubt, both were fair in complexion and had come from well-to-do families. Each of their families was cultured. However, admittedly Mohini's family background was more akin to western culture than Venkatesh's. As Mohini's father lived in a colony of Christian houses and as he loved western civilization more, he gave much freedom to his children that included his only daughter. So under these circumstances, Prakash and his sister Mohini were in love with things foreign. They loved European dress, European art, European music and European ideas. Like Mrs. Mahindra of V.S. Naipaul's *An Area of Darkness*, or more like Nirad Chaudhuri, Mohini liked Western style of life, Western style of functioning. Certainly she did not shun westerners' free sex habits. She admired European life based on the tenets of Liberty, Equality and Brotherhood. Mohini loved a democratic society where no prescriptive behaviour existed, while Venkatesh was all for a good tradition and an order. So in reality Mohini and Venkatesh walked in opposite direction as far as their ideologies were concerned. But her love for him was deep and genuine.

Truly Venkatesh and Mohini studied together. Seeing their teacher, the other research scholars did not like to come there when Venkatesh and Mohini sat there. Consequently Venkatesh alone had been left behind in the room with the newly-appointed lady lecturer. The days brought them love and fragrance. Each of the two respected and helped the other a good deal in moulding their career. In fact, together they studied and dined and chatted. However, Mohini considered him her future husband, Venkatesh did not. Whatever the woman considered him in terms of love or wedding, he did not. But finding it rather more convenient, both lived as friends much to the surprise of their colleagues.

Right from the days of his boyhood, Venkatesh had, for a greater part, been a man of decent behaviour, uprightness, humbleness, wisdom and humour. His modesty and intelligence attracted everyone who encountered him in any walks of life. Besides, his charm and fair complexion impressed those who liked such qualities. His outspoken manners and helping nature earned him a good name. Again needless to say he had become a model to the surrounding wherein he was placed naturally.

It was these qualities of the man that enticed Mohini, the fair-eyed maid. No doubt, like him she too had been fair and social enough to adjust with any sort of people. No matter whether or not he loved her, she treated him her dearest. She was close to him and romantic. However, Venkatesh bore her only on the ground that both studied together.

One day when it was cool, Mohini came to the department but with an ulterior purpose. Since it was a festival though a working day, most of the teachers did not stay in the department until the afternoon. So were leisure-loving students. But Venkatesh was a man of difference. Unlike others he remained in the department all the day and made a rapid progress in his study. Knowing this to win his heart, Mohini turned up to the office and stayed with him even though others went off. She did it deliberately.

Unfortunate was Venkatesh's coming late. Expecting none in study room, he stepped in shyly. Surprisingly he saw there a rare lady with her tiffin box quite big. Soon after a chat she invited him for meals. The togetherness gave them much entertainment. They sat close to each other with sumptuous food before them. He ate the food as she did. Both ate the delicacies with an apparent relish. Leisurely they chatted. So many things were focussed upon in their discourse. But no other issue engaged their undivided attention more than the emancipation and empowerment of women.

'It's my sincere wish that woman should be liberated from the shackles of man. What d'you say?' Mohini asked him.

'Of course; but they shouldn't be liberated completely,' he embarrassed her.

'Why?' Mohini questioned earnestly.

'Because, most women are unbearable. Or you can say that they are more emotional,' he replied firmly. But it took her by shock.

'I know men hate women and they don't allow her as much freedom and equality as they enjoy,' she turned complainingly.

'You're mistaken,' Venkatesh continued. 'I don't think that women are always reasonable. Many times they turn objectionable, emotional, hysterical and bring disasters.'

'I hope you're partial,' she quipped him. Satirical was her voice occasionally.

'See due to lack of modern education, most of women are short-tempered, narrow-minded and cynical.'

'Oh! do you think men are free from these calls ?' she spoke wryly. Her words were scornfully charged.

'Men are not exceptional to this. But they commit less blunders than women. Therefore, men are not yet ready to recognise women as their equals,' he admitted menfolk's parodox. 'Until she gets good education, woman should not be given complete freedom.'

'It's unfair...unfair,' she burst then. She wanted to say something.

'Besides,' he began,' it's because of emancipation and empowerment of women, the rate of divorce has been ever on increase. I hope you've noticed this,' he turned proud as if he scored a point against her.

'That's in Europe,' she smiled.

'Not only in Europe where women are as equal as men but also in India these days,' he returned her a derisive smile which she loved.

'Then what are your views on love and marriage?' she put him a surprising question.

'In this regard I'd like to tell this much only that love instead of caste or status, should be made a basis of marriage. And boys and girls must be allowed to meet each other before they would marry. This might help them avoid their future frustrations,' he elaborated the crux of his theory.

'That's true. What d'you say about men who marry many times, while they disallow their wives to do so,' Mohini burst into a peel of laughter. She hoped this time Venkatesh would not answer her satisfactorily.

'It's true. But it's been followed by men unfairly,' he expressed it as if he was defeated in the deal.

'Therefore, I tell you men are known for their chauvinistic strategies,' she smiled upon him mockingly who sat calm but composed.

'See if I say I love you, I don't think you'll accept it suddenly. On the contrary you expect me to accept you when you love me, don't you?' she spoke intentional surprising him.

'Sometimes it happens,' he broke helpless.

There was a pauze.

Venkatesh was merely taken aback by her ire. He wondered at her constancy and boldness and frankness in love-making. He knew she was not telling this without a purpose. He was simply surprised by her heartfelt emotion. Already both had finished their meals. The chatting begun a long ago continued still. Since Mohini had given him a dinner as a token of her goodwill, Venkatesh did not like to upset her by his frankness. But he did not know how he became a Joseph Andrews. No doubt, his experience with Karisma, his aunt, had made him realize the nature of weak women.

'However, you don't answer some of my questions, I love you deeply,' Mohini spoke turning keen to know his reply.

'I don't dislike you, but my mother may.'

'Wonderful! What d'you mean by this?'

'She's a very traditional woman who can't like a lady like you to become my wife.'

'Is it?'

'Indeed.'

'D'you think I can't adjust with her?'

'I think so.'

'May I know anything that downgrades me?' Mohini, demanded an explanation.

'See my mother is a conservative. She likes a humble girl who can follow her both in faith and practice. She loves a nice girl to become her daughter-in-law. Besides, she hates highly educated woman or woman who live like Europeans with her liberty, equality and free sex,' he stopped for a breathforce.

'No matter how I'm now, in future I'll adjust with your mother's likings. So let's marry.' Mohini held him dear to her. She was very glad to become his wife but with all her youthful whims.

'Let me consider the matter,' he consoled her.

'No unless you promise me I won't leave you,' Mohini held him in her arms. As she was equal to him in might and right she caught him tight jovially. Or, it could be said, by chance he fell in her bondage of love. But he had not yet fallen himself. Instead she had given up herself to him. So for a while both sat body to body enthusiastic.

'Can you kindly leave me Mohini,' he asked humbly to dodge her.

'I don't leave you unless you promise me,' she continued her grip over him.

'How can I promise you without my mother's consent?' he burst adamantly.

'Ah! D'you love me only with your mother's permission?' she questioned him.

'No; but in regard to my marriage I'm supposed to have her consent.'

'Then I've to wonder whether you practise what you preach?' she criticised him.

'Of course! In some matters we've to follow a tradition. In this regard, I'm helpless.'

'But in case of your wedding, you must be free to take your own decision my dear,' she kissed him. All the while the love-affair had been still a one way traffic. He had not yet kissed her. Nor did he love her with a view to making her his life-partner. After a while, he was let free and he felt happy. Thereafter, they talked about the nature of Shobha. They talked a good deal about their families. Mohini narrated him about the social background of her family as much as she heard of Venkatesh's mother's tragic life. But throughout the discourse, she kissed him occasionally and at the end she renewed her desire to marry him. Mohini had been a woman of persuation.

Next year Venkatesh completed his study and found a lecturer post in the same department. Like most others he too felt elated. By then it could be said no other person was happier than Mohini about his appointment. She was gladdened by the event and looked more cheerful. She fancied that in case Venkatesh's marriage with her was materialized, she would be the happiest woman in the world. Unknown about future, the woman in her youthful fancies built a castle in the air. Mohini did not know that Venkatesh disliked marrying her for some ulterior reasons as he had already narrated her a year before. However, the young dame's faith was immaculate. She held the view that Venkatesh would not go for another lady while she had already been in the garden of his heart. The other side of the picture was unknown to her. Nor did she make any honest effort to know his mother's intentions? She knew nothing of his parents though she aspired to become their kindred in the days to come. She thought of him alone, a happy-go-lucky-chap; and she worried about him. Mohini saw him everywhere — in reading room while reading, on roads while walking, at table while dining, in bathroom while bathing and in bed while sleeping. He danced in her. Even she was not new to conversing of him. One day when she was at bed past midnight, she found her mother questioning 'who is Venkatesh?' as her mother knew nothing about the man. Only after a due enquiry, Mohini came to know the reason as to why her mother inquired her. It happened thus. The moment she was asleep in an adjoining room to her parents, she conversed 'Venkatesh I love you.' No doubt her mother heard it twice and could not help questioning her daughter. This made Mohini struggle hard to find a reply soon. Thereafter, the daughter was keen enough to avoid such absurdities.

Indeed as Mohini did not know it, Venkatesh had already seen a lady for his matrimonial alliance. But he did not find her suitable to his taste or temperament. Thereafter, Sadasiva, their kin at Banahatti, assured his mother to show him a good girl for his bride. Besides, the mother too wanted to find him a nice girl and had made her own efforts tirelessly. However, she showed him two girls both of PUC education, she found him unhappy about their physic and complexion. Gradually more aware of his refined taste, she suggested him to see brides himself elsewhere. For this she entrusted Sadasiva. So both Sadasiva and Venkatesh first made an observation, then initiated an enquiry and finally attempted to get particulars about brides. However, non-conservative, they searched for one who could perfectly suit Shobha's house. Understanding the matron's suggestions they chalked out some plans.

Once again Venkatesh and Sadasiva were entreated by Shobha that her future daughter-in-law must be modest, adjustable and virtuous. 'No matter,' the matron cautioned them, 'whether or not, she is a town girl, she should be from a good stock. Let her be suitable to him in physic and appearance,' she told, 'Don't deny the factor of good-lookingness. She should be radiant and pleasant in behaviour. What I want is a good wife for my son and a good daughter-in-law for myself.' I don't like to see only one of these. I'm in need of both. Sadasiva remembered the elderly lady's advice, while the very man in need of a wife shunned some of her ideas. As he knew it, Shobha expected a good amount of dowry also. Although she did not herself give it to Harish, she desired it in consideration of Venkatesh's education. Or, it could be said, like her own father who bore marriage expenses, Shobha expected new relatives to bear marriage cost.

On the appointed day the bride-seekers went to Athani. They had learnt that a newly joined lecturer of a local college was to be seen. After learning sufficient things about her caste, age, colour, Sadasiva and Venkatesh got to the taluk headquarters. As Sadasiva knew the details of the house and its master, he led the boy towards the destination. On the way they made a local phone call and after half an hour later, they trode to their house. They were given a warm welcome. In the beginning all things turned well and good. The house master Mr. Gururaj was very hospitable; he treated them warmly; and he talked to them about the groom and his family casually. When all preparation was over, both Sadasiva and Venkatesh were taken to a big hall where important neighbours of Gururaj gathered. One of the male elders had been his brother and the female eldest of the folk had been his mother. The hall had been well decorated. It had all the furniture one could imagine or expect. The photos of ancestors, calenders of beautiful deities and scenes, trophies Gururaj and Pornima earned had been hung on walls. Menfolk sat on sofas and chair, while womenfolk rested on matress cross-legged. Although sufficient furniture for them had been placed, they prefered floor to furniture which to them seemed artificial or too much dignified. The air-conditioned hall kept them cool.

Mrs. Gururaj who so far guided her daughter on the eve, sent her to the hall. Miss Pornima who looked five inches taller and three years senior to Venkatesh sat on a chair meant for her. Immediately an elderly lady presented herself near her and placed a banana bunch and other articles which had been brought by bridegroom party. It was observed as a matter of custom.

Then she returned to her seat gracefully as if she finished her service. Shantavira, Gururaj's brother who had been a primary school teacher then came near the spot. Already Sadasiva had looked the hands of the lady to observe whether she possessed any ill marks. He saw her palm, turned it left and right and read something without any articulation. Nor did he tell others about it? Soon he too returned to his chair.

'What's your name?' Shantavira, an elder of the bride party asked Venkatesh.

'It's Venkatesh Pattan,' the twenty-eight years old man replied without any reticence.

'May I know your name madam?' Sadasiva burst out as if in retaliation.

'It's Pornima,' the lady sitting before everyone like a musician with large audience, responded gently. There was some smile on her face as an indication of hopes.

'Are you in service?' Gururaj asked.

'Yes,' lecturer in Pampapattan University,' the newly-joined scholar replied.

'Oh! you're a lecturer!' Shantavira looked pleased. 'Then it's a nice thing because our daughter is also a lecturer.'

'Is it?' Sadasiva replied happily though he knew it before.

'May I know where d'you serve?' Venkatesh asked Pornima for the first time.

'I serve in a local college here,' she said without detailing further.

'Is it a permanent job?' Venkatesh asked her earnestly.

'No; but chances of absorption are there.'

'Your subject?'

'Economics.'

'Where did you do your M.A.?'

'I did it in Pampapattan University.'

'When did you finish it?' Sadasiva who was clever in tracing the mysteries of her age put a question. He knew it well that by saying that Pornima was just twentyfive years they lied them. However Gururaj manipulated false details in regard to her age, he was not shrewd enough to tell her to distort the year of her M.A. final.

'1970,' Pornima replied shyly. This established the fact that she had been five years senior to him.

'What're your hobbies?' he asked her.

'See,' she started imposingly, 'I'm an expert in cooking, embroidery, tailering...' She laughed then in response to an elderly woman's comment on her all-roundedness. This time she smiled well and her face seemed beautiful with all its comely features. There was a radiance in her eyes and her lips looked neatest. The complexion was nearly fair. Besides, the gorgeous blue saree, a blouse of similar tint and golden ornaments added much to her heavenly beauty. Moreover, the light contributed its own share in enhancing the dame's contours of prettiness.

'D'you have any hobbies?' Pornima questioned him though traditionally no lady dared to do it. This amused the gathered.

'Yea, I'm interested in sports and literature,' he said in a voice that sounded pleasant.

'What about your family?'

'My parents are lecturers in colleges. My house is in Banahatti. I've a brother and sister both junior to me,' he finished it with a warm smile. In fact, he told her a brief history of his whole family.

'I'm glad you're a lecturer,' Pornima added it at the end. On the ground of his sociability, she anticipated him to be her future man. But she did not know how an unknown force was to work against her without any regard to her wishes.

Pornima went indoors. She looked aged but beautiful. Her body had not yet lost its youthful vigour and her face had still retained its primal beauty. Being a woman of culture, she had good education. She was social enough to talk frankly.

When Pornima's beauty struck his heart Venkatesh toyed with an idea of making her his wife. In fact, her oldness did not matter him. He knew elderly wives were sweeter than youngerly. But his mother, he thought, could not accept it. Besides, her imposing behaviour was there to displease both.

Thereafter, tea was served to all. Menfolk began their casual comments and remarks. They talked about climate, rainfall of the year, standards of university education, scarcity of jobs, difficulties in getting higher education etc. Both the parties spoke to each other freely. When the high tea was served, Sadasiva expressed his gestures of departure. This made Gururaj to summon him to his study room where as it was found later, he gave him details pertaining to his house, his daughter and dowry and asked him to reply about their acceptance. He also took some details of the bridegroom.

Striking enough within an hour the men were on road. Presently they began their discussion about the family, the bride and the way they were respected. No wonder, the distortion of maid's age and the delay of her marriage boggled them.

'D'you think she is of my age?' Venkatesh asked the other anxiously.

'I don't think what they said in regard to her age is right. But as per her M.A., she'd not be less than thirtythree.'

'You're right.'

There was a pauze.

'What might be the possible cause for the delay of her marriage though she's quite beautiful,' Venkatesh asked his companion.

'I hope her marriage is purposively delayed. D'you know how some parents dislike marrying of their daughters who're in service?'

'Venkatesh nodded him simply like children meekly listening to fairy tales.

'This is because of economic reason,' replied Sadasiva.

'Either for living on daughters' salary or to avoid parting with them; some parents don't marry off their daughters,' he finished his say.

'It's possible,' Venkatesh replied shortly.

'Why possibility, it's a reality.'

'Yea,' the young person nodded again to admit his lack of practical wisdom.

'Don't you know Mr Siddappa, my neighbour. He has not yet married off his only daughter however bridegrooms come and go frequently.'

'It may be due to his affection.'

'No affection, but for the sake of salary.'

There fell some silence.

'Similar is the case with Rayanna's daughter,' Sadasiva continued another tale of woe. 'D'you know his daughter Nirmala's case?' Even without allowing his companion answer his questions, the elder continued his convincing business. 'He didn't marry off her until she became twenty-five years old. Consequently, the annoyed lady developed an affair with a neighbour. D'you know what happened then?' Sadasiva spoke vehemently.

'What happened?' Venkatesh broke curious.

'One day Rayanna himself saw his daughter with her paramour. The event shocked him. But he didn't question her. Immediately he arranged her marriage with a high school teacher of Bijapur and closed the matter peacefully,' Sadasiva felt an elation in convincing Venkatesh about the futility of late marriages.

The first time the bride-seeing had become futile in part due to the mismatching details. During the second, when Venkatesh and his uncle went to a house in Bijapur, the things moved smooth. Subha Rao, his uncle from his mother's side, once invited Venkatesh to see a bride for him. He had got enough details of the family. Keeping in mind Shobha's suggestions for a dowry, he was glad to bring a matrimonial alliance between him and a rich party of Bijapur. So on the appointed day both Subha Rao and Venkatesh went to Shridhar's house. Shridhar had been an MBBS, but he did not run a clinic. Since he had been a wealthy person with twenty-acres of grape-orchard, he managed his business without sticking to any particular profession. Presently he had asked Subha Rao to strike a matrimonial alliance for his daughter. So on a fine April day, soon he was informed, the doctor arranged a show.

As expected by Shridhar both Venkatesh and Subha Rao arrived at his house in time. The welcome was warm. The house of bride party had been palatial. It was built on a two-acre plot in a suburbia. It had all modern amenities the science and technology had promised. Around the house had come up a beautiful compound wall. The house looked grand. It was a solid RCC building with three bedrooms, a big hall, a godwon, a big store house, a stable, a parking etc. The house had been grandly decorated and well maintained. The servants both men and maid, the supervisor of orchards — all under the grand aegis of their patron worked for the prosperity of the establishment.

Soon after tea, a bride, a girl of twentyfive years, in all her choicest golden ornaments, finest clothes and aggresive behaviour came out to adorn a special chair specially placed for her. Venkatesh saw her head to heal. He made a special observation, for he had thought of the family very highly. As he was already informed by his uncle about the wealth of them he had till then entertained an idea of marrying the lady if she was pretty enough. He had learnt the fact Shridhar could give him any amount of dowry, a good bridegroom could expect. But soon Venkatesh saw the bride, like the butter in midday sun, his hopes melted away. Instead he felt disgusted. Nor was he happy of her behaviour which was rude and uncouth. Because of great affluence, she prided on her family wealth. She did not know wealth was not all in life. However he was persuaded to take some dowry, Venkatesh stood for a good wife.

The questionaire was over within a short span of ten minutes. Unlike Pornima, this girl had been too proud of her status, but she did not know she had been a Nigress. Nor did she answer his only question ? She declined to do so on the count that she did not like it. Her pride, crow-colour and her immodesty made Venkatesh to think the try was not worth. After the girl went in, tea with snacks was served and Venkatesh and his uncle left the place unhappy of the affair.

Disappointed by these unfortunate bride shows, the affectionate mother took the whole issue in her own hands. On one fine day morning the mother and son left for Pampapattan on her friend's invitation. First, they went to the house of Radha who wanted to help Shobha. It was a May Monday, apparently summer. Shobha and Venkatesh were warmly received by their host. After a dinner, they decided to go to see a bride. As per their plans, they went to the bride's house at six o' clock.

The threesome were welcomed by Ramayya. After a preliminary acquaintance, instead at the end, tea was served in the beginning. This was done on account of Radha's familiarity with the family. Ramayya was a thorough gentleman. A highschool teacher, he had two daughters — both graduates. Since his was a middle class family he could not give either dowry or marriage expenses. What he could do to the son-in-law was just presenting him some ornaments of gold and dress with love and respect. As he had already incurred much expenses because of his first daughter's marriage the previous year, financially he was not sound. But his daughter was a beauteous Sita. Anyone who saw her could like to marry her. But those who wanted dowry or marriage cost, hesitated a little. However, the custom the bride party had to give either some dowry or bear marriage expenses was not acceptable to him. Then who could marry ladies who could not do either? No doubt, rich people who wanted beautiful girls could adjust with such cases. But Shobha's case was different. However, matching the maid might be, she was firm to take either marriage expense or dowry. Or she could ask the bride party to arrange the wedding either. In fact, due to financial tightness, it had been indispensable for her. Nor was it not a part of the tradition?

People assembled in a hall. The girl dressed handsomely and adorned in jewellery, sat upon a chair. The elders particularly those who took the lead asked her some questions. The whole folk were happy solely for the reason that the marrying looked very matching. A cross-section of the kindred felt that they were like Rama and Sita, an ideal match. But they had little idea of other factors that went in finalizing a marriage.

'May we know your sweet name?' Shobha began first.

'It's Ashwini,' came a sweet reply.

'Your education?'

'B.Com.'

'Any hobbies?'

'Tailering and computer.'

'Very good! You've learnt Computer also,' Shobha said it gladly, while Venkatesh was happy, for the bride had an advanced knowledge. Indeed, he knew the importance of computer education.

'Today world is a computer world, sir,' a neighbour interrupted smilingly.

'Hundred per cent true.'

There was a silence.

'Can I ask you to read an English newspaper?' Radha still a traditional woman poked her nose.

'Everyone reads English today,' Shobha put it humorously.

'Alright,' Ramayya controlled the situation that was emotionally charged.

Immediately the girl was given an *Indian Express*. She read a brief paragraph. Her reading was clear. The gathered found it pleasant and they were happy about her grip over English much sought in India.

'Your reading is just like Rina Kanha's,' Radha complimented her to offeset her question.

'She's good at studies madam,' the girl's mother supported her daughter proudly.

'Is she a convent school product?' Shobha could not help questioning this as she admired the dame's talent.

'Yes madam,' the house master replied politely.

'Now you may go indoors,' Radha told Ashwini being satisfied. Thereafter, the bride stood up shyly to rush in. She looked, indeed very beauteous in red saree she wore. Her speech was as sweet as a melody. Her face was round shaped and each of her limbs natural. She did not look obnoxious. The finest attire, the choicest jewels and the fairest complexion were enthralling to Venkatesh. The moment Ashwini stood, Radha threw a glance at Venkatesh who sat next to her gazing at the vanishing figure. Shobha who noticed her son fascinated by Ashwini looked happy. She took it for certain that he liked the girl best. Soon another round of tea was served. As a matter of custom, the elderly people spoke of the standards of education, job opportunities and the importance of computer education. At the end Radha was called indoors by Ramayya, while Shobha relaxed still. After a brief closet, she came out satisfied. So within five minutes, the guests went home.

The two parties were optimistic over the deal and about the match of bride and bridegroom. Many ideas occurred to their parents about the vivid future their kids could have. If Shobha thought of a good daughter-in-law as well as an ideal wife for her son, Ramayya thought of a good son-in-law for himself. But their alacrity had a short life. They did not know how one or the other criteria could obliterate them.

Found happy about the bride and her family in consultation with her son, Shobha asked Radha, her friend to know whether the other party was happy about the issue. If so, she told her to ask them whether they were capable of giving them minimum fifty thousand rupees of dowry or arranging the wedding.

Radha sent the news of acceptance first. Subsequently after an hour or two, as she said she informed the conditions to the bridal party. She rang them up again to know whether they can meet the demands. But to the disgust of all Ramayya frankly declined to pay any money. Nor was he ready to arrange the wedding himself either? Naturally since he had got his daughter well-educated, he did not like to incur any financial losses. This cold move stunned the bridegroom's kinsfolk. In fact, dismayed by the hostile response, Shobha disagreed firmly to talk on the matter further.

It was felt the whole day was a sheer waste. Neither Shobha nor her son looked cheerful anymore. The fate had conspired against them. During the first and second bride huntings it was the bride who mismatched the situation, but during this time, both the parties found each other pleasant. However Ramayya's adamancy proved displeasant. 'At least,' Shobha thought to herself, 'he should've agreed to pay some dowry.' While her friend added 'he'd have agreed to pay at least a small amount.' Mr. Venkatesh supported them by saying 'Ramayya's reply was a hard way of saying no.' All talked freely. But the issue looked displeasant and inappropriate. Particularly Shobha who had greatly suffered due to her husband's indifference found herself on the verge of sobbing. Venkatesh consoled her saying that in case one needs both money and beauty, suffering was unavoidable. Admittedly Shobha retorted him about his impracticability. She said, 'the cost of wedding would be enormous. Anyway she would have a good husband in lieu of some expense.' Radha too supported her. Moved by the genuine issue of her guests, Radha proposed them another alliance. By this happy became the mother and son who till then sat dejected. Consequently, Radha rang up the man concerned and told him of the proposal.

As planned, all the concerned, mentally prepared themselves. On the appointed hour Radha hired a taxi and with her two children in order to make the number five, they went to the house of engineer Shrishail. Like Shridhar the present central government employee had been rich enough to buy a good son-in-law. He did not consider dowry-giving an offence. He overlooked it. Certainly he was a wealthy person. His house had been in a posh area and nice was his family background. He educated his only son and only daughter in a way nobody could object it. They had sufficiently been exposed to western culture and civilized manners. Indeed on seeing the house, its richly decorated floorings, walls and ceilings, Shobha turned delighted. This time the ladies had been quite optimistic. As Radha had already briefed about the nature, culture and background of this engineer, Shobha had been invariably optimistic of the whole deal. Only the things as an ideal mother or an elderly person, she wanted was to find the bride to her expectation. Now, after an hour, the master had readied the things and within a minute or two, the traditional show ceremony was to take place.

However, one person unlike all in the house of Shrishail had been in utter dismay. It was their daughter who was shortly to be exposed to the groom's party. She had been in a state of worry, dejection and turmoil. Now she felt the most uncomfortable or disinterested figure in the entire household. On a close observation of her displeasure, no doubt, the mistress of the house with her held a discussion.

'May I know why you look unhappy today?' her mother put it enquiringly.

'Come to my room mother, I'll tell you something,' the maid whispered the elderly lady. Both rushed to a corner as if they were to discuss some significant matter hurridly. In fact, it was not a trivial matter to anyone who knew the hearts of the youngsters stolen by their sweethearts.

'I don't want to appear there,' the girl said vehemently.

'Surprising! Don't you want a wedding?' her mother put it in a huff.

'Yes; but I've my colleague in the department and I should marry him only.' There was anxiety on her face. She waved her hand towards the concerned department of Pampapati University.

'Wonderful! Shall I know his name?' Mrs. Shrishail asked her shocked.

'Don't be upset. He is a lecturer, a very dignified person... A man of our community. If you see him, I don't think, you'll dislike him,' she disclosed the thing threadbare.

'Anyway since they've come here to see you, attend it. No matter, you like him or not, showing yourself does not mean fixation of wedding.'

'No *ma*! I don't like this.'

'You've to appear. No argument further,' the mother persuaded the dame.

Right at the stroke of six in the evening when all kith of Shrishail gathered in the hall and the bridegroom party had taken its due place, reluctant Mohini appeared before the august audience. But a surprising situation caused her to burst gladly. So much good had come to her out of evil.

'Hallo! you Mr. Venkatesh,' said Mohini overjoyed.

'Ah! Yes,' Venkatesh smiled at her cheerfully. No doubt, this surprised the conscious gathering. Each of the relative and related was taken aback by the familiarity that had persisted between Mohini and Venkatesh. The said familiarity looked anarchic. All were spellbound by the alacrity of the young persons. Even to persons like Radha, Shobha and Shrishail, the whole situation looked like a cinema scene, surprising and esoteric. So for a minute or two none talked. Dead silence prevailed there as never before.

'Are you familiar to him?' Shrishail asked his daughter surprised. So were others.

'Yes daddy. He's Venkatesh, my colleague at Kannada Department, Pampapati University, a nice person,' Mohini burst joyfull. Now she looked the happiest person of them all. Indeed, Indra, the love god had sent her the very man she wanted these years.

'How d'you do?' Venkatesh spoke nicely.

'I'm fine. How d'you do?' she put it in turn

'Alright,' he felt enlightened. But he did not know how it all embarrassed others.

'Why didn't you inform this to us before? Did you plan to take us by surprise?' she questioned him calmly. She was all but gay now.

'Not like that. To be sure I didn't know it's your house. Only because of Radha aunt's goodwill, we came here,' he said her pointing to the lady beside his mother.

'D'you know her already?' Shobha asked her son.

'Yes mother, she's my colleague,' he could not avoid smiling now which grossly annoyed the sensitive woman.

'Then I need not introduce you to her,' Radha cut it jocularly.

'You're right madam,' her counterpart Mr Shrishail supported her.

'Alright now we've come to your house to see you for him,' Radha began the formality.

The wonderful aspect of this bride-seeing had been Mohini's frankness in behaviour. However it looked obnoxious to Shobha, Mohini did not change the nature of her demeanour. Of course, her father did not mistake the way of her conduct.

'May I know your name?' Shobha enquired the brimming bride.

'It's Mohini madam,' the lady in blue saree replied the lady in red humbly. Her tone was clear but proud.

'So you're a student in Kannada Dept?'

'No; like Venkatesh, I'm a lecturer. Don't you know we work together?' she asked the elderly lady overconscious of her position. Shobha who so far knew nothing of her by Venkatesh, now began to suspect his character. Indeed, she threw a fierce glance at him who but did not notice it. She found herself odd to have found in that company, while Radha was hopeful of a matrimonial success.

'Shall I think now you're busy in bridehunting?' Mohini asked Venkatesh fearlessly. She threw a smile upon his face. There was a fascination in her glance. It was a rare scene.

'It's the first attempt,' Venkatesh tried to avoid unpleasantness about his futile bride-huntings. This time he could not help smiling upon her.

The nice saree she wore, the coloured blouse which covered her melons, the fair face and its fairest complexion looked relishing to all looking at her. The jewellery that adored the bride, and the cheerful face that earned her respect and her jubilant love sounded exquisite. With all these features she looked an apsara. Her sociability, frankness in behaviour, smiling face had already struck Venkatesh. Besides, her pleasant company and her urbanity had captivated his heart years ago. But on the ground his mother had been conservative, he had not decided to see her for his wife. Who knows the divine predilection? If man proposes God disposes. Fate, the perblind force does harm or help according to its whims without any regard to human wishes. Although he had determined not to wed her, destiny had brought them together today.

Therefore, Venkatesh blamed his fate as much for the reason as Mohini revered it. What he wanted not, she wanted; what he desired to avoid, she sought always. Fate had given each of them something they liked or not liked. It had brought them certain mystery.

On the other hand, Mohini had been extremely happy. She knew that he would certainly marry her. Now she found things surely happening in her favour. No wonder, her position was like that of Karimkhan who had got a goldern axe for the one made of iron. Like Karimkhan, Mohini who disliked an unknown fellow to become her husband, found a well-known, a familiar, indeed, a much sought after person, as her beloved. Her joy was untowering.

The only one of the group unhappy was Shobha. She doubted her son's plotting against her in order to marry the one he loved. She guessed he had already contacted her for marriage. However, she did not show any anguish on the eve but found Mohini too urbane in behaviour and too superficial in taste. Really she did not believe that she would become her perfect daughter-in-law.

On the daughter's insistance the all loving father arranged not anything short of a dinner. The people gathered took tea and the guests were requested for dinner. Meanwhile Shobha, Radha and Venkatesh were taken inside and they took a look of the house. Everyone felt at home. Mohini who led them in her house, when chance favoured did not hesitate to touch him. She found the greatest satisfaction during this spectacular occasion at her house.

Back at home the squabbling began. A skirmish started between Shobha and Venkatesh. The son felt, the mother was conspiring against him, while the mother misunderstood her son's familiarity with Mohini. They accused each other and cursed their ill-fatedness. If she said she was unfortunate in marrying Harish, he told he was unfortunate in seeing brides and getting none selected. He was glad of Pornima whose father declined the offer as his mother became commercial. But in the case of Mohini though her son was willing to marry her, Shobha withheld her consent on the sole ground that the dame could not become a good daughter-in-law. She had a wrong notion in her head that wives of love-marriages will be good wives but bad daughters-in-law. Here she resembled Gangamma, Harish's late mother. Mohini's intimacy as had been explicit at the eve of bride-seeing disheartened the matron's human understanding. Much against her wishes, Shobha found the lady outspoken, social and aristocratic in life. Her fear was that Mohini would not respect her. Her understanding was that more disrespect, more disharmony, more despair, more failures in family life. Indeed, it milled the melee of her mind.

'D'you know whether such ladies obey their elders?' Shobha asked her son like a school teacher questioning pupils.

'I hope she's humble enough to respect you mother,' he said humbly.

'Even I wonder whether she can be a good wife,' the mother broke cynically.

'Then let's search for another bride,' he spoke passively.

'That's nice. But I don't think we can have a different chap again,' she burst uncertain.

'Then shall we do one thing?' he began hopefully. You give up the idea of taking dowry or asking for conducting marriage. So I'll marry Pornima whom anyway you've liked,' Venkatesh, the wise, told her the only way left.

'Oh! you want a beautiful girl, a useless family! That's impossible. Still you know, I've to marry Ashok who is already twentyfive. Kamala is also there to be married off shortly. So I can't help taking dowry,' she spoke firmly. This disheartened her son.

'Then be contented with Mohini either,' he insisted it like a diehard. Sure he was much in want of a wife. So was his mother much in need of a good daughter-in-law. The riddle simply lay the other way. She was also in need of dowry. Of course, it was indispensable. Discontented were the Pattans because the girl whom they liked was unable to bring them anything, while the girl whom they liked or not, was ready to bless them with fortunes. However, Mohini was not in Shobha's district of likings. So the cold war between the mother and son continued until Radha's phone sounded a solution.

'Hallo!' went a voice distantly.

'Is it Shobha?' came a remote plea.

'Yes, Yes, Radha, it's I,' cried Shobha curiously.

'How are you?' broke the other.

'Nice; are you well?' Shobha spoke back.

'Alright; how's Venkatesh? Is he happy about his Rani?' Radha spoke benevolently.

'Absolutely. Because he's to get his loved one,' Shobha burst unwillingly glancing at him closeby. Venkatesh was naturally attentive to their conversation which was about him only. At his mother's decision, presently he turned delighted.

'I wonder whether you've discussed the matter with him,' Radha interrogated her friend.

'It's already done. He says he's to marry her. You know how he's deeply fallen in love with her?' Shobha finished her say.

'Doesn't matter. It's a good thing. Let him do so. Already I think, he's not less than thirty. Quite a marriageable age, isn't it? May I think whether you've any objections to his decision?' Radha enquired her friend openly.

'Not at all, Radha. But...' Shobha hesitated to express her doubts.

'No matter whatever it may be please tell me. Come on. What's that irk in your voice? Is it about the girl's character?' the invisible voice interrogated Shobha with a benigh concern. The distant voice assured her a promise, a hope, a future.

'Shall I think the maid is too urbane for us?' Shobha shot her arrow of disbelief.

'Of course! She's urbane. But your son is not a country boy to be overruled by her. Don't you know that already he's her friend? Naturally he must be aware of her character, isn't he?' Radha persuaded the other.

'Of course he is! But to my satisfaction, can I take it for certain that she will live upto my hopes?' Shobha spoke for certainties.

'Ah! Hundred per cent,' the Pampapattan voice not seen but familiar enough resolved the heartfelt doubt of a Banahatti elderly woman.

'Alright! Then how much dowry they desire to give us. Or can they conduct the marriage?' the matron changed the subject of her talk.

'They're ready to pay you fifty thousand rupees dowry excluding the jewellery for the bride and groom. Or they can conduct the marriage themselves. Which of the two you like more?'

'Let it be the latter,' Shobha smiled, while her son who heard it patted her gently.

'Oh! don't disturb me,' Shobha told him.

'What happened?' asked Radha astounded.

'No nothing my happy son is patting me,' Shobha burst into laughter.

'Oh! Nice. Nice to see him happy,' Radha exchanged moments of joy. There burst in an air of tranquility.

'So you want Shrishail conduct the marriage?' Radha asked her friend for confirmation.

'Yes; also tell them that we'll present the girl jewels and dress as they offer him the same,' she spoke decidedly.

'That's imperative.'

'True, but I clarified.'

'Alright. Then would you accept October 10 for wedding?'

'Ah! Mostly yes.'

'Better you make it clear. It will be a Monday.'

'Let me ask the chap. Is it okay for you. As it occurs in the vacation, I don't think you'll be disturbed. Shall I agree?' the mother receiver in her hand enquired her son hurridly, while he simply nodded her every time.

'Radha October 10th is good for us.'

'I told you that's a nice day.'

There was a silence.

'What about the ring ceremony? Are you happy if that is arranged the previous day of wedding?' Radha spoke for more details.

'Yes, certainly.'

'So then the problem is over,' Radha was shortly to close her talk.

'I wonder whether we'd do this without you,' Shobha expressed her thankfulness.

'God's great Shobha, Ok... Goodnight.'

'Thank you very much. Goodnight; Shobha finished the talk in a befitting manner. Neither she showed her displeasure about Mohini nor she hated her son for his preplans. This, no doubt, convinced Venkatesh of his mother's conservative nature. He appreciated her benefaction. Presently both looked happy over the deal.

Things moved in a way planned by Shobha. But the master of the family had not to be involed in any part of the deal. Now, for many years Harish had also not frequented Shobha's family. Nonetheless Shobha scolded Harish for his chauvinistic measures, she forgot his visits and non-cooperation. She hated him for the way he committed blunders. In fact, she was all an enemy of him now. At times she also envied her sister's malefic designs against her, her wooing Harish and her sexual tactics. However, Harish married two women both of a same breed, he had, for certainty, not been happy either. At times he felt dismayed to have committed the mistake of polygamy. He realized the truth that two wives though sisters could not live together. It looked to him mysterious but gradually real and natural. Over the years on account of Karisma's son's growth and schooling, his responsibility was increased. Besides, he developed literary activities to keep himself in good spirit. Now after many years of toils, he struggled to achieve something. His collection of poems entitled

The Hero of Misfortunes earned him a name. Likewise his efforts in writing critical essays was going. As the family burdens grew, Shobha too could not help tolerating his absence. He became more mellow now. Most of his sadistic designs were melted away and he became a bit human. His lustrous designs were on decrease. So was the case with Karisma. She turned sober. Gradually, they were making a move to unite with Shobha and live together. But the latter's haughtiness was as usual. So hopes of unifying the two families was still a distant dream for them.

As the days passed can October 10th be far behind? Preparation on the part of parties was complete. Shobha bought gold and clothes and readied necessary jewellery. Sufficient objects of wedding were prepared. Even Shobha was meticulous. Minimising her expenses wherever she could, she readied all essentials for Venkatesh's wedding. Already invitation cards were given to people. Venkatesh and Kamala visited their father and aunt and invited them. So far they had not seen a happy event at home other than Karisma aunt's marriage years ago. Karisma, happy of Venkatesh's education and happier of his wedding expressed her heartfelt joys. Harish-Karisma assured Ashok that they would attend the function. Although already a gap between Harish and Shobha had crept, he did not express his displeasure for the occasion. Nor did Karisma do it either about her sister's adamancy or her own contribution towards Harish-Shobha's spoiled relationship? Both parties had equally erred. But Karisma and Harish blundered first in denying Shobha, a coveted justice. Similarly when Harish desired her own sister in the larger interest of the family Shobha had to allow it. But already the things had become parts of history irrevocable. A kind of conflict persisted between them making them live at enmity.

The poet said 'if the winter comes, can the spring be far behind?' So the 10th Oct. hurried to the earnest. The previous day Pattans went to Pampapattan, the historical town well-known for its tropical climate and enlightening atmosphere. The city had two good Universities, a big belt of industries, vastly extended suburbia, old port, good municipal systems, hi-tech infrastructure. It was also a high seat of socio-religious activities. But it was more known as the centre of higher education in north Karnataka. People loved Pampapattan for other reasons too. If the young loved it for education, the retired and old loved it for retirement life, while the learning-oriented lived there for their intellectual make-up. In this climate people thrived happily and their longevity increased. Less number of people suffered from diseases common or fatal. Minimum dust, optimum heat, moderate rainfall, tolerable weather and beautiful sky went in making Pampapattan an ever lovable city. Wide gardens, beautiful parks, tall buildings, tipsy-turvi hills wholly covered by giant RCC structures, the dense woodland lent their own colouring to the town. Besides, coconut, mango, guava, chicko tamarind, sampige and other trees decorated her as beautifully as the choicest jewels could do a fairy queen. The Railway Station, the big central busstand, Radio Centre, public offices and numerous other locations trimmed Pampapattan. The enormous roads which spread over the city like central human nerves system, helped its dwellers to speed up their work, while like a plait of woman's hair, the national highway added its own sublime to the urbanscape dividing it evenly. The whole city was growing and developing every year without any precaution for the fast increasing immigrants, children population, dependents, idlers, beggers and swindlers.

It was a 10th Monday. The day dawned calm and the sky was clear. The morning weather was tolerable though humid. The sun was rising in his sphere of sky with his golden rays spreading everywhere so warm as morning tea. Birds were chirping in trees which stood like Wordsworth's daffodils. In fact, to a stranger, the whole city looked like a thousand hecters plantation. Only on the basis of big buildings, tall towers and sound and noise stemming from industries, one had to guess Pampapattan to be a city. Presently the people related to marriage parties came to the hall.

The wedding hall named Shantiniketan had been the biggest one there. It was built on a five acre plot in a strategic area. It had a large number of lodging rooms, a big kitchen, WC, spacious halls for dining and other functions. All the modern facilities were available. Seating arrangement for function and standing arrangement for dinner were graceful and spendid.

The marriage preparation had been over by eleven in morning. The wedlock ritual was scheduled to take place exactly at twelve. Everything had been ready. Everyone invited had come. As it was the wedding of Venkatesh, a brilliant scholar, with the celebrated engineer Shrishail's only daughter, each and everyone invited did not like to miss the opportunity. So by twelve everyone neat and handsome in dress, fresh and cheerful, had adored his chair comfortably. People's eyes turned to the bride and bridegroom at times and again naturally. When a music band began its melody, the priest started chanting. The assembled womenfolk particularly the kith performed whatever their tradition imposed.

The scene on the podium was gorgeous. It looked as if it had been the only one-exceptional. The pair looked brilliant, perfectly matching and beauteous. The bride appeared in her richest saree, loveliest blouse, freshest flowers and choicest jewels. Her flapping hair lent her a cine look; while the jewels increased her gandharva qualities. Exceptional to all these was her fair colour which lent her celestial maidenhood that was till then the monopoly of woodland nymps alone.

No less striking was Venkatesh's handsome personality. He appeared in red sapari; the costly diamond ring and gold chain decorated him. Titan like physic he had. The liberty shoes gave their own grip to his legs while walking. His oval face, neat nose, fleshy cheeks and little mouth, wide forehead, black hair and the like made him look like Rama of our Indian mythology. No doubt, people admired the newlyweds' matching and they never failed to compare them to any ideal couple they saw, read about, or heard of in their life.

The wedlock ceremony was over in time. Soon people, particularly the outsiders rushed for dinner which was well-prepared and delicious. Never was seen such a rush. The moment it began all people hungry or otherwise walked fast to the dining hall. While most others mostly the supervisers and relatives struggled to manage the situation.

Presently none was happier than Mohini. Admittedly she was the happiest because her challenge was won. Besides, the man she chose was brilliant and she had loved and married than married and loved. So on and so forth. This fair eyed beauty adored Venkatesh like Parvati adoring Shiva. Occasional was her romance with him. It was sure Mohini was engrossed in her own district where she could find only one man Venkatesh, her everafter hero. Venkatesh too was not an exception to this. But he was caught between two things, how to strike a balance between his wife and mother who expected him to be careful. Although Mohini was greatly with him upon the chair because of her sociability at times she incurred his mother's wrath. However, he did not worry much about the vexing issue there and then.

'Hai... ai...i,' a voice heard from behind.

'Oh!,' Venkatesh exclaimed.

'Very nice, very nice, beautiful,' the woman who saw the newlyweds smiled upon them.

'It's my aunt,' Venkatesh introduced Karisma to his wife.

'Is it?' she spoke briefly. Mohini was struck by Karisma's urbanity.

'It's my father,' the son introduced his father thereafter.

'It's very nice to see you, sir,' Mohini spoke to him with courtesy.

'How are you my son?' the oldman looked at Venkatesh like a grandshire.

'Well,' came a polite reply.

'May I know where's the sister?' Karisma who stood beside Venkatesh, enquired him.

'Oh! She's there busy,' Venkatesh replied her waving his hand towards his mother afar.

Never occurred a moment so enlightening in the history of Harish's house which could excel Karisma's embracing Shobha, her sister. The time she left the newlyweds on dias, Karisma rushed to Shobha and embraced her in consideration of her magnanimity. This she did as a measure of acknowledging the responsibility for the disturbance she caused to the old lady in regard to her life with Harish. No wonder, already the young woman had been tearful which indicated her defeat. The eyes, the cheeks, the vanished radiance highlighted her regret and repentance. Beside her stood her only child like his mother mischievous. But far away from the wives stood the man spellbound who managed them both in his fall and spring. His face evinced his grief, anguish and fatalism either for blundering against the wishes of his first wife or for marrying the second. He was in his utmost self-alienation. He had much grieved of his lust of the yester years, sadism of current times and uncertainty of a future union. The people who stared at them rarely seen together spoke themselves variously. Some reproached him and others blamed the illfated couple of their misfortunes. They said the faults were mostly created by him. Nay a few disliked the fallen hero for his Epicurian tastes. However, for everyone's satisfaction the newlyweds held the day.

The next day of wedding the couple went off to Hyderabad for their honeymoon. They booked a fine lodge at Koti. On their arriving at Bhagyamati (Hyderabad), they chalked out their programmes about their tripping, sight-seeing and film-going. A car was hired. They began their sight-seeing carefully. They saw Birla Planetorium, Salarjung Museum, Tank Bund, Golkonda Fort, Nehru Garden, Charminar and other places. On the roads, they saw Telagu speaking people, nasty monkeys at play in every tree, tallest buildings, high-tech buses, biggest shopping complexes, widest roads, rocky uplands, deep canals of Musi and the like. They mused with each other and mused over and again in

Osmania University Garden. The happiest moments of their life thrilled their young souls. They were all ideal, all gleeful, all enthusiastic, all set earnest and all curious. Mohini enjoyed him hand-in-hand, skin-to-skin, heart-to-heart. But the ecstatic moments of life for them occurred at their beds heavenly and thrilling.

'I'm very happy about you,' Mohini complimented the other in their bed bare-bodied.

'You're selfish in saying so,' he alerted her.

'Why?'

'Because I'm also happy to have got you.' Mohini admired his wittiness while he loved her fidelity. Both continued their merry chatting. Often they smiled and at times they laughed. They saw each other, touched their respective body and felt the ripples of ecstasy. Never they had felt such a touching, such a stir; never they had found so much joy in seeing each other and never they had been fully immersed in the emotions of each other. Indeed, they forgot God at the occasion. Only the concern of each then was bestirring of their hearts, capturing it, entering in it and living in it as long as they could, or as they desired. Mohini saw him, felt his body's warmth, entered his heart, no doubt, as much or more, as he did hers. Like the bees in honeycomb or the ants of juice, Mohini in him and Venkatesh in her immersed completely. After an hour of this unification attracted by the magnetic power of love and its emotions, they fell in each other's arms. So within a moment or two each was perfectly locked into the other.

When the charm of their premiere was over with its curiosity, touchingness, joys and feelings, the newly-weds settled down in Pampapattan calm and passionate. Now, a month or two later, Venkatesh bought a new house in the saburbia of Pampapattan University, Pampapattan. His house was very near to the famous Pampapateshwar temple on a hillock. The houses around Venkatesh's residence were many in number but most of them were secluded. The extention area was growing gradually with an ever increase of population. Anyway the municipal facilities were given and no problem abouτ water or electricity persisted. A good garden near the temple was a place for entertainment. People who went to Pampapateshwar rested in it a great while. A calm resting at the shrine increased their patience and purified their afflicted souls. Of course, chatting or merry-making people were not a rare spectacle to be beholden there. They talked over the joys of their workaday life. Pattans' house was a nice building with all its homely atmosphere. Solidly built in RCC, it had all facilities one could expect of a modern citizen.

The newly married ones had been happy of their setting up of a family in a convenient place. They continued their service in the University. During holidays they went to Banahatti in response to Shobha's affectionate wishes. In fact, they stayed there a month or so. Mohini too had no difficulties to start with. However, to live an ideal daughter-in-law, she needed much more time than she herself thought of.

Mohini's life in her mother-in-law's house had no starting troubles. She helped the elderly woman in every domestic work. She was also good at hearth. No doubt, never either by chance or by circumstance, she annoyed Shobha, the eldest in the family. In fact, they worked together. Perchance a sort of perfect harmony persisted between them.

However in regard to her social behaviour, an air of uneasiness prevailed between the younger and elderly women ever since Shobha first saw her. The matron was a total conservative in spite of her best university education, college profession and marriage to a man of equal social rank. Whereas Mohini was liberal, utterly modern and completely out-spoken. She was an extrovert, while her mother-in-law lived an introvert. In social behaviour, they differed from each other markedly. They tended to be poles — apart when they reacted to an outward anomaly. If Shobha remained in the confines of tradition of Indian womanhood, Mohini aspired for the western style of life. Or, it could be said, due to her superurban culture and parental support, she lived that kind of life which was approximate to Europeans particularly in matters of socio-cultural aspects. No matter, Shobha liked it or not, Mohini did not mind it whenever Venkatesh's friends or her own friends came home. She behaved very socially and mingled with them freely. Be it as it may when she went outside she preferred lady pants and shirts to sarees. She was pond of jeans. Due to his practice and liking, Venkatesh too did not chastise his wife which his mother expected greatly. True Mohini was outspoken and she was never shy or reticent. She spoke freely, and fell in revelry with Venkatesh as well as his friends. This hurt the oldwoman and her hatredness of such things nearly began. For evidence, an incident took place to mortify everyone and severed the things cordial.

'Don't wear jeans when you go outside,' Shobha advised Mohini once.

'I love it and I can't do without it,' humbly spoke the young dame.

'Doesn't matter,' the mother reverted.

'When you think I'd wear it?' the young lady asked the elder annoyed. There was anger in her voice.

'I mean, you'd not wear men's dress at all. Now you're married. You serve in a University. You've a husband. More importantly you're an Indian. Such dress does not look nice to ladies,' Shobha burst wild.

'Sorry aunt, I can't help it,' Mohini expressed firmly. When she made a move to go away apparently in that dress with Venkatesh who awaited her outside for a movie, Shobha called him loudly and he rushed in at once.

'D'you like Mohini go out in jeans?' she enquired him sternly.

'Yes, I like it mother,' he said.

'You like it?' she repeated her query accusatively.

'Yes; what's wrong in it?' he broke.

'It doesn't look nice. Tell her to go in saree,' the oldwoman spoke in an air of finality.

'Why?' he tried to defend his wife.

'I don't like her going out in jeans which angers public mind,' Shobha turned adamant.

'This is very common these days mother. Since we've got University education, it doesn't look bad for us,' he tried to convince her. Meanwhile he gestured Mohini to wear a saree.

'Oh! You're the only persons who've University education,' Shobha shot ironically.

'Of course, you had it, the way of life you lived then has undergone a sea change now,' Venkatesh spoke.

'Sea change?' the matron giggled.

'Indeed.'

'Indeed?' Shobha's bitter feeling was voiced again.

Meanwhile in obedience to her husband's motion of advice, Mohini though unwilling, changed her dress and both went off. However, the resolve she took then to alienate herself from her mother-in-law's clutches had been finalized. Venkatesh too took it for certain that that would certainly divide the family. Mohini began hating Shobha as vigorously as the latter had already started doing so. If Mohini's disliking had just begun Shobha's had begun right from the time of her meeting Mohini years ago. Unfortunately, the family harmony was broken. Thereafter, Mohini insisted upon her husband not to take her to Banahatti. When he went to Banahatti she left for her parents' house in Pampapattan. No wonder, in the upcoming years the women met each other only for a few times and they spoke to each other rarely. They loved each other's absence in their respective houses but the adverse effect of this disharmony and alienation on Venkatesh and his children had been worse to think of.

Over the years, Venkatesh's horizon of knowledge about human existence, his level of understanding and his quality of thought developed markedly. He reoriented his creative energies, streamlined his thought process and struggled to do whatever he could in the larger interest of others. He determined to help those who were in distress, gave cooperation to anyone who was in tune with his theory of life. He loved and respected those who deserved it. He became more practical and humane. At the same time he did not overlook human limitations. He had a clear vision, clarity of thought, perfect ways towards happiness. He thought and acted rather than acted and repented. His clearheadedness, linguistic competence, ability, integrity, hardwork and patience went together in moulding his personality. He rarely had any dichotomy between his words and deeds. A good husband, an able lecturer and an ideal citizen he became thereof. Unlike his father more he aged, mellower he turned. The qualities of his head and heart reached a maturer stage. A perfect man of social conduct and creative genius, Mr. Venkatesh Pattan turned an asset to the department where he worked. His was a rare service to the University.

One day when Venkatesh was lecturing his students he found one of them yawning. This hurt him and he desired to chide the boy. The class was full and both the boys and girls were equally numbered. However, all the students listened to his teaching with joy and dedication. None created any noise or talked needlessly. Nor did they abstain from his lectures either? They were happy to attend classes which were informative and enlightening. But this time when Venkatesh found a boy sleepy while he was teaching Wordsworth's nature poetry, he could not help warning him.

'What are you doing there?' he asked him.

There was a spell of silence.

The boy who mistook the question for someone else remained neutral.

'Stand up,' Venkatesh ordered.

The studentfolk found the situation tense and serious. They looked at the professor only. No doubt, at once the boy stood up.

'Shall I think you're here.'

'Yes, sir,' the boy took it literally.

'What are you doing then?'

'Sitting.'

'What for?'

There prevailed silence again.

'Unless you're interested in classes, you'd not come here,' their teacher clarified.

'Sorry, Sir,' the boy obeyed promptly.

'It's not a matter of sorriness. You'd listen to us carefully. Otherwise you'll miss the fragrance of life,' he said firmly. 'D'you know the way you've to behave, or attend classes, do your assignments, taking notes, maintaining good relationships with teachers and others and make out a successful career for yourselves? Students'd be like explorers of truth, light, nobility and beauty. You must be humble, hardworking, honest and sincere. It's not all. You'd be scientific in thinking, correct in action, sound in judgement and sharp in sensibility. Otherwise how can you make your life so sweet a tale for others?' he stopped.

'Well,' he continued his lecture.

'Wordsworth was a high-priest of nature. He wrote on nature and he lived amidst her. He's a nature poet par excellence. His idea of nature is that nature is our mother, teacher and deity. She is the creator, the preserver and the destroyer. She's, he says, a perennial source of all things meant for human existence. Indeed, she's a book written by God for our instruction. It's said God first created the Garden of Adam and Eve which is nothing but the world of nature. Nature is the outward form of mother earth and finally of God. Man is a part of this. Like poetry and music nature gives us joy, peace and beauty. That's why Rousseau says 'Return to Nature,' Valmiki says, 'A river or hill, a tree or cloud indeed, any object of nature inspires man to worship God.' According to Sita, 'forest is a garden of delight.'

Nature provides us everything. Such is the mother's alchemy. Indeed, she's an agency of God for our survival.

Now listen to some of Wordsworth's stanzas of nature poetry I read out :

One impulse from a vernal wood
May teach you more of man,
Of moral, evil and of good,
Than all the sages can.

Wordsworth loved nature. So did Tolstoy and others. Tolstoy says 'if man's existence on earth should not be ceased, his harmonious connection with her should not be broken.' Similar are Gandhi's views and Tagore revered Nature in all of his melodious lyrics.

Really to the romantic poets the woodland, the birds and beasts, the whole biological millieu appeared an indispensable part of life. The cuckoo, the nightingale, the skylark heralded them messages of hopes and brought them visionary tales. See how Wordsworth sings of a bird.

Though babbling only to the vale
Of sunshine and of flowers,
Thou bringest unto me a tale
Of visionary hours.

Romantic poets loved nature as heartily as they loved wine and woman. Even the Victorian and modern poets like Hardy, Auden and others wrote of nature in superlative degree. For example, Hardy describes man's link with founa as an inevitable one. His poem 'Weathers' illustrates the point in question.

This is the weather the cuckoo likes,
And so do I;
When showers betumble the chestnut spikes,
And nestlings fly.
The citizen dream of the south and west
And so do I.
And rooks in families homeward go,
And so do I.

See how man's life with objects of nature is closely associated. Not only the birds and animals, but also the plants, trees, creepers find a beautiful place in man's heart. Look at Chorley's 'The Brave Old Oak.'

Then here's the oak, the brave old oak
 Who stands in his pride alone;
And still flourish he, a hale green tree,
 When a hundred years are gone!

The strength that lay in age, experience, bravery is apparent in this poem on Hearty Oak. Likewise you too should acquire strength, grace and patience over the years lest you cannot find nobility and greater consciousness. Nor can you explore the domain of truth and beauty of human existence,' Dr. Venkatesh lectured the students for long.

Now he finished his class. Already his energies had been sapped. Nor had he any time to drive away the truth of life further. So walked he to his chamber.

Venkatesh had become a savant in every sphere of his life. Already as a teacher-scholar he had earned a good name. Most of his critical works helped the scholarly-reading public. His collection of poems *The Mercy of Creator* had evoked a sensitive cross-section of the reading public. The poetry of this book was about heavenly bliss, eternal light, divine power, noble life and immortal love. The protagonist of the lyrics asks the almighty for bestowing upon him joy, peace and prosperity. He asks the Lord to provide man an order of life, sweetness and light and power and glory. He asks for more peace as it is the secret of life. The hero representative of mankind implores the Godhead to save his soul and protect him until he retires to grave all pasions spent.

An account must also be taken of Venkatesh's administrative ability. Over the years he became the Head of Department, the Dean and once a Syndicate Member. Everyone became Head of Departments but only a few of them led an intellectual life. Almost every chairperson of the University departments either gave up himself to the VC or followed him in every possible manner. The heads had no courage to talk to him boldly. Whenever they met the Vice-Chancellor in regard to their academic activities or BOE, BOS, BOA works they simply followed the VC's suggestions in spite of the VC's polices malevolent and humiliating. Many times the heads yielded to the VC's whims and caprices. This downgraded the education standards. It substanderdised the system. Besides, whenever the VC mismanaged things none save a very few, protested against him. Either because of fear or for the sake of favour every chairperson acted in tune with the authority. This was a characteristic feature of meetings and discussions of Deans, Academic Council, Senate and Syndicate Members. What the VC said went there. Upright people were not included in any committees. This was a mark of gross irregularity. This happened for the reason the VC had to retrieve the investment he made while he was appointed. It was just like 'throw money and grab money.' Gone were the days of dignity and fairness in university administration. Or had there been any people who would create a democratic atmosphere in the campus. A type of feudalism had come back there. Rules were arbitrary and people in power turned every odd to their advantages. Good people, or intellectuals had tough days in store. Faithful people or virtuous, indeed, had no days. Even truthful and sincere teaching staff had their decline. Only those who were known for their intellectual arrogance, nepotism, flattery, paper eligibility, muscle power and the like flourished. No matter whether they taught their students sincerily or not, they were the people who in part due to their politics gained power, had accessibility to authorities and contributed towards the downfall of sanctity, disappearance of standards and absence of democratic principles. It was due to lack of moral standards, clear-cut rules and regulations, most of the university staff was corrupted. None seriously bothered of duties. What they had to do they did not do. Nor did they avoid what they were not supposed to do? Faithlessness and dishonesty danced threadbare in the scuffle of uncertainty and misrule. Those who came to university either to teach or to be taught with a sound belief in it, soon found themselves disillusioned. Though university was the highest seat of learning, the highest quality of education did not exist. Either because of lack of intelligence or because of maladministration, justice was not given in a way people justly expected it. Particularly in regard to results misappropriation swept. Those who should get ranks did not get them due to wrong assessment or owing to the injustice meticulously meted out to them. Most of men in power did everything arbitrarily and they did whatever they could to strengthen their socio-economic ties.

In this kind of hostile or feudal atmosphere what can a few good people achieve in univeristy? No doubt, people truthful, intellectual and bold had no chance not only in Universities but everywhere. Neither they were encouraged in their enterprises nor they were supported and appreciated for their works of eminence. Gone were the days of students openly supporting them. Like most of elders, most of students were also insincere and indifferent. This was an unfortunate phenomenon of modern times. Besides, good people were suppressed, hated and opposed by the bad at times and again. No doubt, they were avoided from works wherever finance was involved, policy matters were undertaken and status was attached with. Indeed, sense of excellence was judiciously murdered in the whole set up.

Prof. Venkatesh had been one of them who were excluded wherever status, money and power were the matters of concern. But he was not a man who could mind of his exclusion in administrative matters. However, whenever he was included or ordered to do something, he never cared for nopotism, partiality and misrule. He did whatever he had to do in the purview of rules and regulations.

One day, Prof. Venkatesh was called for a meeting at about eleven in morning. But as per the order he had to attend it at ten o'clock. Of course the very order for him was given at eleven delibarately. Indeed, he went to the VCs meeting hall. Already every member of the concerned committee was present and the discussion was underway. He knew it best as to why the VC as well as others who hated him did this intentionally. No sooner Prof. Venkatesh went indoors the discussion hall than the VC turned wild at him.

'Oh! you're coming now?' The VC spoke in an indifferent tone.

'Yes, sir.'

'You're coming now... too late... disobedience,' the presiding figure shot orderly.

'Yes I've come now as I received the order at eleven,' Venkatesh returned to his mood of anger.

'You've no rules?' broke the VC accusatively.

'I wonder whether you've any rules,' Venkatesh exchanged heat for heat.

'What rules?'

'The rules of system and order.'

'D'ye know at what time you'd to be present here?' Dr. Gopal, the VC turned vulgar.

'At ten,' spoke Venkatesh bravely.

'But at what time you've come?'

'At eleven.'

'Why?'

'D' you know at what time you'd to send me the order?' Venkatesh's question turned the other spellbound.

'What time...?' the VC sat in confusion.

'Yes; at what time you'd to send me the order?' Venkatesh held the ground.

'Didn't you receive it yesterday?'

'How could I, when it did not come my way?' he burst defensively.

'Did you not send him the order yesterday?' The VC asked Registrar who sat close by him.

'I sent it, sir,' the subordinate grumbled to save his skin.

'He did not send it to me in advance. Better you ask the peon Mallanna when he gave me the letter?' Venkatesh, the only opposition member insisted upon the point of accountability.

Soon in came the peon to witness the scene.

'When did you give the order to Prof. Venkatesh?' Dr. Gopal enquired the man bony in body.

'I gave it to him just at eleven sir,' the servant spoke honestly. Therefore he was bony.

There was a pauze.

Now the Registrar's face was downcast due to his callous nature. He had become a party to Venkatesh's enemies.

'Why you gave it late?' this time Venkatesh asked the servant smiling upon him.

'Sir told me to hand it over to you late sir,' he began politely and ended in the same pitch.

'Oh! this is deliberately done. You want to delite democratic principles of the University set up. You are partial and corrupt,' Venkatesh shot at the other.

'Don't talk nonsense here,' the VC in tiptop attire spoke irked by the other's directness.

'I'm talking what I'm supposed to.'

'What, what, what you mean,' Dr. Gopal stammered.

'I mean what I said,' the other turned aggressive.

There was an ire in their tone.

'You're talking too much these days?' the VC retorted suddenly.

'I'm talking it because of your misrule and corruption,' the member spoke still angry.

'D'you have any proofs of my corruption?' the authority shot at the other at the top of his voice.

'Yes,' said he. This startled the VC.

'Then give evidence.'

'Have you not taken fifty thousand rupees in case of Mr. Ramagouda's appointment to Reader post in Sociology? I also know who else have bribed you in appointment cases. I know when they have paid you, how much they have paid you, and why they have paid you,' Venkatesh turned rebellous.

There fell a deep silence. Nobody dared to brake it. All desired to avoid the sensitive matter as it could affect the prospects of many lives.

'You've remained silent sir,' the professor moved ahead the whole discussion.

'Anyway it's not your business to talk of things that are of my concern,' Dr. Gopal asserted his monopoly.

'So you want to do anything to exploit office?' the other turned offensive.

'Don't ask that. If you want to support me, stay here. Otherwise, the door is open.'

'Does it mean that I shouldn't ask about the proceedings?'

'Yes.'

'Alright give it to me in writing,' the other demanded it lawfully.

'Mr. Venkatesh is a wrong headed man sir?' one who hated Venkatesh's uprightness poked his nose in support of VC's assertion.

'Mind you business,' Venkatesh shunned this chap of the committee.

'Alright! I'll give you an order of cancellation of your membership to the committee,' the officer tried to end up the deadlock.

'Why?'

'Because you want to go away.'

'Did I ever say so?'

Again there crept a silence like a village ghost of night.

'No,' Venkatesh replied himself. He knew he answered his own question.

'Anyway I'm unhappy over the issue that you've brought so much of displeasure here. I'm sorry to tell you. Let's hold the meeting on 25th November. You need not worry this time. I'll see that you'll get an order in time. But try to improve your bad conduct,' the Vice-Chancellor told the other authoritatively.

'Take your last sentence back,' Venkatesh retorted.

'No, I'll not.'

'Then I'll stage here a satyagrah. I don't tolerate your stubbornness,' Venkatesh turned wild. He also demanded an apology from him. When all the members began to go out, he held the ground and insisted upon the point. At last the VC could not help expressing sorry. He expressed his regret over the matter. 'But the insult,' he thought, 'he got today had been enormous' . He felt humiliated in the hand of a professor. This, it could be said, emboldened him to chalk out any oppressive measures to suppress his enemies. On the otherhand, Prof. Venkatesh was two fold jubilant. Wonderful enough the whole event spread in the campus. People who loved sanctity in administration loved Venkatesh's uprightness and those who stood for money and matters summarily dismissed Venkatesh as one of the cranks. Prof. Venkatesh too anticipated that the VC would not help him in the days to come. But he was not a man who could easily be disheartened by such evil powers. In fact, he never budged to any one. He prepared himself to brave up problems, to tolerate the inhuman and to boldly tackle his adversities for getting justice though a little late.

Having become a victim of campus politics, Venkatesh became more and more fastidious in his duties, privileges and responsibilities. In spite of this the men who hated him supported authority in tarnishing his image. They were cut-throats, sadists, anarchists. But a few of them knew that he was not a small force to be eliminated. He had his own voice and his voice was strong. More he was troubled, stronger he grew. Greater he faced hideous politics, more he became famous. Occcasional might be, but the pressmen published his views in papers. In turn the whole prestige of Pampapati University was lost in the quagmire of nepotism, backbiting, misrule and the like. But Prof. Venkatesh's image was proportionately developed and the people's admiration for him was enhanced thereafter.

Prof. Venkatesh got a very good image over the years. His virtues were recognised by society. Many town programmes invited him for functions. In fact, he presided over programmes both in Pampapattan and outside. People liked his deliberate responsiveness, essential humanity, rare integrity, talent, creative power and originality. They loved and admired him. But the irony of circumstance lay just the other side. The VC and his followers did not like him. Nor did they talk to him either? This was the result of his flawlessness in his style of functioning.

Venkatesh hated immorality, partiality, falsification. Whether in personal life or in social, he was a gem of virtues. He tried to enlighten and sweeten his environment. Of course, his exposition of other's bribery or their vices made him unbearable. But he never harmed anyone unless he found it essential.

It was a Wednesday evening. Venkatesh was on his way home from the city where he had a social function for the emancipation of woman. On the way, he found his peon arguing with someone beside his house. Soon Venkatesh heard it coming loud and louder. Mr. Indran, a Tamil outcaste who had been a peon in Pampapati University had been presently quarrelling with a man of the town. But the hustle-bustle went beyond normal and when the parties involved in it were likely to exchange blows, the peon's wife rushed to Prof. Venkatesh. On hearing the matter, Mohini asked her husband who had by then reached home to help the poor fellow in getting his problem solved.

'What's the matter?' Venkatesh enquired on reaching the spot.

'Sir, this fellow has molested my wife,' Indran spoke angrily while the other figures stood speechless. Of course, no outsiders heeded the event as they were not there in the surrounding. Indran's home was in an isolated area. This helped him carry on his cathouse business.

The professor was taken aback by this.

'Sir, this rascal has molested my wife,' Indran told to Mr. Pattan again in expectation of his support.

'Is it true?' Pattan asked the novice.

'Yes sir but it's done lawfully,' the other defended himself.

'Molestation...lawfully... impossible,' Pattan thought firmly.

'Yes sir; they are playing a game.'

'What you mean by this? Tell me as I'm at a loss to understand it,' said the eldest worried.

'When I first met Ammukutty, Indran's wife and struck a deal, it was proposed that I should pay her Rs. 100 everytime. This way I sleep with her. Sir, it's also known to Indran. No doubt, he has permitted her thus to earn money. Already I've slept with her nearly for twenty times and paid her Rs. 2000 honestly. But today I don't know why he has turned indifferent,' the businessman who loved Ammukutty for her seducing countenance finished his say. Particularly her radiance and the melons of her blouse had bewitched him.

This business man of Pampapattan used to come to Indran's house once or twice a week. After an illegal accord had been struck between Indran and his wife, Ammukutty kept on inducing rich men and just for money she lifted her legs to them any time. But whenever Indran found a particular man unwanted either because of his arrogance or because of his dislike for him, he trapped him. It was his policy to threaten the man and exploit him to the fullest extent. This way or that he exacted five to ten thousand rupees from each of his client. Thereafter, did he or she abstain from such brothel house activities? In appearance he looked a chaste husband but in reality he permitted his wife to earn money by any means. As they belonged to a down-trodden caste, they did not hesitate involving in cathouse business. On several occasions he himself brought such men and offered them what he had not to do. No wonder, people with Mrs. Indran slept instead of convincing him, while he kept a guard on outsiders. People used to think it might have been a guest at Indran's house. Already many men but all prosperous were lured by Indrans and lately he had become a prosperous person in the colony where he had lawlessly built up his hut.

Currently, Venkatesh who did not know the vagaries of Indrans stood spellbound by these sordid affairs.

'Sir, tell him to offset the event by money,' Indran sought Dr. Pattan's support.

'So you mean he has to pay you to have molested her?' asked the savant.

'Why not sir?'

'This is the business he carries on here daily,' the townsman interrupted smiling upon the University Professor.

'My God !' Pattan stood silent for a while.

'Alright give him some money, and kindly don't indulge in such business hereafter,' Pattan spoke over the disgusting business. He wished that he should have not been there.

'Sir, I've already given her a hundred rupees,' the other held the ground.

'Pay five thousand rupees. Lest I'll hand you over to the police,' Indran apostrophised. He turned kindless.

'See this is a very sensitive matter. Adjust with any amount he gives you. In fact, you'd not take anything because the fault is as much of yours also. If you go to station, all of you have to be imprisioned. None likes this.'

'What, sir?' Indran interrupted.

'Immediately he'd give you some amount as you demand it and you'd bear the ills. If the topic is closed soon, it's good for all,' Venkatesh said nobly, 'Bear it also in mind that I can't wishstand this kind of scene. So I'll go.'

'Please sir stay for some more time at least for God's sake,' Indrans implored. The haggling continued and the educated man stood neutral to the ugly issue. Oddly enough Ammukutty, Indran's wife who ran the commerce did not feel sorry of her filthy affair. On the otherhand, she had been happy. Firstly she got money; and secondly or more significantly, she enjoyed forbidden fruits officially. She knew her husband was not able to gratify her. She gave the money to him while she enjoyed the clients for herself. Occasionally she exploited people for more money. No doubt, her feminine grace, her bewitching look, her readiness to cope with any one... anywher :nytime for the sake of money brought her certain wealth which was the only monopoly of prostitutes. This pleased her like anything. Prosperous in her business at times she found her husband dislike some of her clients merely on the ground that they did not respect him. 'Why should they respect him when she was paid?' It was her current view. The present case was the same and it irked her naturally.

'I don't accept anything short of five thousand rupees. otherwise, you know how I'm terrible. I'll report it to police,' Indran continued threatening the other.

'Pay something and go. See that next time both of you don't involve in this dealing,' Dr. Pattan suggested the other who was standing at the mercy of Indrans.

'Scoundrel. Take two thousand rupees,' immediately the man threw a bundle of notes and went in a huff.

This is the worst business I imagine. I don't know how daring you're to carry on this. Don't you know you are a university employee? I never like this. You've forgotten *character is lost everything is lost.* Please don't see me again. Yes both of you. Don't come towards my house either. Nonsense,' Venkatesh told them angrily. Quickly Dr. Pattan left the place in an utter dismay. The whole affair of Indrans looked filthy to his righteous nature. Dr. Pattan had not seen such a couple. Of course, he had heard that there were women who lived on others he had not known a case like Indrans.

Dr. Venkatesh came home dejected. He was unhappy of the day's event.

'What's the matter?' Mohini asked him when in dispair he got indoors.

'Ah! That's a disgusting affair,' he stepped in in a mood which Mohini never witnessed before. Understanding her husband on the basis of his mood, the landlady did not dare to enquiry him for the nonce. She followed him to bed where he was meditating over the evils of human society.

'You look dismal dear. May I know what troubled you?' Mohini made a gentle interrogation before she could give him a cup of tea.

'It's the degeneration of human values?'

'Let it be succint my lord.'

'See that man Indran, one of the peons of our university, has turned an evil-doer... He is hiring the body of his wife to any people who pay him...'

'My God!'

'It's not all. He also plays with the prestige of those for whom in lieu of money his wife lifts her legs.'

'Is it? Wonderful,' Mohini spoke astonished.

Came in a deep silence.

'Certainly that's the worst thing one can ever think of,' Mohini stopped sipping her tea. Nor did she see the other doing it either? They were engrossed in the matter. What a wonderful scene? They were worrying about the evils of their society.

'The bloody bitch too does not know the importance of her character. She's forgotten that 'character is everything,' he reproduced the details.

'I wonder whether low caste people can think of such matters. They're essentially dirtiest,' Mohini consolidated the matter. She cooled him.

'Indeed, they carry on any sorts of evil-tapestry,' heaved he a sigh of relief.

Then the door was closed. Mohini sat closeby. Venkatesh was taking rest. Meanwhile Sidhartha, their only son turned in from playing. There was a maid servant to look after the kitchen affairs, house-cleaning, gardening and the like. Sidhartha who had by then been ten years old, had been in his fifth standard at St Joseph Convent School. He was a beloved of his parents as well as his teachers. His wittiness and sportiveness made him a loved one, a miniature hero. He was an exact replica of his boyhood grandfather. He had inherited his grandfather's aptitude for study and his father's qualities of head and heart. His parents virtues were to be descernible in him. A pretty face, red complexion, nice nose, charming cheeks, dark eyes and robust health smarted him. He looked like Lava, the son of Rama. The way of his reading, writing, speaking, playing, thinking and finally acting had been pleasant and flawless. Often his maid servant exclaimed, 'what a lovely child he was!' Not surprising, his mother loved him more than his father, his grandfather loved him more than his mother, his grandmother loved him more than his grandfather. His grand mother whensoever she came there was greatly pleased by his composure. In fact, he made her forget Mohini's indifference. She kissed him with all her affection. Harish, the boy's grandfather had taken a photo of him with himself. No wonder, everyone wished that he or she should get such a child — handsome, intelligent and hard-working.

No other phenomenal event disturbed Harish and Venkatesh, than their family disharmony ever afterwards. If Shobha hated Harish, Mohini hated Shobha. Although, Harish's visits to Shobha at Banahatti had been irregular he had not stopped visiting her altogether. Similarly due to Karisma and her son borne to them, Harish could not be perverted in his moods and musings.

Nonetheless, he kept a balance between the first wife and the second. Once a week he definitely visited Shobha and passed his time with her and her children.

Presently the typicality of Ashok had become a story of the town. Everyone knew Ashok from close quarters. They knew he was a prank, a rogue, a village vagabond. But like a paralysis attack to a young man a sudden metamorphosis had occurred to him. He had turned overreligious. But his mode of life had become more superstitious than spiritual. Often he wondered whether he could survive in the fabric of society and live upto the general expectation of his mother.

Needless to say Ashok had developed a sort of nature placatory but unreasonable, religious but inconsistent and traditional but objectionable. He lived in loneliness and spent his time in religious austerities. The extremity of his rogury had created a kind of reverse emotions in him. As a result, under the influence of a swami, he underwent a sea change, but he had picked up considerable excentricities. He stopped entertaining any friends for revelry or otherwise. Lost the companions he had earlier and he gradually turned more a *satwik* in nature. Again his *satvikness* had been different from the *satvikness* of others, the *satvikness* of swamis or of the particular swami who had brought a sway upon him. Too much is too bad. (ıdual change in mind changed his dress, manners, diet and speech habits. Instead of roving in the company of wastrels, he went to a math, an asylum, a temple. He stopped wearing jeans; began using orange cloth which was common to sadhus. Gone were the days of his eating chicken and mutton, or enjoying fish and egg masala. Begun were the days of two squaire meals made of bread. He ate no delicacies modern hotels provided. He stopped card-playing, drinking and frequenting brothels. Ashok abstained hurting others. He did not annoy even his mother either by his speech or action. His rapport with materialistic house-holders was limited only to his mother and a specific kindred. He began wearing ashes on his face and body. Often he was only in his lioncloth either at home or in math. He sat barebodied while counting a chain of beads or a chain of wild nuts. What a marvellous change ! He had turned a sadhu like figure. But his relationship with his wife now a second one continued. As he could not lead a household life with his first wife, on one bitter morn, she had left him. Thereafter, more by his mother's persuation than by his own accord, he married a village woman who was junior to him almost by a decade.

The gloomy person in the house of Ashok about his future had been neither Ashok nor Vanita, his wife, but his mother Shobha. It could be apostrophised, Shobha had been the unfortunate woman in the world. She got a husband who did not remain constant to her in love; she got a brilliant son but because of a remote place job he remained inaccessible; she got a daughter-in-law but she alienated herself from her; and now she had Ashok, a second son who turned a rogue-rishi. He had become a duplicate Sadhu. As a sadhu, he lost his first wife who divorced him accusing him of impotence. What a shame! What a sin! What an insult to Pattans' family! However her great virtue was patience throughout these days of suffering as ever before. If she lived, she lived for Ashok. However he was a waif, he was her son, a young son and a only son after Mohini had snatched away Venkatesh. Now, after these years of trials and bitter moments of life, Shobha was doubly bent in body and she was strained in mind. Her only hope was to see Ashok get to the right track of life. In this regard, many questions occurred to her inward eyes. She thought of his future and the future of his wife, a mere girl of twentythree. Ashok had no job, no asset as such save the house and no sound education that could help him for a living. Nor did he possess any skill to labour for survival? Still he was fortunate because he had no issues either by his first wife or by his second. Certainly in part due to barrenness, his first wife had divorced him. He could not help accepting it meekly. The cause of it was not his impotence however, but his first wife's desire to live with her paramour.

When he did not live to her expectation, the mother believed, Vijaya found her own ways towards happiness. Equally the position of his second wife was not different. She too did not have any source of livelihood. So uncivilized were Ashok and his wife to live upon Shobha, the sole bread winner of an uprooted family.

But happy was the man who lived elsewhere. Harish bothered about none except Karisma's family. He knew Shobha managed her children well. A lustrous man addicted to avarice, sex and sensuality, he aspired for a luxurious life. In ease and comfort, he lived with Karisma. After all they had only one son. Harish did not mind Shobha's problems, her children's education, marriage. In this circumstance only the mother and her eldest son married Ashok and Kamala. Of course, Ashok's first marriage had been a failure and he married for the second time, while Kamala was married off to a prosperous zamindar. She got a good husband and a good future. Only a bad spouse means a worst life. Even Harish did not attend the wedding of either Ashok or Kamala. Did he help them financially? A barbarous fellow. He went scottfree. He escaped his great responsibility. He became ever a happy-go-lucky-chap. Under the earthly influence of Karisma, he favoured her party and he spoke jovially that 'the sons of Kunti will get nothing.' But he was oblivious that both Kunti and her sons were wise to mould their future. Harish was vindictive. His ambition as Karisma taught him was to see that her son would excel Shobha's. But it was a foolish idea and a mere caprice. How can an orange become an apple. Impossible. Harish was not a man of down-to-earth reality. Misguided by fleshly ills he got merely thistles for figs. Wasted was his life. A terrible thing to hear or see was his spoilt personality.

Harish was basically a man of no character. Essentially he was hedious. Equal was his adamancy and dare devilry. His love for melons was horrible. It was because of his obsession with Karisma, he incurred Shobha's wrath. Incontrovertible was the fact that people hated him for his womanizing habits. Therefore, the times when in her company, Harish appreciated westerners' free sex, Shobha recollected him the commandment that 'everyman should have only one wife.' She was correct. She was right because people like her husband in India did not allow their wives to dally with their menfriends. Even Shobha had questioned this. To a little extent she was radical and rebellious. She faced his bravado. She rebelled against his male-supremacy. She challenged him. His curtailment of her freedom was really the point she hated him for. She knew Harish did not allow her to be social always. The moment he found her talking with others, particularly with men, he saw her with contempt. Stark was still his negligence of her children.

He had his own stand against Shobha. He hated her challenging temper. Her directness alone damaged his love for her. But it was inhuman on his part. He did not like his wife's rebellion. He loved her own sister, while she expected him to be fair in the matter. Shobha's hatredness rose out of her family background, university education and new mode of life. Harish also hated Shobha for her unadjustment with Mohini. He thought Mohini disliked the oldwoman on account of her traditionalism and imposing behaviour. He knew on no occasions Karisma erred more than Shobha, and her erring, he felt, caused a ripple of dismay in the district of their kinship.

It was on the eve of Ugadi, Venkatesh invited his mother to his newly-built house in Pampapattan. Ugadi was Hindus' grand religous festival. In fact, it was their new year eve. It could generate hopes of constructive activities. All good things were to begin from thereafter for the next year. When Shobha now a woman of more than sixty years came, by chance, Venkatesh was not at home. None went out to welcome the oldwoman either! As light was not there, the bell too did not work. But Mohini did not open the door initially in spite of hearing the sound of door knocking. This hurt the elder. She knocked the door again. As a result a hoarse sound was heard in a hurting manner. But within a few minutes the door was opened.

'Why late in opening it?' first spoke the annoyed woman.

'I was far in,' the younger replied falsly. She did not welcome Shobha which was unthinkable in Indian context. The old woman came herself in the house with a sense of remorse. She placed her luggages somewhere before she could rest. Venkatesh however arrived soon and he was glad to see the arrival of his mother. Unfortunately he could not understand the reason for her dismay.

'How are you mother?' he burst joyous.

'Well...' Shobha spoke dismal.

'You look unhappy?' He enquired her.

'Yes my son.'

'Why mother?' the son spoke lovingly.

'I don't like to tell it to you now,' she said. Meanwhile Mohini was overhearing the oldwoman and she was seething with anger. She knew well the nature of Venkatesh and his anger in case he found anyone disheartening his mother. So she sensed something undesirable during the upcoming days until the old lady could disappear.

'How is Ashok?'

'Fine, but not working in the factory where he could earn his livelihood. Recently he left it,' Shobha heaved a sigh. She was peevish.

'Why?'

'He wants to live in a math and he wants to serve a swami,' broke she worried.

'Wonderful!'

'Really.'

There was an overbearing silence.

'Then what of his family. None is there to earn a living for his wife,' Venkatesh spoke with concern.

'They'll live upon me,' the matron spoke derisively.

'Of course! But how long?'

'Until I die,' she laughed at him.

'Nonsense. He'd know that he'd live.'

'D'you think we can do something for him?'

'See now I'm happy here. Tell him to join us with his wife. They can reside in the other portion of my house. I'll buy him a vehicle. Let him run it for hiring,' he resolved to help his brother.

'True it's a sound idea. But that chap may not undertake it. I think,' the mother continued, 'you have already written him a letter in this regard.'

'Yeah. D'you know what he's replied?' the son threw a glance at the oldwoman curious, while the latter was patting Sidhartha, her grandson beside.

'Can you read it to me?'

'Wait...I'll bring it here.'

Venkatesh went in to bring the letter. He was all earnest. He went in first to his bedroom. He began searching a bundle, while an unhappy figure behind him whispered something.

'Why she's come here?' enquired Mohini.

'Nonsense,' Venkatesh quipped her at once. 'A stupid fellow. You've no respect for my mother,' he expressed his anger as she had disrespected his mother. But without standing beside her long, with the letter in his hand, he hurried back. Shobha sat still where he had left her. She was happy about Sidhartha, now a good-looking boy, quite lovable. Venkatesh resumed his dialogue.

'See, it's his letter. I received it just the other day,' he heaved a sigh of relief.

'Let me know the content.'

'Yea,' Venkatesh began reading it :

Dear Brother :

I'm happy here though others think I'm not. None knows me well, nor I myself. Only God does it. You know life is an accident, an illusion; it lures us utmost but we'd not give upto it. We've to avoid the inducements, the ambition and the sense of attachment. We must be contented with whatever we find. Greed is a cause of misery, misery is a cause of death, a bad death is a cause of rebirth. In turn rebirth leads to relife which is again a vicious circle. Therefore, we've to pursue a path of truth and nobility. For this I've turned a yogi, a man of religion, a man of God — one with the oversoul.

With Best Wishes.

Truly Yours,
Abhayanand.

(Ashok Pattan)

'An excellent letter! Wonderful! Look at his determination, his ideas and goals. What a nice name he has adopted! Does he tell us anything about his family, of his mother if not father, of his wife if not others,' Shobha expressed her long standing grief.

'I wonder whether he can become a real monk!' Venkatesh exclaimed.

'Did you wish him become a sadhu?'

'Never mother.'

'See how you're wrong when you think he's doing some business, while he thinks of God and religion alone?' the ailing woman spoke back.

'Yea, mother. But as a brother it's my bounden duty to worry about you and him. Since father left us to our destiny, how can we neglect our interest. We're human beings. Since we're endowed with reason, we'd think in a right way,' he finished his say, while his companion sat happy of her son's concern for the family.

'Still d'you think we can do something for him?' Shobha optimistic of things asked him again.

'He'd do something as we guide him.'

'What's your plan for him.'

'Let him come here. I'll buy him either an autorickshaw or manage to set up an STD booth just in front of my house. So that he can manage one of these without any burden,' he looked at her in expectation of her response.

'A very good idea. But the chap is quite thick-skinned. He'll not follow us,' she spoke hopelessly.

'It's his badluck then.'

'That's true!' the old lady heaved a sign of relief.

Then all turned for a dinner.

The horizon of Venkatesh's knowledge had improved, elevated and standardized over the years of calm as well as storm of his strife. The struggle he made ever since his birth till today had taught him a vivid and authentic experience. But the experience he had got had been bitter though as such it had given him an expected satisfaction. Like Ashok, the king, he realized the fact happiness lies in sorrow. The happiest song of his life had been a tale of his saddest thought. The indifferent father, the docile but traditional mother, brother rogue turned rishi, the belligerent university set-up where he worked had taught him bleak realities of human existence. Besides, social evils, evil-doers like Indrans, nepotism, corruption, avarice, immorality, cheating, gossip mongering in the surrounding were injurious. Often he wondered as to why man troubles his fellow beings. Father's indifference towards his mother, his wife's rebellion against his mother, Ashok's spoilt-career shocked him. Besides, his colleagues' professional jealousy, their slanderousness, the indifference of officialdom, the deterioration of social-values enerved him and often he thought of death. Life seemed a long labour in the thoroughfare of sad humanity. He thought the world is a welter of futile doings. He saw everyone unruly in behaviour, ignorant of his individual limitations and commercial in attitude as never before. He was hurt by man's inhumanity and lack of harmonious man-woman relationship. Nor was he happy about the discordant man-social relationship which had been worsened because of man's evils. He knew man was going to dogs because of the excesses of his nature. No doubt, he found Camus, the existentialist writer right when he said life is an accident in a purposeless universe.

Venkatesh's creative as well as critical writings had already been bulky both in quality and quantity. He had authored five books and each of them had greatly contributed towards the enrichment of Kannada literature. Most of his works had gained a high reputation and all of it had been translated into Hindi and English. As a man of letters, his name was familiar to the vast reading public not only in Kannada but also in other vernaculars. *Critic*, his first book, a collection of literary essays had become almost a reference work; the second, a collection of short stories was enlightening; the third a novel called *Sangharsh* portrayed human strife; and the fourth *Dispersed Meditations,* a collection of popular essays dealt with themes varied and mind-boggling, while his fifth *The Discovery of Human Mind* that depicted the shape and size, the colour and contour, and the ebbs and tides of human mind in the vast ocean of life's joys and sorrows. This last one caught the minds as a hot cake. The ideas, thoughts, new insights it explored and exposed brought a new name to its author. The book *The Discovery of Human Mind* had been both psychological and philosophical probing into the deep waters of life. There was also a touch of religion, ethics, aesthetics and the like and different stands of thoughts were enshrined in it. The insights it displayed were few, but they were very new. The nature of Venkatesh's ideas, the scope of his work, the new bearings for which it stood, made a revolution in the domain of ideas. The discovery of man's mind, heart, soul and inner furies either that signified anything or nothing represented a kind of double vision of Venkatesh, the writer-thinker. The book showed Venkatesh's mind as an empire of ideas. It vivified his exploration of truth and beauty, nobility and consciousness. Besides, the greater vagaries of human nature, the cause, growth, spread and decline of them were succintly analysed.

It was an April Monday. Apparently a summer day with its clear sky and warm weather. The time was five o' clock evening. The sun was still settling down in the horizon of western hemisphere. The sky looked blue with no stars yet in its fold twinkling. There was no dust, no storm, no noise, no rustle. The atmosphere was calm, tranquil and lively. Now, after the sun got a little down or the earth moved in the other direction, the sun's rays all scarlet turned golden. He looked clearest and blessing.

The western sky looked beauteous and the big buildings and tallest towers spread their ghostal shadows in the surrounding. Presently men, women, coolies, professionals, craftsmen all were homeward bound. Shepherds stood on hillsides herding their sheep, cowherds gave them company and the stray animals were wandering aimless. The songs of birds, the cool breeze and the glow of stars began the moment the sun went down in the western valley.

While it was eventide, Venkatesh, Mohini and their son sat before a television. A TV serial had begun. They watched the struggle of a man for eking out his livelihood. Afterwards at seven, the news of Doordarsan started. What a wonder! What a surprise! What an achievement! The third news item of the evening had been something about Pamp Award for the celebrated Kannada works. No wonder the announcer read out, a short while later, the item 'the prestigious Pamp Award for Prof. Vankatesh Pattan of Pampapati University.' In the details, the news said, the 'award was given to his work *The Discovery of Human Mind*. Thereafter, it was said it was given to this particular work in consideration of its in-depth thoughts and brilliant psychological insights it probed and generated. It was made clear that the work produced a new wave of thinking and an excellent inspiration and guideline to those who wanted new clues for exploring the unknown territories of human mind.

Hardly it was nine o' clock when a telephone message came. The secretary of Pamp Award Foundation said Mr. Venkatesh Pattan what the news had detailed was true. He rang him up solely for the reason Venkatesh should be confirmed about the news. The Award consisted one lack of rupees, a citation and a statue of Pampa, the first poet of Kannada literature. Meanwhile many more phones from friends and relatives, men of letters, admirers came one after another. People congratulated him in the morning, in the evening and at the day time. They admired his quality of thought enshrined in the award fetched book. Indeed, they appreciated Venkatesh's flawless genius.

Next day at the tme Venkatesh was about to go to University, Radio and TV interviewers arrived to his house. They were welcomed and given hospitality. Thereafter, admiring the writer-scholar, they took an interview.

'Sir, we're happy, for you've got the prestigious Pamp Award,' a TV reporter burst gently.

'Thank you.'

'We congratulate you on the occasion,' the Radio interviewers told him happily.

'Welcome,' spoke Venkatesh politely.

'May we know the central idea of the book?' the TV reporter asked him and the Radio man gestured in support of the other.

'See my book *The Discovery of Human Mind* explores the deep nature of human mind and its mysteries. It is an in-depth study of man's whims, ideas, thoughts, emotions. At the end, my book advocates man to refine his sensibility, sharpen his intellectual fibre and to think in a right way for the sake of meaningful life. Thinking is very important as choosing is based on it. In turn, choice leads to action and action to responsibility. As a result we find results good or ill. It can be said, what we sow, we have to harvest,' the celebrity stopped his say.

'That's right,' the elder of the two admitted the truth of his assertion.

'You're a University Professor, a distinguished man, a scholar, a writer at that. Most of us know that University is the highest seat of learning. Shall we think that the highest thoughts for the advancement of mankind are really generated there?' a reporter shot at him.

'A good question. See Nehru says a University stands for humanism, for reason, for adventure of ideas and for search of truth. As I view it, a University stands for the onward march of mankind. If Universities plan good education and impliment it adequately, it is well and good. In case they do not do this, or they go a wrong way, they become organized anarchies or man-made jungles. You're eager to know whether Pampapattan University is doing this. My answer to this question is that because of the campus politics and intellectual arrogance Pampapattan University is not contributing properly to human welfare,' he finished his views.

'Really, sir,' one of them admitted it.

'It's what the Universities are doing today. They have become dens of intellectual villainy,' the TV man spoke accusatively.

'How you think of the award?' the Radio interviewer made an earnest enquiry.

'I'm happy about it. But receiving the prize means an increase of my responsibility. Of course, an award is an indication of my talent, a recognition of my merit, a sure encouragement to me for further creative writing,' the man who sat gracefully before the interviewers and their mikes asserted gently.

'What're your next plans?'

'Now I want to set up a Kannada Institution with the help of this award money and I'll encourage young writers by holding seminars, workshops, symposia.'

'An excellent idea,' the TV man burst.

'It shows your concern for the cause of mankind,' the elder of the two spoke honestly.

'Thank you,' the professor broke smiling.

'Ok sir we congratulate you once again.'

'Thank you,' Venkatesh nodded.

He thanked them heartily.

Presently the TV and Radio interviewers stoppped their recording. They were given tea. Soon with one more round of thanksgiving, the outsiders disappeared.

The next Sunday, all the newspapers, regional and national published the news of the award given to Prof. Venkatesh Pattan. Even the press-persons rushed to his residence. No wonder, the whole month of November, Venkatesh busied himself replying, answering and supplying information to the mass media.

It was the month of December. A Friday morning. Dr. Rajanna and Prof. Venkatesh had been walking towards administrative building in the compus. Dr. Rajanna had been a friend and colleague of Prof. Venkatesh. They were talking about the Award, the criteria for it and the status of one who got it. In front of them, came a huge figure aged sixty-five. The man had been in full suit, tie, shoes entirelly well disciplined. There was a suitcase in his right hand equally aristocratic in look, and his left hand balanced his marchfast. He looked taller as well as fatter than Venkatesh. However his physic was strong, he did not look like Venkatesh's father, but like his elder brother. The friends walked and the gentleman marched ahead. He approached the other two, but showed no gesture of familiarity or any marks of smile. Hardly both the parties had been not afar, the gentleman who had been Harish, Venkatesh's father stopped his walk abruptly. It was his visit to his son, a visit after a gap of eighteen years. Now, nearly after two decades, he had come to meet his son and show his repentance and thereby regret over his spoilt life. Of course, he had come to congratulate Venkatesh who had recently got a great literary award.

'How are you father?' first spoke the son with all humility.

'Fine.'

'How are you?'

'Nice, you came just now?'

'Yea, where are you staying?'

'In my house very near here.'

'I heard the news of your success and watched the TV news. A brilliant success. What I could not do, you did or what I wanted to do you did, my son,' spoke he emotionally.

'Something I did. Well, let's go home,' the son asked his father glad.

The son took his father home and Rajanna turned back to his department. The father and son, now going together looked more like brothers than what they had been. However, the oldman looked less educated than his son, and he looked an obnoxious figure due to his way of life akin to European. He did not please anyone as profoundly as his son did. He looked essentially a bad character. A man of worldliness, he lacked spiritual poise, grace and ultimate strength. The Gandhian soul-force lived in him not. Because of the impact of western life-styles and culture he did not adjust with men of his faith nor he loved them. He had become rootless.

'You've a fine house,' the father spoke. He knew he did not do such a thing in life.

'Something is done daddy just to find out a way towards happiness,' his young companion broke humbly.

'Very good.'

'Is that car yours?'

'Yes, recently bought.'

'I hope you have used the award money for that,' the oldman spoke envious.

'No; my own money. The award money is kept for setting up an institution,' Venkatesh spoke sincerily.

'An excellent idea,' shot the other.

There was a pauze.

'How are you Mohini?' Harish spoke to his daughter-in-law on reaching home.

'Nice, How's aunt?' enquired the dame.

'You mean Karisma?'

'Yes... always...'

'Unlike the other, she's well and good.' Here the 'other' was Shobha. Harish hated her ever since she disliked Karisma's loving him. He called her a self-opinionated woman-always ego-centric and traditional. Soon Sidhartha came in and the oldman passed his time with the fifteen years old guy.

'How is the grandma?' the boy asked its grandfather.

'You mean Karisma?' Harish asked him the same question

'Which Karisma?' shot the young. The grandfather was pacified by this.

'Oh! You mean Shobha?' Mohini laughed at her son's nobility, while Venkatesh enjoyed the situation.

'Yes, yes,' the grandfather told the boy recollecting Shobha.

'She must be nice.'

'Did you not come from there?'

'No; I came from Belgaum.'

'Oh! You don't live at Banahatti?' the boy surprised the elder directly.

'Yea...' There was a guilty consciousness in Harish's face. This made his face downcast occasionally.

'Mother had come here recently,' Venkatesh changed the matter.

'Did she, a bloody woman?' His father broke.

'Yes she stayed here for a fortnight.'

'How is she now?' Harish grinned.

'Not unwell. But she's all worried about Ashok, the spoilt brother,' replied he.

'Is it true that he's become a sanyasi?'

'Not so. But every mark of that is imminent in his character now.'

'I knew it. It's nothing but that woman's impact upon the chap,' Harish accused his first wife. He was angry about her always.

'What's your next plan? Where d'you want to settle down?' Venkatesh enquired his father while the latter sat on a high-heeled arm chair.

'I want to settle down at Belgaum,' replied the elder with certainties.

'Dad better you come here. So we can live together. I'll also ask the mother to join us,' Venkatesh spoke with concern.

'Then what about the house and Naresh's education,' his father worried of his son from his second wife.

'Let me take care of it here.'

'You're known for harbouring good ideas,' the husband of two wives thanked his son. Harish found happy about Venkatesh's assurance. He knew his son was not an ordinary person. Already his magnanimity was known to the world.

I'm happy of you. Although I didn't take care of you sufficiently, you educated yourself and you found your ways towards happiness,' Harish admitted his failure in caring his family. His face was dismayed. There was a regret in his tone and a repentance in his heart. He knew that he did not do any justice to his first wife and her family.

Soon all of them got up for dinner. Mohini happy about Harish's decision to settle down with her, served them well. As she hated Shobha for her sheer traditionalism she loved Karisma and Harish as her true parents-in-law. Venkatesh alone understood the broken heart of Shobha, a suffering soul never to be seen elsewhere.

Years elapsed. The events turned good or ill, but unfavourable to Shobha, now a woman ten years retired, fragile in body and pessimistic. However, she was unhappy while all her kindred were happy. She was unhappy because Ashok did not become a man; and did not make a living for himself. Besides, he got no issues. He married twice but made no move to live with either of his women. When he did not lead a married life with his first wife, she abandoned him. Now, he had Vanita, his second wife, a poor creature. Like him, she too had been jobless. He had turned a wastrel additionally. He showed no signs of get togetherness. Even he did not come home regularly and if came did not satisfy his wife. Neither he gave her any money nor showed her an ounce of love and sympathy. Like the predecessor she turned frustrated. Already a twenty-five year old woman, how can she live happy without her husband's love, or company. Admittedly he did not support her. He let her to his mother's care. He did not come home daily and he lived in a monastery. Shobha, the mother-in-law looked after her. In fact, Shobha cared the daughter-in-law as a mother. She advocated her to be good in matters of life. She told her to be strict in regard to any worldly allurements. However, she had worried of the daughter-in-law because the latter though had been very humble looked to have developed an affair with Vasu, Ashok's boyhood friend. Vanita tried to the best of her abilities to control her passions but ultimately she succumbed to it. Though they had been married for the past six years, she had not yet enjoyed her husband. As Ashok had turned a sanyasi, she thought her life became pointless in the modern world of science and commerce. In spite of the fact that she had to obey her mother-in-law in every matter, she failed in sexual gratification.

Indeed, she wanted to cool the heat of her body at least secretely.

Vasu had been Ashok's good friend. Although both had been together, Vasu disliked Ashok's hatredness for worldly life. He knew he could not do it. As a matter of fact often he came to Shobha's house. He found Vanita, a bird utterly neglected. So he desired the abandoned fruit naturally. Although Shobha anticipated something wrong in their relationship under the impression that she would be at home always, she did not undertake any precaution. Admittedly the two hungry souls desired each other and planned to do something towards finding some outlet. They knew they were badly in need of it. They met at temple, they spoke to each other and they exploited the absence of the oldwoman. As Vasu had been one of the parishioners, he found her company at least once a day. When he found Ashok, turned spiritual, he pretended to be his best companion. But his designs to exploit the situation were fertive. He became a well wisher of Shobha. Really he helped her in any physical works the circumstance demanded. This way or that indirectly the ground for the courtship between Vanita and Vasu had been in full spring. Naturally the flirtation flourished and reached an alarming stage when it was shortly to find an exploision.

Indeed an opportunity came when the fair of Kadasiddeshwar started in Banahatti. During this festival people went to the temple in large number possible. As the temple had been the biggest religious shrine in Banahatti, the devotees or others, all went there and displayed their devotion and jubilance. People gathered at the temple and proffered their devotion. Every sort of shows, markets, entertainments, eatables, sellings and buyings were carried on. The children of the town and outside made their merrymaking, a success during the event. If children enjoyed toys and revelry, elders exchanged their joys and sorrows. They prayed God for peace and prosperity. There was a carfair and it was pulled by hundreds of devotees as it was done at Puri. Besides, during the car procession crackers were set astounding. The young and old entertained others and got delighted. The festival had been a rare event in the surrounding.

Naturally like anyone of the faith, Shobha, the theist went to the temple. She had already been fragile in health. Her life had become a sort of struggle or a pilgrimage none could like to follow. She lived a life of suffering, hardship, sacrifice and sorrow. Good or ill, she led a sixty-eight years of life single-handedly. Mostly she could still keep on struggling happy did she have no problems regarding her young son. Or it could be said, she could like to live upto a hundred or more years if Harish had been a benevolent husband to her, or Mohini would have not harboured any ill-will towards her. Shobha knew it well that it was Mohini who came on the way of Venkatesh's love for his mother. Therefore, she hated the eldest daughter-in-law. But she was all an affection, love and concern for Venkatesh and his son. She loved Sidhartha as he was the only grandson in the province of her kinship. In fact, she loved all, though some of them disliked her.

It was six o'clock evening, a Monday of January. Most people had been joyous and contented with their earthly lot. She had already performed her worship at the temple. By the time Shobha turned homeward, the car procession had been in full swing. More than a hundred people — all devotees were pulling it. Tenfold of that number was following it. Children were picking up sweet meats, dry fruits, coins thrown over the car, by the wealthy, religious and noble-hearted. The bells of the procession and the bands of music therewith accompanied produced its lilt and melody. There were thousand rejoicings. People laughed, they enjoyed the scenes and they felt the heart-stirrings of a religious fair such as this. Already the western sun had gone into the horizon afar. He was sinking rapidly. The golden rays he created had disappeared with his setting down. The evening stars had not yet made their dimly presence. Dark had spread everywhere. There was no calm, no light, no rays of hopes and even no assurance of good days for Shobha. The sunshine of her life had vanished by the midday storm. But no beams of tranquility, optimism and joys seemed in the district of her ending life.

Everything, everyone whether kindred or unkind did not seem supporting her. It seems the whole world of hope and happiness had disappeared for the grieved old woman.

Shobha walked home lonely. None consoled her for her misfortunes. Nor was there any companion to soothe? Now she was alone neither her husband nor her sons walking beside. Even she did not have a single grandchild to assist her in old age. Her husband had already deserted her. So what of the eldest son? He had well-settled down somewhere where she could not go often either because of Mohini's indifference or because of her own dislike. Ashok had joined a monastary throwing away the clutches of life and responsibility, while his second wife was counting the last days of her exile.

Shobha came home by six-thirty evening. As they left for the fair the neighbours were rarely seen. The whole atmosphere was tranquilized. As all the boys had been at car-procession, the suburbia wore a stunted look. The house looked abandoned in the absence of its dwellers. The dark night had spread its ghostal shadows. Her own beautiful house too had its door closed. This puzzled the old lady. She wondered whether Vanita had gone anywhere to pass her time. Shobha stood near the door and knocked it twice. But oddly enough she found the door bolted inside. Nor did she hear any voice coming out? She was astonished because the inside bolt had been latched though none could be seen there. To explore the truth, she trode some steps sideways and presently she stood exactly in the same place wherefrom many decades ago she caught her husband in her sister's sarees. The atmosphere recollected her the old event. Indeed, what she anticipated just came true. Now she saw Vanita and Vasu sleeping together. They were in each other's arms fucking. Shobha was shocked to see it and at once she fell down crying 'God save my soul.' Immediately the two lives locked in each other inside, hurried out and found the old lady unconscious. But after a while she returned to life and by that time, Vanita's paramour who sensed the danger had disappeared never to come back to kiss Vanita's neglected heart.

Found guilty of the whole situation, Vanita first managed to get the dying woman inside. Shobha almost broken-hearted took rest and relaxed on the same bed whereupon she had slept with Harish, Harish had slept with Karisma, Ashok had slept or not with his wives and presently Vanita-Vasu had misused it unable to bear the heat of their bodies.

It was one o' clock midnight when Shobha got up unable to sleep any longer. Her mind was seething, her body had produced an anguish. The situation around her turned unbearable any longer. A question occurred to her sensitive mind. It was not an ordinary question. Extraordinary one. Right...Serious...Valid... Meaningful. Indeed, she questioned herself, 'WHY I'D LIVE? FOR WHOM ?' Presently she changed the syntax of it but at every modification the meaning remained Unchanged Futile...Nothing...Zero. She found no justification for further life. Presently she came near a table and found tablets. They were sleeping pills. She took three of them in her hand; she had a nice look at them and she counted... counted... counted them. But the number was always three (1) the tragic birth... (2) the tragic suffering... and (3) the tragic death... What a rare combination!!! Life looked to her nothing but an enigma... an illusion... a veriegated *maya*. The lota of water lay just beside. Shobha recollected her God, she remembered her sons Venkatesh and Ashok and Kamala, her daughter. Finally she recalled Sidhartha, her grandson. All the loved were remembered and the unloved lost. Now she took the three tablets and slept down soundly never to be disturbed by Any One... Anytime... Anywhere... The morning came when the eastern sun withdrew the hideous dark curtain. Again the evening came. So the days began running. But it was not different... The sun was the same. The same wind danced every here and there... The trees... The flowers... The birds... The people around the Pattans' house — all looked the same... unchangeable ... monotonous. Already Vanita guilty of the blunder and betrayal had fled away to her village far away. While the house stood stockstill in the compound and its door was unlocked, the tresspassers, neighbours and children thought that somebody must be there. None desired to disturb the tranquil air... the settled dust... the ailing calmness. All passed on the way with or without the reservation of their candid remarks.

Tuesday passed. So did the next day of January. January was January. The Happy New Year Was Not Her Happy New Year. However, it was a modest beginning in the scheme of stellar universe. The suburbia was the same place. Presently it was Thursday. The people in the neighbourhood then smelt something stinking. The right side neighbour who identified the stink, alerted the left side colony men. Satamma of Naganna's house, Bhima and Ravi and others consulted each other. All under the aegis of Srinivas, the aged neighbour after an hour long serious discussion decided to check up the house. They wasted no time. They came to the house, saw the door unbolted and entered it but only to find the filthy carcass. An ugly smell had spread out of the dead body and it had legitimately covered the surrounding. Presently they learnt the tragic end of the old woman — very good, sympathetic and human. Immediately their eyes trickled the drops of sorrow and their hearts beat fast — a beat of regret. Srinivas asked Bhimu to ring up Venkatesh, while he sent someboy for Ashok. They learnt Vanita had disappeared never to return. They informed Venkatesh first and within four hours the whole family of Venkatesh and Harish rushed to Banahatti regretting for the lost lady. Already Ashok had come and had informed his kindred about his mother's demise. All relatives gathered by the late afternoon. Thereafter, Harish decided to take up the body for funeral. Already the eldest son and his only son had wept bitterly and they found themselves very unfortunate regarding the calamity. The most tragic man had been Venkatesh who could not bring a reconciliation between his mother and wife. An in-depth despondency stunned him. Sidhartha the boy understood his father and mourned over the death of his truest grandmother who sounded most beloved to him everytime. What a remarkable scene! What an ideal son and a loving boy! The combination had been Shobha — Venkatesh — Sidhartha. Each of these loved the other two beyond the ken of their memory. Whereas Harish stood aghast but his wife Karisma wept bitterly over the death of her sister. But Ashok sat in a corner all passions spent. Some people thought Ashok should have died instead of his mother. There was a grain of truth in this remark. He did not know how his mother cared him greatly. In another corner Kamala squatted in full tears. The villagers, one upon the other, by mourning over the demise shown their respect to the departed matron.

By four o' clock of the saddest day, the burial ceremony had been over and the people save the kindred went homes. Harish, Venkatesh, Ashok with others of their family gathered in the hall of their house. They sat there together though they could not. It was for the first time in the last decade, Ashok saw his father. This was also true in the case of Kamala. It was not less than twenty years afterwards Karisma spoke to her sister's children. What a trial, what a strife life looked to them really! Never the less, all loved their life and all lived it in accessible distances, not a single soul of them tried to meet each other and add sweetness and light to the pale life of theirs. Most of them misunderstood each other and missed the fragrance of joys. All except Venkatesh were the alienated souls living apart. The things fell apart as the centre could not hold them. If Harish had behaved strangely with the children of his first wife, Mohini annoyed the late woman. If Karisma spoiled her sister's joyous life and prosperity, Ashok took wrong moves in life ruining himself. While the two successive wives of the rogue-turned-rishi erred because they could not withstand the fury of their nudity. Each severed his links from the rest and lived like separate orbits free from the region of other's smells, touch and air.

However, the unhappy person of the house was Venkatesh again. He alone knew the scientific formula that 'happiness lies in sacrifice and it lies in unity and strength. He knew the mission of life to live and let others live as happily as oneself. The point *Paropakararthavidam i shariram* had been his credo and accordingly he helped others to the best of his abilities. The life's fetters and agonies, ups and downs were known to him more accurately than to his father though the latter had turned grey-headed. His father though an educated did not know what was wheat and what was chaff. Indeed he exchanged figs for thistles. His only mission in life was physical happiness, material prosperity and the here and now. He never worried about the hereafter. Nor did he try to discover his own self. But Venkatesh had been cost in a different hue and he stood distinct from the lot. He trusted himself; discovered his self and strove thereby singularly. What his father failed, he achieved and what he wanted to obtain in life, he did. He stood for humanity, for an order, for a mission and found truth, beauty and nobility which many of his lot missed miserably.